TREAD

Clayton Lindemuth

Hardgrave Enterprises
SAINT CHARLES, MISSOURI

For Julie, my wife,
whose unending support and belief
have made everything worthwhile
in my life possible

MY COUNTRY'S MADE ME ITS ENEMY.

IT'S FORMAL, NOW.

—NAT CINDER

Chapter One

Flagstaff at sundown. I drink a quarter of my flask of Jack in two gulps. There's a crew of secessionists in the cabin behind me, bitching about the same old. It's endless, and that's why it's got to end.

I'm on the porch wondering when I should tell the boys to get lost. They got guns but won't use them. They got the same reasons to be pissed as I do. A tax code seventeen thousand pages long, for shit's sake. But they'd rather suck beer and fart than defend themselves against the almighty Machine. And what am I doing? Sitting here drinking whiskey and thinking about a dead woman's feet.

One more gulp of Jack and I'm going in. The only one that has any stones is George Murray—the bastard's lugging around a set of cannonballs. The IRS closed his bait shop and he's stockpiling black powder. He's raising a fuss and I want to hear it.

"We ought to firebomb 'em," Murray says. "Hit the IRS, courthouses, Fish and Game. Then they'll know what we're about."

I stand at the door beside a floodlight swarming with moths. Murray and Charlie Yellow Horse, a white man with a sixteenth of Apache blood on his mother's side, are nose to nose.

"Fucking moron," Yellow Horse says.

"Talk! Talk! Let's blow some shit up!"

It's about damn time they show a little spirit. So far all the boys have done is snivel. They come from all over. One smokes Dominican cigars and the rest chew Copenhagen, but when it comes to bearing arms, they each take their panties off one leg at a time and when their asses are bare, they bend over.

Except Murray. Praise Jesus.

The fire lights surrounding trees in an orange glow. I get the feeling we're not alone. Might be a chipmunk in the leaves, but this kind of group attracts attention. All we do is talk, but it's the wrong kind of talk.

Tree branches break the outline of the moon and the breeze carries a storm. The sky flashes but no clap follows. Electric is in the air.

Murray talks and my head snaps back to the show.

"I'm sick of being a goddamn government mule," he says. "Any of you ever have the IRS chain your shop shut? Pay this, pay that! I'm sick of it!"

"Why don't you do something about it, shithead?"

"Well, well. The Indian who dyes his hair black is talking tough. Why don't you reach down and see if those wampum nuts of yours are big enough to join me?"

"Behold the modern White Man," Yellow Horse says, and jabs Murray's shoulder with his closed fist. "Talk."

Cowboy boots shuffle on the plank floor as fat men slide back in a hurry. Yellow Horse shoves Murray through the screen door. Murray stutter steps past me and falls off the porch. He's a heavy man, but Yellow Horse has thrown him. He rolls and leaps to his feet.

Yellow Horse steps outside and they square off in front of the fire. Someone cries, "Whooo-hooo!"

Yellow Horse is quiet now. He wishes he was a real Apache starving on lichens and grass, killing men with knives, flitting across the rocks like a ghost. Instead, he's a grad student at ASU writing papers about the evils of assimilation, wearing a leather necklace with a silver arrow as the jewel.

Murray puffs his chest and throws his shoulders back, fists high, arms parallel, like an Irish pugilist. And I know Yellow Horse is praying to Red Cloud to make him a man, just one damn time.

Murray has the pounds, but Yellow Horse is sinewy and lithe, his stance like a coiled spring. His hair catches firelight and the illusion is strong. He circles Murray.

Yellow Horse lunges. They lock arms on shoulders and dance around the fire.

"Gittim Murray!" Merle cries.

In a minute they're gasping tired and I imagine this fight will reach the back-slapping, good-buddy stage before anyone bleeds. Sure enough, Murray steps back and drops his arms.

"You don't know when to stop running your dick-licker," Yellow Horse says, and drives his fist into Murray's jaw. "Maybe if I bust it, they'll wire it shut." He throws another and the sound is wet with blood.

Murray touches his mouth and his hand goes to his chest like a man patting a wallet he can't feel.

Yellow Horse sends a flicker of a look to me. Our eyes lock.

Yeah, I saw it.

I watch the woods again; hair stands on my neck. You get a sixth sense as a Ranger; I have a seventh.

Yellow Horse charges and grabs Murray by his arms and jerks him forward. Murray falls and throws him with a practiced move—the kind you see on TV. They roll and Yellow Horse is back on top with his knees pinning Murray. Yellow Horse punches him below the right eye. Murray bucks, but can't marshal the strength to throw him. Yellow Horse thumps him again.

Maybe there's hope for this group.

I take a couple slugs of Jack. I'll need a refill soon. I've felt like I've been in a river for the last fifteen years, sucked along to a destiny that includes this kind of action. Maybe these men have something to do with my end, after all.

Yellow Horse sits on Murray's chest and gives him a sudden jerk like a dog snapping a rabbit's back. Murray's shirt rips open and a flat black rectangle is taped to his chest.

Yellow Horse tears it off and tosses it to me.

"Gee, Murray. This ain't too good," I say.

"It's a voice recorder," Yellow Horse says.

"You didn't get this gizmo at Radio Shack, didja?" I say.

Murray coughs bloody spit and hocks it to the side. "Just trying to protect myself."

"How's that?"

"I was afraid y'all'd say I was instigating shit here."

Yellow Horse pops Murray in the jaw. His knuckles glow red when he pulls back and wails one more time.

"You was the one talkin' about blowin' shit up. Wouldn't that be entrapment? Murray?"

Yellow Horse looks at me and his eyes pass to the group behind me.

"You're under arrest for conspiracy and sedition," Murray says.

"Sedition? They didn't even get the Rosenbergs for sedition," Yellow Horse says. He grins; he's holding a law enforcement officer's life in his hands. He's lost himself and in this moment has a chance to measure against an old standard.

The group has ten members. We haven't named ourselves a militia or printed some redneck banner to fly on our Jeeps. We haven't voted for leaders, though they all know I'm the one with the dough. None has ever taken action on behalf of the others, save springing for a kegger. And yet the central government—the Machine, as Yellow Horse calls it—finds us dangerous.

It's the worst confirmation. My country's made me its enemy.

It's formal, now.

Yellow Horse watches my face as fire reflects little orange dots in his eyes. His jaw is frozen: a white man transforms himself into the savage he always wanted to be. He's fluttering on the cusp of metamorphosis, and just when I think his courage will fail him and leave him with nothing but a good story, his hand falls to his side.

I jump. "No!"

With blurring speed Yellow Horse unsheathes a boot knife.

His arm whips forward and he slices Murray's throat. Murray writhes and gargles blood; Yellow Horse flips the blade in his hand and drives it into Murray's forehead. He stands and turns to the rest of us, trembling with courage.

"Jesus," I say, though the Almighty had nothing to do with it. One of the boys behind me throws up on a lounge chair.

Murray is dead but shaking. I smell piss and blood and remember Gretchen, my wife, suspended above me in a flipped Ford Bronco.

The smell just about breaks me and I turn aside.

Yellow Horse watches me. I finish my flask and wipe my mouth with my sleeve.

"Well," I say, "they're on us. This group is done."

By dusk the temperature had fallen from mid-afternoon highs of one hundred-twenty to a reasonable hundred-five. The crowd cheered Governor Virginia Rentier as she cut the yellow sash. It fluttered to the ground and she stepped to the surveyor's mark, cognizant as kiln-baked clay pressed pebbles against her soles.

Mick Patterson, Chief of Staff, placed the handle of a round nosed shovel in her palm. The crowd stilled.

"Here?" She indicated a stake with a pink ribbon. A bronze man with day laborer shoulders and a black five o'clock shadow nodded.

Holding the shovel vertical, she dropped it. The earth rejected the point without a chip.

"Eh, Meez Governor—you wan mi hombre bust ee dirt?" A different man from the crowd spoke. He wore ragged flannel and his back was stooped. Even in the purple street-lamp glow, his face was crinkled like the scorched clay underfoot. Rentier followed his eyes, trod a few steps, and returned holding a pickaxe level at her hips.

The second man nodded at her. The first grinned.

She swung the pick overhead; her left hand slid along the shaft and she whipped her back and buttocks. Her heel broke. A small cloud of dust popped free as the metal shank plunged to the rounded swell of the handle. Vibration stung her hand.

Holding the man's eyes, she lifted with her knees and pried loose a heavy chunk of baked clay.

The stooped man smiled wide and his compadres cheered.

Votes.

Rentier held their eyes, pair by pair, until she owned them. Finally her gaze settled on Dick Clyman. The Republican Minority Leader of the Arizona House stood with the others, his pale Anglo face distinct from the Hispanic throng, his mouth lopsided in a Dick Cheney grin.

This wasn't his kind of event, and Rentier was suddenly aware that she stood lopsided.

Her fingers closed toward an old burn scar high on her right cheekbone. She swept the willful hand through her hair, waved, and kicked off both shoes. The group erupted. Photo bulbs flashed white under the streetlamp glow. She steeled herself to step across the sharp pebbles.

"I—"

A frenzy of cheers silenced her.

She passed the pick to Patterson, took the shovel and tossed aside a spade of loose dirt. Camera flashes sparkled like a Flagstaff snowstorm.

"I am honored," she said, and waited for their whooping and clapping to subside. "I am honored to break ground for the Arizona Center for Undocumented Americans. Across the street, the Chavez Center stands as a proud reminder of the Hispanic community's contributions to Arizona. Now the ACUA will join the fight to expand the civil rights of the Undocumented, hear their voice, and amplify their voice."

More cheers.

"The Arizona legislature will soon pass the Vallejo Bill, and I will sign it. I will take your fight all the way to the White House. May God, Arizona, and the United States bless you!"

She stepped away. Patterson and a contingent of state police security men shepherded her toward the limousine.

"Governor!"

It was Clyman.

Chief of Staff Patterson stepped forward to deflect the minority leader. A state trooper opened the limousine door and Rentier slipped to the seat. She watched Patterson and Clyman between elbows and torsos that gathered at the vehicle until Patterson leaned close to the window, his blank eyes searching the darkened glass. She lowered it.

"Clyman wants a meeting tomorrow morning," Patterson said. "It's urgent."

"I can't. You know that. I'm with the Girl Scouts tomorrow morning."

"Governor, you need to see him."

Patterson's Marine Corps bearing, like his flat top haircut and Hitler mustache, touched a nerve. His cropped grey hair often made her think of the day her father burned her—it was one of the reasons she kept Patterson around.

She touched her cheek. Plastic surgery, concealer, foundation, powder, and still her fingertips found the shiny-smooth cigarette scar.

"Mick, it just struck me you look like Adolph Hitler. Shave your moustache."

"What?"

"Tell Clyman to get in. He can ride back to the tower with me."

Patterson's jaw clenched.

"What?" she said.

He turned away.

A moment later Clyman was beside her. His arms poked from his barrel chest like legs on a blood-gorged tick. He'd escaped a childhood in Jerome, Arizona with his closed mind intact—before gays, bikers, and painters made the mountain copper town chic. He was a lineman on the Sun Devil football team in the seventies, then matriculated to a Catholic law school in Pittsburgh. Now he was a fat Republican who panted after climbing into a car seat.

He was too close. He regarded her with wide-set eyes that lorded a secret.

She drew her knees together. "I hope this isn't about Vallejo."

His lips thinned and the right side curved upward. She'd seen that look years ago, when he defeated a minimum wage increase she'd asked a junior representative to submit on the House floor. The same leer graced the front page of the Phoenix Times when he lambasted her for visiting Mexican President Vicente Fox. Behind those pinprick eyes, his brain was as tight as a sparrow's ass. Why did conservatives elect such ugly men?

Clyman shifted. "I have information that might help you avoid a public relations problem. Thought we might come to an understanding."

She caught the driver's glance in the rearview mirror. "Mitch, I'm sorry. Will you raise the divider?"

The window climbed and nestled to the roof.

"What are we talking about, Dick?"

"Veto Vallejo."

"No way. That bill has a long history, and I'm going to be the governor that signs it."

"It'll kill the state."

"Only a Republican would say more power in the hands of the people is bad. Or are they the wrong kind of people? We've argued this to death in the papers. Talk radio. The House floor. Why stake a proslavery position? Twenty-two states in the past had no citizenship test to vote. The country did fine."

"That so? I have a different story. My mother—seventy-five years old—comes home from the grocery store. Finds two spics busted in. They knock her around, tie her so tight her hands turn blue and rob her blind. When the police catch the perps, not only are they illegals—they've been caught and released twice before! Like goddam fish!"

"I didn't know about your mother."

"She had gangrene. Doctors had to amputate her hand to save her life."

Rentier drank water. Stared forward, then at Clyman.

Clyman's face changed. "Let me do you the favor of being candid."

She waited. The car turned to a highway onramp and accelerated.

"There's photos floating around," he said. "You know, queer stuff. No one really cares when a woman eats pussy anymore, but the compromising stuff is who the pussies belong to. Now, if word gets to other Republicans—hell, Democrats—they'll cry for impeachment. That's the last thing I want. I think you and I can work together. Am I communicating with you?"

Rentier studied his face. Clyman smiled.

The Secretary of State—who became governor if Rentier became incapacitated—was a Republican. Clyman didn't want her removed because he thought he could control her.

"And you can make this problem go away?"

"No; I don't have the photos. I'm not even sure they exist. Let's say if you and I were allies on Vallejo, you might assume my help in this matter."

It was her fault, in a way. Heat flushed her face; her scar pulsed. She rapped the glass divider and it lowered. "Pull over."

The limousine stopped a mile short of the Executive Tower.

"Dick—I appreciate your candor enough to return it. Put those pictures in your personal collection, right next to the Vaseline. It's the best use you're going to get out of them. Now get the fuck out of my limo."

Yellow Horse drives a pick into the ground. We've been up all night and I'm running on fumes. We took Forest Road Forty-Four deep into the woods outside Flagstaff; I looked at his gas gauge to make sure we'd make it out. We came to a place so arbitrary and lonely it seemed fit for a clandestine burial.

The pick wedges between a rock and a root. "Son of a bitch," Yellow Horse says. He pries it loose.

The body rests under a tarp on the ground, one leg splayed and visible in the moonlight.

I didn't used to be like this. Before Gretchen died I managed a section at Honeywell. Had an MBA and a secretary named Cyndi.

I left for work at four a.m. and always kissed Gretchen's forehead. That last morning she had her leg kicked out from under the blanket. I passed around the bed in the dark and her toes caught my suit pant. I rubbed her sole and along her outer arch. Her feet always hurt, maybe from the weight of being pregnant. Her foot was soft as her inner thigh. She died that night.

I kick Murray's leg under the tarp.

"You could've let him go," I say.

"And let the Machine grind me to dust? Inject my veins with poison?"

"They don't do that for talk."

"It was the wrong kind of talk."

I drink from my flask. "Keep digging. It'll be dawn soon."

Murray's blood has curdled in the bed of the truck; the clots glisten like cherry pie filling flung with a spatula and worked with an oil rag.

"No problem," Yellow Horse says.

"They have chemicals that make blood show up."

"Not after I take a torch to it."

"You might try Clorox."

He shakes his head and his eyes light up; they don't fit the face of a man that just murdered another. "This is a 1972 F-150," he says. "It gets burned."

"I figure you have a couple of hours. I'm surprised they weren't on us when you stuck him."

"It was a recorder, not a transmitter," he says.

Yellow Horse grabs Murray's arms and I get his feet. His ass drags as we work him to the pit. The body's getting stiff. We drop him in.

"You better pull that blade out," I say.

"Why?"

Doesn't seem right to send him off with a knife in his forehead, so I jump in the hole and yank at it. His jaw falls open and each pull pumps dead air through his lungs. It stinks. I climb out.

Yellow Horse shovels dirt on Murray. I suppose he thinks he'll be able to tuck away the killing in a corner of his mind. Or maybe he thinks he'll revel in it. But human beings aren't built that way. He'll be running from the law and himself the rest of his life.

We cover the grave with dirt and pine needles and soggy oak leaves, then get in the truck and head back to Flag. Last night's storm fizzled at the damp wind stage. Wet air collects on the windshield.

I look at Yellow Horse and wonder if he's plotting his next moves, maybe running to Mexico this afternoon.

I'm going to sleep. No one but Yellow Horse knows me as Nat Cinder. The secessionists think I'm Tom Davis. When I get out of this truck, Tom Davis disappears, and Nat Cinder never heard of him.

"You can drop me off here," I say.

Yellow Horse pulls to the curb two blocks from the house where I left my bike—where I plan to spend the morning in the arms of a skinny blonde named Liz. She lives with Rosie, a big-boned woman liable to quote the Constitution the way some women quote psalms. I hear "we the people in order to form" and I get a chub like to club a seal. Liz and Rosie are rednecks, bar girls prone to throaty laughter; they view tattoos as the same kind of vanity as big earrings and big hair. They embrace all three.

I stand beside the truck with the door open. The sun's been up for hours but the air is brisk and damp.

"You'd best get out of town," I say. "See what shakes out."

"There were a lot of witnesses," Yellow Horse says. "Eight, counting you."

"And half of them fairly new to the group. We're gonna have to start over. One person at a time. Work in cells."

I expect him to turn away when I open the door, but his eyes are narrow. "You gonna be alright?"

"What do you mean, Charlie?"

"Last night. I don't want to have to worry about you."

"Wait a good while until you get in touch."

He pulls away and I walk toward the house. Under leafy maples, shade outweighs light and brief splashes of sun warm my skin. I need sleep and I think of Liz. It ain't love but she beats Miss Palm and her sisters. I see her like I remember her, legs spread, and just as I can damn near smell her musk, tires squeal and two brown sedans swerve front and back of Yellow Horse's truck. They skid to a stop. I'm fifty yards away. Four guys in suits jump out waving guns. They wear sunglasses in the shade and they converge on the driver's side door.

Yellow Horse bolts from the passenger side and sprints across a lawn to the woods behind. The men fan out and chase. After a few seconds the trees hide them, but their shouts mark their paths.

There's no one on the street either direction; no parked cars. I trot across a lawn and behind a house. A Rottweiler lunges but a chain jerks him short. I jump a half-rotted fence that almost collapses and cross a lawn to a parallel avenue. FBI men bellow in the distance. Yellow Horse used to be a distance runner and I have the feeling these patent-leather chumps will be sucking wind inside a mile.

Liz and Rosie live in a small house with sooty white siding and a rusted bike collection under the eaves. I approach from the back yard and push my Triumph from the porch. It's a coldblooded machine and I choke it. While the engine steadies out, I rap the back door.

Liz stands in her underwear and a shrunken T-shirt with a mug of coffee. Her legs bear the sheen of a fresh shave and I take a third of a second to debate whether I should save Yellow Horse's ass, or pound hers.

"You better clear out," I say. "FBI was layin' for Yellow Horse. They'll be checking houses if they don't get him. They were outside, so they know this place."

"You takin' off without a goodbye kiss, Tom?" Liz says.

Rosie watches from the kitchen window, her face illegible.

I give Liz a peck on the lips and she grabs my mess. She smells of cigarettes.

"Get out," I tell her, and drink from the mug.

"How much time do we have?"

"Not much."

"Can't I ride with you?"

"No."

She slams the door and the pane rattles.

I told her my name was Tom Davis when I met her at a bar a couple years ago. Thomas Jefferson and Jefferson Davis. I'd been scouting Flagstaff to get an understanding of grassroots thinking on secession. I had the time and the bucks, and figured other folks saw the same freedom meltdown. After Ruby Ridge and Waco, you don't let government know who you are or what you're doing. I set up a fake name and did a few credit card transactions to support it. I have two more identities, unused.

One more gulp of coffee and I climb on the bike—a Triumph Rocket. It has a car-sized engine but no cup holder. I take a final drink and toss the mug to the lawn, then cut a mark across the grass and over the sidewalk.

At the junction with Maryland Street a black sedan pulls to the corner on my right. A suit watches me from inside. I drive straight and the car turns left. He stays in the open, an FBI harassment technique. It's also what disinterested strangers do.

I take Madison and then Santa Clara; the car falls back but remains in sight. He weaves. There's no traffic so I figure he's fiddling with the radio or a cell phone. Checking his email. One more turn and I'm on the road to Interstate 17. I've made a loop and I'm parallel to where Yellow Horse left his truck and sprinted into the woods. If it was me, I'd be sticking to the flat ground and making distance. He's covered a mile and a half, if I'm right.

Soon the houses thin to one every hundred yards and the pavement weaves between a dirt bank on the left and a hollow on the right. Tall trees choke the undergrowth with permanent shade. It's like driving through the dank air of a tunnel.

Yellow Horse runs like a raped ape to my right. The air whips his hair and I recall last night, when the illusion was strong. He's in his element. If he lives only ten minutes, he'll be glad these were his last. I'm not as exhilarated.

Three men follow at a distance; their white shirts flash through the trees. I bump my horn and Yellow Horse angles to the bike. The sedan behind me accelerates.

We meet fifty yards ahead. I skid on the pavement and Yellow Horse leaps aboard, rocking my balance. I pop the clutch and the bike rights itself. The engine screams like a dago tenor with a wine bottle rammed up his ass. I yell, "hang on!" too late and Yellow Horse claws at my side to keep from falling off the back. The bike explodes. The rear tire chirps; the front tire lifts. It's as close to instant travel as man can come. I push it hard—the car is right on us and there's a hand with a gun sticking out the window.

We bank right and left and when we've gone a mile I swerve on a left fork and press the bike again. The wind has fists and bugs feel like sling-shot rocks. Yellow Horse doesn't have sunglasses and he buries his face to my back. I come to another turn and take it. We've lost our pursuers and I skid to a stop.

"If I was you I'd visit Mexico," I say.

"If I was you I'd get rid of that yellow flag."

I look at the back of the bike where I've mounted a small yellow pennant—the Gadsden flag—with a coiled rattlesnake and the words, DON'T TREAD ON ME.

Yellow Horse slaps my back and disappears into the woods.

I figure every federal dick in Flagstaff and Phoenix is scouring the land looking for a Triumph Rocket. They have cars, motorcycles, and thanks to Janet Reno, Abrams tanks. They probably have helicopters after us by now and I won't be shocked if the NSA offers up a satellite. The sum of the facts is I'm not taking Interstate Seventeen back to Phoenix. I wouldn't make it to Mund's Park.

I head down 89A through Oak Creek Canyon toward Sedona and mix with tourist traffic. The famous red rocks stand bright in the sky; grass ripples as cars pass. The double lane winds along the creek. I'm behind a string of cars a mile long—people that saw the Grand Canyon yesterday and will visit the O.K. Corral tomorrow—when a helicopter flying NAP of the earth pounds overhead. I hunker down without thinking and when I look up I'm under heavy tree cover.

The bird continues along the road and by the time it banks right it looks more like a dragonfly than a chopper. I can't see any markings. Mountain-sized boulders block the left, Oak Creek the right. Every turn dead-ends in fifty feet. I go straight but watch the sky.

One of the witnesses called the FBI. Like Yellow Horse said, Murray wore a recorder, not a transmitter. Unless it had GPS, which I wouldn't put past the wily sonsabitches, there's no other way they know Murray's dead.

I could turn on Yellow Horse and save my ass, but what kind of choice is that?

Break things down to black and white, the grays have to pick a side.

Two miles before Sedona, on the right, a stone wall gaps at a driveway with a twelve-foot gate. The top of the worked iron rolls into an eagle crest. Wings spread as if braking for prey; outstretched talons hang ready to rend whoever passes unauthorized through the gates.

A hundred yards distant, at the top of a knoll, a log cabin with a wraparound deck peeks through the trees. It dates to 1891, built by one of the first settlers in Sedona. A later owner planted an orchard on the field to the right, and between us, Oak Creek gurgles over rocks.

The governor of Arizona, Virginia Rentier, escapes the desert here. She could be inside right now, cutting a deal with another cutthroat or scoring a business transaction. A security element patrols the cabin whether she's there or not. I've mused about this ranch.

In Sedona, tourists fight for parking spaces and wander with cameras and plastic shopping bags, searching for meaning at souvenir shops, tarot readers, psychic healers, and food service joints. Want a genuine Navajo trinket? From China with love.

Nobel Prize-winning economists tell us the global economy is a good thing; it isn't a zero-sum game. But deep inside, I can't help but think there's something good about being able to make our own trash.

Tree cover thins after Sedona. I follow 89 to Cottonwood and cut across to Jerome. The old copper town tugs at my heart; climbing the switchbacks I pass eight biker bars. The air chills and my hands grow stiff. I stop at the rest area at the crest and take a leak, then replace the lost fluid with fresh Jack Daniel's from my flask. Back amid trees, I park the bike in the sun and think. I'd be smart to hole up. I'm confident they don't have my name, but my bike marks a trail like fresh blood on snow.

I have a place near my trailer on the outskirts of Phoenix. Maybe I'll make it.

Chapter Two

Washington Street ended with a round, thermometer-bulb turn a few yards from the double glass doors of the Executive Tower. Six square columns, three on the left, three on the right, spanned from ground to top, reinforcing the image of executive strength and balance. A phalanx of administrative buildings shot horizontally from the base and a dozen acres of parking lot and lawn made the tower a bastion of executive authority. In the morning sun the building seemed to strut with purpose.

On the ninth floor, the highest, Virginia Rentier stood at the window and turned as her assistant, Jennifer Sprague, crossed the hall. Rentier's gaze landed on the athletic fold of her knee.

"I need my notes for the press brief—and will you get Patterson?"

Rentier looked out the window. Men and women scurried from their cars to the buildings that constituted the executive branch of Arizona government. It looked immense and noble, all these people working to manifest better lives for others—but to Virginia Rentier, their number was paltry in comparison to those they supported with their efforts. There could never be enough government.

Mick Patterson rapped the door and whirled around the corner.

"Why can't we get a vote on Vallejo?"

Patterson stood at the center of Rentier's office. "I talked to the Speaker this morning. She's one vote short and still talking incentives—"

"Fuck carrots. Tell her to use a stick. And sit down. We'll be a minute. Ask her what pressure the Executive Branch can bring—if she doesn't have enough of her own muscle."

Patterson nodded. "I'm worried about the Senate."

"I have friends in the Senate. It's the House that's a bunch of cannibals." She paused, sat in the chair beside Patterson. "You know this bill is important to me. Not just to the state, and eventually the country, but to me."

"Maybe we should leak something to the Times. *Governor works behind the scenes...*'"

"Remember the brunette who did the exposé on gun violence? I want a few minutes alone with her."

Patterson stood.

"Sit."

He slid into the chair. "That thing with Clyman was odd. What's that about?"

Rentier looked across her desk and gazed at the horizon. The sun inched higher and grey morning haze resolved into smog.

Her past had twice intersected Clyman's. She'd met him at Senator Brownward's Arizona presidential campaign headquarters in 1988. Fresh out of law school, the bell curve of her sexual dynamism had just lifted from the plane. Clyman had a wife and a daughter, a reporter Virginia's age. Clyman made a pass at her but his daughter stole her breath.

That didn't work out at all...

His daughter's death catalyzed him.

Clyman quit his public defender's job, switched to the Republican Party and slicked his way into a chief of staff position for Senator Willard. Within three years Clyman won election to the Arizona House, and spent two terms accumulating power as an aw-shucks bullshitter. When his party lost the majority, Clyman emerged as the strongest Republican standing.

Clyman had learned the game in Democrat trenches but had spent most of his political career with Republican devils, and that made him dangerous. He wouldn't risk concrete knowledge of the photos. His chief of staff, Preston Delp, had to be the starting point.

"This problem doesn't get solved without trust." Rentier faced Patterson. "At the beginning of my term I had an affair. Someone took photos. I received an anonymous call, probably from a person working for TetraChemical, demanding I veto a pollution bill. I was three weeks in office and I didn't have any machinery in place, so to speak."

"You vetoed that bill."

"I did."

"Once you give a bear the honey …."

"There's no honey here, and don't presume to lecture. As I said, I didn't have assets that could take care of the problem."

"Yeah, but that was then. Clyman's a puss."

"You'd be surprised. He demands I veto the Vallejo bill. If we were allies, I could expect his help regarding the photos."

"Did he say he had them?"

"He's too coy for that. It has to be his Chief, Preston Delp."

Patterson inhaled deep and released. "You know, there are only two ways of dealing with this. Stay bought … or …"

"I know. I'm interested in 'or.'"

Patterson nodded. "I'll talk to Buffa." He lifted a folder from the floor. "May I place this on your desk?"

Rentier nodded.

Patterson landed the file and flipped the cover, exposing a photograph. "The inmate I mentioned."

Rentier studied a photo of a man with RGT tattooed on his forehead. His teeth were half-rotted black and he'd pulled his hair tight against his scalp in a ponytail. His nose was narrow and hooked; cheekbones rode high above a whiskered basin that extended to his jawbone. His narrow eyes reached across twenty years to warn, *don't fuck with me.*

She placed the photo on her desk and rifled through the folder.

"Rudy Ging Theen," she read. "All three names—just wonderful. Out of a hundred and fourteen death row inmates, you pick a guy who actually sounds like a serial killer."

"That's an old photo. Check the bottom of the file."

A different man looked back at her: hair trimmed and combed, pulled forward to hide the tattoo. Clean-shaved face and an engaging smile. A crucifix dangled from a thin gold chain around his neck. Virtuous energy illuminated his eyes, like he and the cameraman had just shared a joke about apple pie or a sinner standing at the Pearly Gates.

"This is from the back cover of his last book for teen boys. This is what God did for him." Patterson said.

"What's the evidence against him? Details … quickly—I hear Girl Scouts gathering outside the door."

"Charged in 1984. One man dead in a gas station holdup. Theen matched the description given by a pair of witnesses. The jury deliberated forty-five minutes."

"Murder weapon?"

"Snub thirty-eight, found in his apartment."

"Motive?"

"The prosecution said drug money, but there's more to it than that."

"That's good enough. Any other crimes in his background?"

Patterson hesitated. "Possession of cocaine."

"The ten-gallon hat demographic won't understand a pardon."

"Of course they will. For the left, government rehabilitation was the first lucky break the poor bastard caught. For the right, the very hand of God saved him. He leads bible study in prison. He writes books for teens about living clean lives. He even had his teeth done. He can change hearts and minds."

"I'm on the fence."

"He'll be handy in a pinch."

"We have Buffa."

"Buffa betrayed you. Theen won't. Before he wrote boys' books, he wrote a memoir. He took responsibility, but it wasn't him that needed the drugs. It was his mother. A woman that burned him with cigarettes and put clothes pins on his testicles. Yet when she was dying of cancer and no prescription could ease the pain, he jacked a gas station to get her some pot. Things went sour—but his motive is telling."

"She burned him? And he loved her?"

"He's like a savant."

Patterson waved the first photo of Theen. "Can this guy get a good paying job? Can this guy buy expensive painkillers? In the book, he said his mother gave him life and he decided before the crime that he would do whatever it took to save her."

"Whatever it took."

"The prosecution painted him a drug-crazed addict and that went against him in sentencing. The truth would have gotten him a life sentence, but he never mentioned his mother. He could be loyal to you, either way."

"What if the Attorney General's office signed off on it?"

"Why would Lynwood insulate you?"

"Just ask her to do so. Tell her it's of utmost importance, and that I know she'll back me. And we're going to need help with the Times. They run that picture, we're in trouble. Dammit."

"What?"

"I don't have hiking boots."

Joey Buffa drummed his fingers on the dash, thumping dust into the air. The parking meter clicked down to five minutes. He reached for another quarter.

He sat in a black Jeep Grand Cherokee by Washington Street, outside Congress with the engine running. Even with the a/c, it was fuckin hot. Phoenix hot.

He got the call an hour ago to tail Preston Delp. His client believed Delp possessed information that could be detrimental to a very important somebody. Buffa assumed that somebody was the governor, and he had an idea the 'information' was carnal photos. More instructions would follow. For now, his job was to keep track of Delp.

Was Delp the same lard ass he was four years ago?

Johnny La Rue sat beside him. Like Buffa, Johnny came from Philly. La Rue fidgeted with his hands a lot and sometimes had a tick.

"So how'd you get out from under the Boss?" La Rue said.

"That's a story." Buffa took a swig of Coke and remembered the Boss, Dante De Luca.

Buffa did freelance security work. His card read "Security Consultant." His enterprise flourished with the patronage of a few key clients—one of them, the Arizona state government—although his meetings with the governor's chief of operations were never recorded in any official itinerary, and he never received a check bearing the governor's seal. He didn't take checks.

It started with handyman jobs. Fresh from Philly, his voice had enough olive oil to make a neophyte lawbreaker feel safe about hiring him. He kept his rates low and the business rolled in. Some guy knock-up your baby girl? Need his leg broke? An easy five hundred. Photos of a hotel love affair? A grand, flat rate. A burial in the Sonora Desert? Fifteen grand, plus a risk premium. Simple. He ran a referral business and protected himself with a dead drop system for instructions and payments, like the CIA. Over the years, like any client-focused entrepreneur, he earned repeat business.

He didn't choose to work for the state; they chose him. Eventually he realized his unique appeal to members of government: sometimes politicians, for the good of the citizens they served, needed to augment their legitimate power.

"Simple. I told him I wasn't fuckin workin for him anymore."

"Yeah, but there's a story, right?"

"Yeah. There's a story." His eyes never left the window. "The Boss had a runner—a new kid named Rummans. The kid stole from him and you don't steal from Dante De Luca. He told me to bust him up good, yeah?"

"Yeah."

"So I bust him up good. Fuckin sweet. Next thing I know, I'm in front of a judge. Gimme a smoke."

La Rue lit one and offered it. Buffa grabbed the deck of Marlboros from his hand and took the lucky one La Rue had flipped in the middle. "Like I'm gonna take a smoke you dick-lipped. Gimme your lighter.

"All right. I'm in the courtroom and they wheel in this fifty-two inch, the prosecutor screwing around with leads and shit, then Rummans shows on the screen. He's lying there in this full-body cast, and some guy's off-camera asking questions. 'What's your name? Why you in the hospital? How did that happen?' And then, of course, 'what do you want to say to Joey Buffa?'

"'He can see me, right?' Rummans says. He looks straight down the barrel of the camera. I stare back, because the judge watches me.

"'Joey Buffa,' Rummans says. 'Look at me. The doctor says I have eight broken bones. I don't know you. I didn't do nothing to you.'

"'Joey,' he says, 'you ever gotta piss through a tube? Have some guy nurse wipe your ass?'"

"I try to look sympathetic but really I don't give a fuck—yeah? You don't hold out on Dante De Luca, and Rummans had to learn.

"'Are you hearing me, Joey Buffa?' Rummans says. 'I'm here for three months, but by the time you get out of jail, I'll have had two and a half years at the gym, and the pistol range, and the library.'

"They always like to make threats. But the library threw me.

"'I'm going to fuck you up,' he says.

"'Mr. Rummans—I want you to watch your language,' the judge says.

"'I'm gonna hunt you down and when I find you, I'm going to—'"

"'Mr. Rummans I'm warning you—' the Judge says.

"cut you, prod you, kick you, castrate you—"

"I say, 'Hey!' and the bailiff finally unplugs the tube."

Buffa sat straight and nodded. A man in a suit had emerged from 1900 Washington. He looked like a heavy guy who had some success eating salads, but his face was flabby like a Saint Bernard. Preston Delp. "That's our man."

"So what happened? He was gunnin' for you?"

"Just a minute." Buffa watched Delp descend the steps. He looked back and forth until his eyes landed on the Jeep. His step froze in midair, then he scurried toward the parking garage.

"He's getting away," La Rue said.

"That garage only has one exit," Buffa said. "Right there."

"So Rummans was giving you hell…"

"The people in court don't say anything for a minute, then they chuckle. It's like when your eighty-year-old aunt farts and don't know it. You laugh, but it ain't like one of the boys did it."

"You got hard time, right?" La Rue said.

"Three years. No parole. And the whole time I'm in the joint, I think, he had to say that about the library. I couldn't remember the last time I was in a library. I was awake at night wondering what kind of crazy shit he was learning. I couldn't even make up stuff to be afraid of, because I didn't know what to make up. Fuckin sick.

"Then I thought I was in a library too. I mean, all these fellas around me weren't innocent—not all 'em. I started asking how they got busted. I learned some moves. Most guys got caught because they made complicated plans. It's a simple world.

"Made me wonder how the hell I got caught. One thing I learned, always expect the double-cross. Loyalty ain't a two-way street. That's why I keep things simple. Three years is a long time, and it didn't go fast. But when I got out, I looked back at the twenty-foot walls with barbed wire, and at the rifle towers, and thought they did a hell of a job keeping Rummans out.

"Did you think he'd come for you?"

"Shit. I turned around; he was across the street, leaning against a phone pole. The day I got out! Had one heel hiked up like he was James Dean. He was a big son of a bitch, too. You can put on a lot of muscle pumping iron for three years. He waved at me and smiled real big."

A white Toyota Camry pulled from the garage and drove past the Jeep.

"Just sit like you're supposed to be here. Don't look at him, dumb shit."

Buffa eased out of the parking space and when the Toyota turned onto Third, Buffa gunned it through a U-turn. He sighted the Toyota a quarter mile ahead and followed.

"So he's there on the street." La Rue said. "What happened?"

"So I say to him there on the street, 'You look as dumb as the last time I beat your ass.'

"'I'm gonna fuck you up, Buffa,' he says, cheerful as hell. He stays there leaning on the pole. I keep walking.

"I decide to keep my eyes open, and make sure this guy doesn't catch me by surprise. The fellas I worked with before prison hooked me up with a place to live, and the Boss spotted me some dough. He said I should get on with my life, put prison behind me. Forget anything ever happened.

"So I went back to doing, you know, what I did." Buffa shrugged. "That's it."

"What did you do?" La Rue said.

"You know. The docks."

"Right."

Buffa took the left turn lane to Interstate 10, three cars behind the white Camry.

La Rue lit another smoke from the cherry of the old, and tossed the butt out the window. He offered the new smoke to Buffa.

"Then one day the cops took me to the station. Rummans was dead. They played that good cop bad cop shit for a while, and showed me a book."

"What kinda book?"

"I dunno. It had a cartoon picture of a helicopter on it. I said I never saw it and they let me go."

"He was dead?"

"Would ya shut the fuck up and let me tell the story?

When I pull into my driveway the temperature is a hundred and fifteen. My arms are burned and my hair has enough knots I think I'll cut it off.

I make a pot of coffee and sit. I want to sleep but my mind floats in a zone. I sit at my computer and close my eyes; an endless dotted highway line flashes one yellow strip after another, zipping at me from the darkness like bolts of laser light.

I've been here before, this generic road: a flash of headlights from the right, a crumpled Ford Bronco. Gretchen's side is smashed; the vehicle has rolled, and my unconscious face rests on pavement and broken glass; a smoking bread truck sits catawampus in the intersection.

I'm seat-belted in and hear muffled excitement around me. I don't know how long I've been unconscious. My pregnant wife hangs limp above me, suspended by a seatbelt. As the fog recedes I realize the blood on my cheek is hers.

I'm home. I snap my head to clear the vision.

Paramedics estimated they took twenty-five minutes to reach us. She was gone before I came to. Police never found the other driver, but they didn't look too hard. They had a husband who smelled of booze blowing .028.

I slam my fist on the desk and particleboard falls to my feet; the mouse jumps and my computer monitor comes to life.

Stocks like Google and Apple move fast. Liquid as water and fun to trade. Their options, more so. When I started, the bane of trading, bad news, handed me my ass. CEO Busted for Nailing his Teenage Daughter kind of news. The kind that makes a stock drop thirty percent in three minutes. Lose like that, you find a better way: Index options. With the S&P 500, it would take a dozen CEO's banging kids to drop the market. Not total protection, but better.

I expose myself to risk that comes in bushel baskets. I don't shave profits by hedging. I stand on a ledge with my dick hanging out while the market throws knives. If the market burps, I shit ten grand.

This is what it takes to forget Gretchen.

I open a trading platform and load four charts of the S&P 500. My pulse quickens. We're down three points on the day, trading at the bottom of a range. The glowing green and red tick marks flash with blinding speed and near-random variability. I'm flat right now, all cash, looking for an easy read—a pattern that tells me what the index will do, and how to know I'm wrong.

On my one-minute chart, the last tick bounces from an up-sloping trend. My Fibonacci fan predicts support. The four-period moving average on my three-minute chart is a hair away from crossing over the nine-period simple. I queue an order for a hundred calls. I've got a hundred and thirty grand in one hand, and a pair of dice in the other.

My fingers work a calculator, converting a percentage move into prices. If the index hits my number, I'm in.

I wait.

The S&P moves and I send the order. I'm in. Eight times out of ten, the move will last long enough to make a profit. Four times out of ten, I'll make five grand or more.

The move fizzles and a news alert pops up: Fed Chairman Bernanke has opened his mouth. No matter what he says, the market sells. I exit the position at a four-hundred-and-ninety-dollar loss. I'm flat again and wait to see if I get a move from the last top. I do. I buy a hundred puts and wait.

I'm whipsawed. Bernanke, apparently, believes inflation is at bay. The market reverses, and I've made a mistake I swore I'd never make again. I sell puts to close and do the math. I'm down three grand. Normally I'd decrease my position size and keep trading. The numbers always work out. But today the market holds nothing for me. I'm beat.

My eyes drift across my office. Books, a bright yellow Gadsden flag behind the ancient Zenith floor model television with original remote, a flintlock rifle on wall mounts. All of it reminds me of who I am.

Outside at my bike, I remove the plate that supports my Flagstaff identity and replace it with Nat Cinder's license. I'm me again, better or worse. I remove the registration and driver's license that match the other plate from my wallet.

I straddle the bike and back it out. My arms are red with sun and the sudden heat makes them burn. In five minutes I'm on the Carefree Highway, and in ten, I turn south on Cave Creek.

The Desert Broom branch of the Phoenix library was built in 1998. The abominably modern architecture has won many awards. The façade is rusted metal, and orange wrought iron poles hang like stalactites from the ceiling, stopping just overhead, looking like a prison gate about to slam to the ground as soon as you cross below.

Inside, I pull a familiar volume from the shelf, "Abraham Lincoln: The Death of Federalism." I sneak a gurgle of Gentleman Jack, drop the flask into my cargo pocket, and find a reading chair by the window overlooking Cave Creek Road.

I've been here every day this week.

I'm at my edge.

Chapter Three

Buffa's hands were cold but his back sweated against the leather seat. Buffa and La Rue followed Delp onto Interstate 17.

"North," Buffa said. "He's a long way from home."

"Does he know he got a tail?"

"Who gives a shit?"

They were silent.

"So how did Rummans die? You whacked him, right?"

"I told the detective the truth, mostly. When I got outta the joint, I went back to work at the docks, but I went back to the other work, too. Fresh out, a fella's got to go easy, and the Boss understood. He said he'd start me off with a job at a warehouse.

"I asked what kind of job, and he shrugged. 'Just bust up a meeting. Simple.' I like simple, and De Luca knew it. Rummans showed up outside my place that night, sitting in a Pontiac. I was on my way to the warehouse. I saw him before he saw me, and I went right up to his car.

"'I got a problem with this,' I said.

"'I got your problem right here.' He grabbed his nuts.

"I leaned up to his window and made a grab for him. He flinched back. Next thing he hit the gas and took off up to the corner. 'I wanted to see you one more time,' he said. 'A tough guy.' He burped his tires and took off, yeah?"

"Yeah."

"Before I got in my car, I checked underneath. Maybe he learned to build a bomb; I didn't know."

Delp exited the freeway on Deer Valley and drove east. Buffa turned and let the gap between them expand. "Delp knows we're on him," Buffa said. The road passed a small airport and after crossing Seventh Street, entered a wasteland bordered on the left by an aqueduct behind a chain-link fence, and on the right, shrubs and trash.

"Did he blow you up?"

"Do I look blowed up?

"Boss used to have us sort goods at an empty grocery warehouse. Cops raided it and he found another place. Driving there, I thought about all the things that didn't add up. The library comment three years before; the warehouse job—no specifics. How the Boss had said to use the west entrance."

Delp turned to Cave Creek road, northbound lane. "Where the fuck is he going?" Buffa said.

"This, ah, this goes to Cave Creek," La Rue said.

"You all right? You look jittery."

"No. No. Fine. So what happened? You kill Rummans?"

"I parked at the north side of the building, walked east and found Rummans' Pontiac behind some dumpsters.

"Inside, a row of offices was on the south wall. The truck bays was on the west, and the entrance I was supposed to use was between them. The meeting was through that door and to the right. I jimmied a window on the east side and eased myself in, then made my way up between a couple storage racks. Light came from the truck bays and a flashlight lit the office. There was a blowup black and white mug of me in the office on an easel. I could see it from thirty feet. Maybe they were sitting down, out of view, but the place was dead quiet. A meeting would make some noise, at least. I stood still and listened.

"Ahead, in another aisle, I saw a man's outline against a truck bay window. I waited and the movement didn't happen again. I crept through the pallet spaces to the other side and lined him up with the light from the office window. I recognized Rummans' shape and listened for other movement, other breathing. He was alone, watching the west entrance. Held a pistol in his hand."

Delp's turn signal flashed. The road was a split four lane, and he crossed traffic at a light. Buffa stopped behind him.

To the right a Fry's grocery store served as the hub of a new shopping plaza. Buffa looked at the hot wavering air over the hood of his Cherokee. Must be a hundred ten.

The left arrow turned green and the Camry jumped. Delp did a U turn and Buffa took a left. He U-turned on the side street and swerved back onto Cave Creek southbound, but the Camry was gone.

"You tricky fuck," Buffa said.

"So what happened?" La Rue said.

"I lost Delp. Look for him, idiot."

Buffa accelerated, glancing left and right for places the Camry could have turned.

"Well, Mr. Delp is a long way from home to go to the library."

Buffa turned into the lot and found the Camry in the back, on the left side. He parked at the opposite corner where he could watch the entrance.

A glint of chrome caught his eye. An evil motorcycle was parked about twenty feet away. It looked like a chromed-out school bus engine with a seat and two wheels.

"That's my kind of bike—'cept that yellow flag. Looks queer."

The license plate said, "TREAD."

They waited with the engine running and the air conditioner blowing. "So what happened?"

"Where was I?"

"You was ready to kill him."

"Yeah. I charged, hit him belly-high and drove him sideways into the door, thinkin' I'd bust him hard then follow him to the ground and beat the shit out of him, see?

"Rummans moved at the last second and I hit him crooked. He slammed through the door and I bounced off the jamb. I heard a whoosh sound and saw a black shadow with a silver edge swoop from above. Rummans screamed. It was a blade of quarter-inch sheet metal, about four feet wide and six feet long, suspended like a pendulum from the ceiling. Prolly weighed two hundred pound. The edge facing the door was like a razor. A couple pulleys and a rope linked it to the door."

"Fuckin A," La Rue said.

"Rummans was in two pieces on the floor. The pistol was next to him. His eyes was glassy. His guts was all the fuck over."

"Rummans," La Rue said. "What a bozo."

"'You coulda just shot me,' I said. He was still alive, for a minute, just looking dumb. I wiped off any prints; burned my shoes and clothes thirty miles away, you know the drill.

"So what was the book?"

"The book? Oh, yeah. The whole interrogation thing with the detective was a fishing expedition. I'll never forget the book, The Most Dangerous Game: Advanced Mantrapping Techniques."

"So how'd you get free of De Luca?"

"When the cops cut me loose I went outside. The Boss was parked down the street from the station. I got in the back seat with him."

"What happened?" La Rue said.

"Shut the fuck up. He asked if it went okay. I said, 'I been thinking about that warehouse job, Boss.' I was playin' it real cool. 'That was a present for you,' he says. He crumpled his hands. You know they're lying when they fuck with their hands, right? The driver looked sideways for a second. De Luca said, 'I heard Rummans was gonna be there, and I thought you'd appreciate the chance to put it all behind you.'

"Can you believe that shit? 'Chances like that don't come too often,' I said. I knew De Luca was lying about Rummans. There's no way I coulda been caught three years before without the Boss being involved. I didn't know what kinda deal they had. It wasn't the right time to call him on it, but me and Dante De Luca was on the same page."

"So how'd you get out?"

"I told the Boss I was going to Phoenix. I told him if he sent anyone after me," Buffa stared at La Rue, "he'd better be good and he'd better be fast. 'Cause if I got him first, I was coming back to Philly."

La Rue's hands folded in his lap, except his thumbs. They twitched. "That's killer," he said.

I take a slug of Jack. I'm half drunk and coming down from caffeine jitters, trying to read an eight-hundred-page volume of American history. The author claims Abraham Lincoln was the first and most powerful traitor against the infant U.S. Republic—that he alone returned us to the hands of tyrants. I sample books at the library before I buy them. My bookshelf is high-dollar real estate.

To the right of the printed page a pair of patent leather shoes angle toward me. They belong to a man I've ignored for the last thirty seconds, standing a dozen feet away. He has a flabby face and wears a suit jacket in the summer heat. His head is cocked and he's reading the spine of the volume in my hands. I've never seen him.

The man doesn't fit the FBI template, but he isn't a Jehovah's Witness, either. I glance along the window and down the 900 aisle. Both escape routes are clear.

"What are you doing?" I say.

"Oh, excuse me. I'm trying to see the book spine."

"Why?"

"I saw where it came from on the shelf, and—I'm Preston Delp." He offers his hand, and when I don't move, says, "I'm sorry. I was looking for a title."

He retreats to the bookshelves; I look across the library for other men in suits. Delp removes his jacket, revealing a wrinkled white shirt with sweat-stained armpits. His tie is choker-tight. He drapes the jacket over his arm and I glimpse a sliver of white, maybe an envelope, tucked in the breast.

My eyes move across the page but I watch Delp take a book from the shelf—a biography of Alexander Hamilton I recognize from twenty feet.

He carries the tome to a table, studies a few pages, and hunches over it with his suit jacket beside it. He looks to the library entrance. Then glances behind him, then to me. He replaces the book on the shelf.

"Not what you're looking for?"

"No. It, uh, I don't think I'll have time to read it."

He pulls another volume from the shelf, bigger than the last, and then three more from different shelves, and carries the armload away. I can't see the titles. In a moment he returns each to its slot on the shelf, and walks away.

"I've seen some stupid fish," I say. I go to the shelf and study the Hamilton book without touching it. Delp exits the library. I cross to the sliding glass door. "But that is one dumb bass."

Delp enters a white Camry and circles to the exit. At the same time a black Jeep Grand Cherokee backs out of the space close to my bike. It has muddy wheels, a swashbuckling grill and a Warn winch. I lock eyes with the driver, a dark-haired man with the look of singular focus.

That, I think, is an FBI man—but I'm not his target.

I scan the desert and check the cars in the lot. I'm edgy, on the cusp of transformation, like Yellow Horse with his hand on his boot knife. I've stockpiled ambition and resources for a rainy day, and a big fat drop of water just hit my head. It'll sprinkle a bit, and then the storm will come—and then it'll be time to spend.

Buffa flipped his cell phone closed.

"Who was that?" La Rue said.

"None of your fuckin business."

Buffa gripped the wheel and clenched his jaw. He'd hoped this job wouldn't get too dirty. He could make good money just following the guy around for a few days. The first time he talked to Patterson, it sounded like a simple tail job. Keep track of Delp, see if he was the guy they were looking for. But this last call was more strident. Patterson wanted the photos now. Today. ASAFP.

"We're gonna rattle his cage now," Buffa said. "So when we visit him tonight, he plays ball. Yeah?"

The split four-lane of Cave Creek road couldn't have been worse. Noontime traffic kept all lanes thrumming with cars. Each driver had a cell phone and most phones had a camera. Buffa hated the damn things. Everyone was a journalist, now.

Delp took a right onto Dear Valley, the same road they'd followed from the interstate to get to the library. Perfect. A couple miles ahead the road was slow, traffic rare, and the curves, wicked. It narrowed to two lanes, dipped through an arroyo, twisted back on itself three times. A rock quarry stood on one side and some kind of manufacturing firm on the other.

"Gimme a smoke," Buffa said. "And don't light it."

He took the Marlboro from La Rue. "You know you can kill somebody putting wool in a cigarette?"

"Nah."

"Yeah." He pressed the cigarette lighter. "Makes mustard gas."

Buffa flipped the cigarette and studied the tobacco end, then, holding the lighter to the smoke, he smelled water. He remembered the aqueduct, and powered the window down. Heat blasted in.

"Smell that?" Buffa said.

"Yeah. Smells like an oven. Roll it up."

"That comes from the dam. Must be a leak or something. All these plants."

"Yeah. Makes me claustrophobic."

"I'm gonna go up to the dam this weekend. A little bit of weed and the pussy's crawling all over you. A couple lines of coke'll get you laid all night," Buffa said.

"Yeah."

"You ain't been laid since you got here, have you?"

"Sure. Lotsa times."

"Bullshit. You got any dope we could take up there?"

"I don't do drugs."

"Not for me. For pussy."

"Nah. Not me."

"You like guys, that it?"

La Rue looked away. Buffa laughed. "Fuckin bone smoker. Watch this."

Ahead, Delp's Camry took the opposite lane to pass a bicyclist. Buffa followed, then pressed closer. He'd mounted a grill guard and winch to the front of the Cherokee. Never used them, until now. He gunned the engine around a tight turn and slammed into the back of the Camry at an angle; the Camry fishtailed, then corrected and accelerated.

"Yeah!" La Rue said.

Buffa pressed the gas again. "Just to make sure you know I'm here, asshole."

The Jeep's eight cylinder Hemi surged and again the grill rammed the Camry. Buffa watched Delp through the sedan's back window; Delp raised his hands and waved to add torque to language Buffa couldn't hear. The Camry squealed through the remaining turns.

The two vehicles raced up the exit side of the arroyo and the desolate area ended. New houses, all at various stages of construction, surrounded them. Clumps of dirt littered the road. Buffa hit one and pebbles and dried mud rattled his undercarriage. The road straightened.

A group of bicyclists filed along the white line of the road ahead, their legs oscillating in a rhythmic, relaxed strain, as if connected like train engine wheels. They wore helmets and spandex.

Ahead, a string of cars approached in the opposite lane. The first one's daytime headlights shimmered in the heat. Buffa looked at the cars, the cyclists, and back to the cars again.

He stepped on the gas.

Prison had an institutional smell, not quite as clean as a hospital but similarly sterile and flat. The walls were cement blocks painted tan, the floors linoleum.

Patterson looked at the bulletproof glass partition with crisscrossed metal filaments. The danger in this place wasn't that the killer would strike again. It was that a visitor would claim vengeance. That's why they had the glass.

Patterson looked into the eyes of a murderer, reformed or not. It was repugnant to be here; Patterson's kind of justice would have seen this man dead—and he was here to set him free. Patterson took a certain pride in being able to set aside his convictions when political expediency demanded.

He lifted the phone. "How are you?"

"I get to walk outside for two hours, three times a week. I can't see grass. Just a hundred thousand square miles of kitty litter, and a chain link fence to keep me from it. But I've learned gratitude. When you focus on the good things, like still being alive, it's harder to pay attention to the bad things, like this is no life at all."

"We might be able to change all that."

"You know I have friends on the outside? I've had a website and pen pals trying to get me free for years. This isn't going to work."

"It's already worked. All you need to get out of here is an understanding."

Patterson wrote on a yellow pad and pressed it to the glass. "These conversations are recorded."

Theen nodded.

"When this happens," Patterson said, "and it will be soon, very soon, we need to be clear. Your job will be to find a nice church with a lot of activity going on, and join it, and write your books, and talk to high school kids about the straight life."

Theen nodded. Patterson studied him. He had a sober face, but an unsteady one, as if joy and barbarity danced side by side behind a worn white sheet.

"The governor expects that you will also, when the day comes, be a strategic resource. A trustworthy person—an expert—we can go to off the record."

A small grin crept across Theen's face, and his teeth looked angular.

Theen nodded again. "If the governor was to restore my right to vote, I'd punch the ticket for her every time."

The events of the last fifteen hours are discordant. My sixth and seventh senses tingle, as if my three-dimensional image is this moment being studied six stories underground in an alphabet soup agency in Virginia.

With the Lincoln book back on the shelf I head for the exit. I'd borrow it, but I don't want to create a record for some investigator waving a copy of the Patriot Act to follow. Ten minutes have passed since Delp left.

The sliding glass library door opens and heat hits me like I've stuck my head into an iron smelter. I stride through; after a moment the sting of the sun on my arms chases away the coolness from the air conditioning.

The Gadsden flag is still on my Triumph. I forgot to remove it. Sweat breaks on my forehead and I look at the desert again. The cars in the lot have tinted glass and the sun's high angle makes it hard to see inside. I look for tailpipe exhaust or open windows; no one can survive the greenhouse effect inside a car in the desert. Every vehicle is empty.

There's road noise on Cave Creek and a dead gust flaps the pennant. I cut its plastic staff with my pocketknife and tuck it in my pocket.

I don't want to go home. I need sleep but closing my eyes is more than the conclusion of a twenty-four-hour period—it's a coffin lid slamming closed on a chapter of life.

I have too many secrets; maybe this is a good time to attend to one of them.

My son's name is Josh Golden. He lives with his mother Cyndi, a woman who performed a brief stint as my secretary in 1988 when I was a midlevel manager at Honeywell, two years before Gretchen died. Every man has a libertine inside him; I uncaged mine with Cyndi. She got pregnant and left the company. At first I funneled money to her to help support Josh. When Gretchen died, there was no reason to hide the cash flow, and by then our relationship was fiduciary. Who could blame her? Later I set up a trust and she still draws from it to support him. I'm not on the birth certificate. I am a benefactor, not a father.

Three years ago, I saw Cyndi alone at a grocery store. We talked. She was stiff and angry but ended up pulling pictures of Josh from her purse. His hair was long like mine and he was scrappy. His forehead was high and his eyes brooding. I wanted to know him.

I dated Cyndi for a year, nothing physical. She saw her son entering his teen years and worried the wrong influences would lead him astray. Phoenix offers ample temptations for a thirteen-year-old boy. Maybe I could help steer him toward a clean future. Right. She put one condition on our water-testing: she alone would decide if Josh learned I'm his father.

Josh came home from football practice one day with a bloody nose and a chipped tooth. I asked what happened and he said Coach Nichols did it. Stories are never as simple as a boy tells them, but before I thought, I recouped an eye for an eye with Nichols. I haven't been welcome at Cyndi's house since.

Josh and I communicate now and again. I buy gas where he works. He thinks I'm an old Army Ranger carrying a ten-pound chip on my shoulder, one nut among the many his mother has cracked. Truth is, Josh and I hit it off, and when Cyndi booted me, I let him down.

I head south on Cave Creek. At the rate I'm piling on problems I need to get rid of an old one. I'm like a woman buying clothes, throwing away an old set to justify buying the new. I'm going to see Josh. Call him aside. Level with him.

I may not get another chance.

Turning right on Deer Valley, a news van shoots through the intersection and nearly clips my back tire. I jet forward and it swerves behind me, then accelerates until its front bumper is inches away from my rear fender.

"Jackass!" I wave my fist and ease back on the gas. The bike drifts until I travel the speed limit. The van looms in my mirrors.

The road has a sporadic third lane in the middle. The van engine roars as the driver rushes into the center to pass. I twist the throttle to stay ahead until an oncoming car, waiting to turn in the middle lane, forces the news van to pull back behind me.

"Shit eating bastards!"

The van driver hits his horn and holds it until I salute with one finger.

The problem with modern society is that good people do nothing.

I slow as the road bends hard left. Traffic stands at a stop and I stamp the rear brake and squeeze the front. My rear tire slides and I'm still leaning from the turn; the bike skids sideways. I stop a few inches short of a black car. The van tires squeal and the nose pitches forward.

I pop the clutch in third gear. The Triumph pounces forward and stalls. The van rocks to a stop an inch from my thigh.

It's time for a come-to-Jesus.

I take a quick look around and boot back to the van, rap on the driver side door. "Roll it down, punk!"

Inside, a man with a goatee and glasses turns to a blonde in the passenger seat, one of the newest college girls to land a job pimping highway carnage for the local news.

"Open the door!"

The man rolls the window down a few inches. "I'm trying to get to an accident you selfish bastard!"

I punch his door and leave a dent. "I'll make you an accident."

He reaches for the shifter mounted on the steering column, backs up, rams it into drive and squeals between my feet and my bike. His tire rubs my toes.

The van careens in the oncoming lane and disappears around a turn. Lights flash through the trees.

Cars in the endless string of traffic behind me do three-point turns. Traffic approaches from ahead. The black sedan creeps forward. I want to turn like the others, but more than anything I want to find that television crew and bust glass.

I idle forward, making a game of balancing the bike while moving under five miles per hour. The black car has two men inside. Clean cut in suits.

Behind me a police cruiser weaves between cars in the oncoming lane; the hair stands on my arm but the black and white works past me and around the bend.

I get to the accident and find chaos. A police car with whirling lights blocks traffic; an officer stands before his car making a loop motion with his arm, urging drivers to turn. Three ambulances park at the middle of the scene and two television news vans stake claims at the periphery.

I turn short of the police car; my gaze follows black skid marks angling from the center of the road, cutting gouges through a ditch. Mangled bicycles lay on either side of the ruts. Frantic men and women in uniforms work on twisted, bloody bodies.

The ripped-open ground traces the path of a car that broke through a chain link fence and landed upside down in the aqueduct. Men crawl over the white bumper and scale down the undercarriage, tethered to others with nylon straps. They aren't trying to reach a body. They're readying the vehicle to tow it out.

As I turn, a hundred shards of red taillight plastic glint on the pavement, flashing me back to another accident from years before: a Ford Bronco smashed in the side by a truck. A dead woman. Blood, and enough guilt to drive a man insane.

I drive home, shaking.

I pour a snifter of Jack Daniel's on the rocks and grab the Zenith remote. The picture tube takes a few minutes to warm but the sound is immediate and I turn the volume low. The ceiling fan whirs and the lanyard rattles against the globe.

I see Gretchen. The bourbon's steadying affect spreads warmth through my face and limbs until I lay my head against the backrest, close my eyes, and awaken to the five o'clock news.

"…three cyclists are dead, and the driver of the Camry drowned. Witnesses say a black sport utility vehicle chased the Camry, which attempted to avoid the cyclists, only to hit a car in the oncoming lane. It then crossed back into several cyclists. The Camry crashed into the canal, where the driver drowned."

The television shows an unsteady image of the blonde from the van. The cameraman keeps the cones of her 1950's rack in the picture as he pans to the wreckage behind her. The car—a white Toyota Camry—is out of the water. I reach for the remote but the images stays me.

The screen splits between the wreckage and anchor John Festes. "That's terrible, Isabelle."

"Police are still questioning witnesses, and as you know, with four fatalities, both lanes will be closed indefinitely as the investigation continues," Isabelle says.

"Didn't earlier reports claim the sport utility vehicle rammed the Camry?"

"That was an eye witness report, John, which we have been unable to verify. Police are not elucidating."

"Any word on the identities of the victims?"

"Police were about to release the name of the Camry driver just as we were coming on air, and my assistant, just a moment..." She turns to someone off camera and accepts an index card. "It is Preston Delp, whom some of you may recognize from local government as the state minority leader's chief of staff."

"Terrible news for Arizona." Festes smiles.

"That's right John!" The voice, the rack—she's too perky for this kind of work, but the name grabs me. Preston Delp was the man in the library.

"Do we know the identity of the driver of the black SUV? Any plate numbers, or any way our viewers can help law enforcement?"

"We're waiting for a brief by a police spokesperson. They appear to be treating this as more than an accident."

"Thank you, Isabelle, reporting live from Deer Valley road; terrible news—"

I turn off the television and stare at the dot in the middle of the screen. Preston Delp worked for the Minority Leader.

I've become the nexus of bad things.

Preston Delp's boss, Minority Leader Dick Clyman, was my father-in-law.

Buffa didn't know how it happened. One second he rubbed bumpers, the next, the Camry swerved into oncoming traffic, collided corner-to-corner with another car and caromed across the road. Buffa slammed his brakes and watched the Camry spin sideways over three men in yellow spandex, crash the fence and splash into the canal.

Buffa swerved past the remaining bikers and hit the gas.

"Does this change things?" La Rue said.

Buffa took the next turn, a road that dumped into a residential area, and drove along empty streets with occasional Mexicans building houses. He parked at a roadside portable toilet with *Carter Sewage and Plumbing* on the side and opened the door. The stench of slow-cooked chimichanga defecate hit him like a punch in the gut, and he urinated outside against the blue plastic.

It took three hours to drop off La Rue and get home following only residential streets. The radio announced four fatalities, including the driver of the car. Buffa thought about the ramifications in the sauna-like heat of his garage, as he scrubbed white paint streaks off his winch. Afterward he thought more on the living room sofa with a glass of vodka. After a double, he slept.

He awoke to an throbbing head and a ringing cell phone. He knew it was Patterson without checking. Buffa drank a glass of water with a couple six-hundred milligram ibuprofen horse pills.

He made coffee. Patterson was a Marine with thirty years under his belt. He'd understand collateral damage. Hell, they weren't sure Delp had the photos to begin with. Buffa dialed Patterson.

"I'm in the car right now," Buffa said. "I'm taking care of it."

"How? He's dead."

"I'm visiting the missus."

"Call me on a land line when you have the photos."

The night air was cool after a day in the hundreds; cleaner, somehow, with a touch of humidity. The monsoon was coming. Rain in the desert was seldom a halfway thing. When it stormed, a guy wished he'd built an ark. Most of the time, though, the rain stopped when the bug guts were smeared on the windshield.

A couple of Internet searches gave him Delp's address and a map. State politicians' staffs didn't make enough to live in gated neighborhoods. They were the same as everyone else. Broke and accessible.

Buffa drove past the house. The only light came from an upstairs room—maybe a bedside lamp. Two cars sat in the driveway. One plate was from Nevada. Bingo. That's a five-hour drive. A guest stayed over during the initial days of grief.

Streetlamps cast a purplish glow but a row of maples blocked the light from the houses. Some had floodlights on the garage; Delp's didn't. Buffa drove up the road and back again, studying each parked car for the telltale glow of a cigarette or a silhouette that would betray the existence of a security detail.

No one here for Mrs. Henrietta Delp but me.

He drove a block, turned right, drove another, turned right, and parked. He removed a nine-millimeter from the glove box, chambered a round, checked the safety, and slid the piece into his shoulder holster. The road was still. A bat fluttered below a street lamp. Buffa put a roll of one-inch duct tape into his jacket pocket.

Most houses in Phoenix had tiny yards with six-foot privacy walls. The new, tightly packed houses shared block fences with no easy way to cross. Older neighborhoods like this one pre-dated the construction boom, and an undeveloped square foot here or there didn't trouble anyone. These houses had gaps between the cinder block fences, or no wall at all, maybe just a row of shrubs.

Buffa passed between houses, crossed a fifty–yard grassy depression where people took their dogs to play Frisbee and shit. He counted houses from the end to locate Delp's and scaled the six-foot block fence. Perched on top, he flashed a tiny mag-light to the back yard. No dogs.

He jumped.

His right foot landed on a rock and his left didn't. His ankle popped. A searing pain shot from his right heel through his leg. He gasped, caught his balance and hopped toward the patio—and then slipped and pitched to his rear.

A sound like a small animal issued from the shrubs; a second later, the sprinkler system spattered him with a cold spray. He hobbled to the patio and sat on the concrete, wiping fresh cut grass and water from his hands.

He had hoped this would be a silent, in and out job without disturbing anyone. Break, enter, search the den, find an envelope with a bunch of nudie pictures, and leave.

His ankle might change things.

Buffa pressed the bones. No pain. It was a sprain, a muscle and tissue problem. It would swell, but he'd still be mobile.

The sprinklers switched from the far heads to the near and he was in the spray again, even on the porch. Delp didn't know shit about adjusting sprinklers. Buffa stood and stabilized himself on a patio chair. He shifted to the right foot and took a tentative step. His ankle throbbed.

It was time to pay Mrs. Delp a visit, and that was her bad luck.

Josh Golden was three inches from heaven. Merry Paradise had just crawled into his back seat. The convertible top was down. He wove between the bucket seats and dropped into the back with her. He had the good fortune to lose his balance and land with his hand on her hip and his nose inches from her blouse.

She grabbed his head and pressed it to her bosom.

"Don't say anything." She said.

Josh complied. His mind raced, his hand drifted from her hip. He breathed her perfume and marveled at his mouth's proximity to her left nipple. He felt it stiffen under her top and he clamped easily with his teeth.

"nnnNNNnnn!"

She leaned against the armrest to block his hand and bent his thumb sideways. He pulled it, unwilling to yelp. Success required focus. Tenacity. Moxie.

She was a coldly self-possessed adversary; she never slipped, never let the jostling and touching turn into what he wanted, desperate, hungry, pugnacious sex. Her every move seemed designed by an angry God to both encourage and thwart him, but Josh knew with biological certainty that persistence would grant the ultimate reward.

"Do you love me?" she breathed.

"I thought you didn't want me to say anything."

She mashed his face into her chest again, giggling. Bare cleavage pressed his nose. Breast flesh on his nose! His chest pounded and he felt his pulse everywhere his heart drove blood to meat.

Josh pulled free and rested his head on her lap, looking to the sky defined on one side by the windshield and on the other by her bust. Rain might be coming.

He pulled his hand loose and touched her cheek, then let his hand fall slowly along her neck, seducing inch by inch, until she grabbed his hand and locked it to her collarbone. Josh adjusted his balance, placed left hand at the small of her back and bore his weight on his elbow. He put his mouth to her neck. She rubbed his shoulder. She moaned as his lips fell to the scoop above her left breast. He cupped the other with his free hand.

"Baby," she said.

He cradled it.

"Yes," she said.

He lowered his mouth an inch and pulled her top down. They hung bare for the third glorious time. He sucked her nipple and tried to fit every godgiven square inch into his mouth. He found her panties with his right hand and wiggled underneath them.

She cavorted and bucked. "Josh!"

He slipped a finger inside.

"Josh! Not yet. Josh?"

She pushed him away. "Something else? I'll do something else for you."

Josh sighed and pressed away, wiggled through an awkward moment of rejection and lack of balance in a back seat with a half-willing girl who ought to be all-the-way-willing by now.

This cat and mouse routine was turning into Tom and Jerry. The mouse was kicking his ass.

"What's wrong Josh?"

"I'm just thinking."

"About what?"

"Maybe we should see other people."

Buffa pulled a pair of rubber gloves out of his shirt pocket and slipped them on.

The back doorknob was locked. Gravel crunched under his feet as he stepped around the corner to the kitchen window, wincing with each step.

The window was open but too high to worm through. The next was lower; he slashed the screen with a switchblade and pressed the glass upward. Locked. He cut the next window's screen. Also locked.

Back at the patio door, Buffa removed a small glass cutting device with a suction cup on one end and an industrial diamond glass cutter on the other. He licked the suction cup, held it to the pane a forearm's length from the doorknob, pressed and rotated the cutter, sounding like a steel wheel rim on concrete. He froze.

A car door clanked shut; another followed, and a concentric light beam flashed through the trees in front of the house and traced along the top of the block wall to his left. Without releasing the pressure valve, Buffa yanked the cup from the glass; the window shattered. The flashlight snapped to the house. Rattled, Buffa freed the valve and the glass disc fell to the cement. For now, the wall protected him from the light.

He jumped on the wet grass and slipped, caught himself with his open hand and jumped against the back wall and scaled it. Every other step blasted a stab of pain through his leg. He flopped over the wall and jumped, absorbing the shock with his left foot, and hid behind a narrow row of shrubs. A second flashlight appeared on the opposite side of the house, swinging back and forth. A shadow moved in an upstairs window.

It screeched open.

"Fucking bastard's in the back!" A woman cried. "Behind that bush right there!"

The person with the flashlight on his left trotted along the outside of the block fence, cutting off Buffa from his most direct route to the Jeep. Buffa tracked their voices; the person on the right had circled around the front. The right was clear.

Pressing his body to the block wall, he rubbed the butt of his pistol. A shootout here would be bad news. He hurried along the partition, each step taking him farther from the Jeep.

"He's up by the wall! Get Him!" The woman shouted.

Who carried the flashlights? Cops? Rent-a-cops?

Still moving, he glanced over his shoulder; a flashlight beam projected from the perpendicular wall, sweeping back and forth over a broad range, and returning for a more methodical investigation of the same terrain. The man was cautious.

Buffa might get out without killing him.

He hitch-stepped along the wall. Adrenaline overrode the pain in his ankle and motion loosened the joint. He'd ice it later. Behind, the flashlight beam narrowed just around the corner. Ahead, the block wall diminished into the distance, forming a channel with occasional shrubs on the right, until it abutted against a chain link fence at an old warehouse. The wide-sweeping light beam neared.

Between housing blocks, the wall became a ten-foot iron gate, recessed a foot, over a concrete water drainage chute. He stepped into the setback sanctuary as the flashlight lit the darkness where he'd stood. His adversary swept the light back and forth. The gate behind him was too tall to scale and too close to the ground to roll beneath.

Several minutes passed; his heart thudded and sweat stood cold on his brow. Buffa peered around the corner to check the cop's progress.

Two feet away, around the corner, cackle from a walkie-talkie burst through the quiet. "Bobby—you find anything yet?"

Buffa pressed his breathing to a slow, quiet rhythm. He stroked the nine-millimeter's trigger with his index finger.

"I think she's just a little jittery." The man said, around the corner. "I haven't found anything."

"Come on back," came through the radio.

Buffa remained frozen, ready to step into the open and fire. A minute passed. He peered around the corner. The man who had been on the cusp of finding him turned the corner at Delp's house and disappeared. Buffa looked through the iron gate to make sure they hadn't flanked him, then stepped toward the abandoned building a hundred yards away.

"I'm sorry, Merry."

She leaned against the outside corner of the seat, her head pressing the door, below the glass. She sniffled and shuddered. He touched her thigh and she pushed his hand away.

"How could you say that? You say you didn't mean it, but you said it."

"I didn't mean anything I said."

Josh flopped against the opposite door. Her legs lay across his in the thin space at the center console; his shin pressed and augmented the rolling curve of her calf. She moved and her skin was like silk and smelled of coconuts. Though they'd argued, they remained nestled below the windows in the Mustang's back seat, with the roof open to the sky. Could anything in Creation be as intoxicating?

He had to dig his way out.

She wiped her eyes, smearing mascara. "I think you should take me home."

"I didn't mean anything," he said.

Neither moved for a long while. Merry stared ahead.

In the silence, Josh heard a dragging sound and the stutter of footsteps on gravel. The next iteration was closer.

The car rocked and a man groaned, "Fuck."

Merry's jaw fell open. Her eyes spaced with alarm. Josh raised his finger to his lips and leaned forward to peer over the back seat.

The man on the trunk moved. The car shifted under his weight. His back heaved with labored breaths. He watched toward the houses. "Shit." He leaned forward, supporting his torso with his hands on his knees; after a long second he sat erect and placed his palms on the trunk, arms wide.

Josh saw his shoulder holster set against the lit area beyond the corner.

"You better un-ass my Mustang."

The man lurched and his hand raced for his holster. The black outline of a handgun arced across the sky; Josh leapt from the back seat, tangling his legs with Merry's. She screamed. Josh stumbled over the backrest and crashed into the man at his shoulder, feeling forearm hair on his cheek and smelling sweat.

The man's arm twisted at the elbow, pointing the gun skyward. It fired. Josh's ears rang and the odor of gunpowder filled his lungs.

He tackled the man with all the force he could muster. The handgun flipped to the trunk. Josh drove the man off the Mustang and followed him, legs kicking against the bumper, into the pavement.

The man pushed Josh away with brawny strength. His hand closed on Josh's throat and squeezed; his fingernails dug flesh. Blackness encroached on the edges of Josh's vision and he wriggled to break free but couldn't. The gun flashed into his mind. It was on the trunk. Still on top of the man, Josh reached back, grabbed the cold metal and smashed the butt to the man's face. His head cracked against the pavement; his eyes were wide and empty. Josh hit him again, ripping a gash in his cheek. The man writhed. Josh smashed the butt to his face once more.

The man was still.

Josh stood trembling, gun in hand.

"My God you killed him!" Merry said, on all fours on the trunk. "Oh my God!" She climbed down and stood beside him.

Josh stared and his heart galloped. He stepped away, stretched his arms back and closed his eyes; fresh air expanded his chest. He struggled to let his mind resume control; to let the violence within him subside.

"It's me, Josh. Josh, put the gun down. It's me."

Finally his harsh breaths abated and he opened his eyes. He said, "I'm in trouble."

"We have to get out of here."

"I love you."

"I know. I—love you too."

Cool drops of rain hit Buffa's face, rousing him. The back of his head rested on gravel and his skin was numb. His ankle was swollen and immobile. He fought the blackness of unconsciousness and rolled to one elbow. Blood matted his hair. He groaned.

A security light just around the corner of the building cast a shadow where he lay. His legs stretched into the light. The moon had moved a quarter across the sky. Hour and a half. He sat up, brought his hand to his empty shoulder holster and glanced around. The kid had taken his gun.

The kid had kicked his ass.

Buffa dropped his head. Chilled, he staggered to his feet. His ankle fired a salvo of pain up his leg.

The kid would get it back in spades.

He limped to the Jeep, avoiding Delp's road, glancing ahead and behind for traffic or roving bands of hooligans. His body warmed with the action and his ankle loosened by the time he sat in the driver's seat. He pressed his foot sideways and the bones popped. His face hurt like hell and he flipped the sun visor mirror, scrounged a wad of toilet paper from a roll stashed behind the seat, and wiped crusted blood from his cheek. He tossed the paper to the floor.

A half hour later he sat on a recliner in his living room with his ice-packed foot propped on the coffee table. He watched the iridescent swirls of oil in cheap vodka the way a cave man might have watched blades of fire.

"I could go back to Philly."

He looked at the empty room.

"If I wanted to."

His bedroom pillow was on the sofa and he leaned against it, propping his head on his hand.

"Don't owe nobody nothing."

But a teenage punk had taken his gun and busted his face with it.

He lifted his phone and pressed numbers.

"Frankie? Yeah, I know what time it is. I need you and Tony on a special deal."

Chapter Four

The temperature has climbed to one hundred by the time I return from a run. My knees feel like bone meets bone with sand paper between, and my thighs are broken rubber bands. I am fifty years old today, and I feel as shitty as yesterday—but no worse. The breakdown is incremental, day by day; God phased-in our decrepitness to avoid the rebellion that would follow if it happened all at once, and the Machine learned from Him. Now we pay taxes before we see the income, and a hundred years of legislation has shackled us with too many laws to count. My head aches from it all, including yesterday's whiskey, but hair of the dog is out.

I won't drink before nine a.m. No exceptions.

I drop my Camelbak, half full of ice and water, to the floor.

Deep into heat exhaustion, I sit on the floor under the ceiling fan until the faintness goes away then force myself on wobbly legs to the kitchen for a special hangover-destroying elixir of parsley, carrot, and spinach juice. An old Juiceman sits on the counter. Old, but it still grinds the shit out of vegetables. I feed everything on my countertop through the chute and it spits out a frothy quart of juice that looks like sand art.

Being fifty does feel different than being twenty. It wasn't three days ago that I was a young punk, balls deep into this gal or that, to the sweet sounds of the Lynyrd Skynyrd band.

I log onto my trading system and see what's going on with the equities markets. The message light on my phone blinks.

"Nat. Hi… uh. This is Josh. Something happened last night. I may, uh, need your help. Uh. I'm going to work. Stop by. Later."

I play the message again.

"Must be in a heap of shit."

I didn't know he'd kept my number. Maybe he suspects the truth.

The second message is cryptic and muffled, but I recognize the way he says long vowels. "I'm on a payphone. I came into town just to tell you thank you for the lift. I appreciate it, my friend."

Yellow Horse wasn't built to be a twenty first century law-breaker—that, or he's losing his mind.

I bust a couple eggs into a pan and fetch the local rag from the roadside post box. Modern society requires a right-thinking man to be a chameleon, at times. My subscription tells me what color blends.

There's another good reason to get the paper. I like dark humor. Today, the front page documents the latest freedom march staged by nomadic bands of undocumented laborers, doing the work Americans won't pay Americans to do.

On to sports. Brent Davis, short stop, has a big write up. I scan the article. Baseball's as entertaining as watching a javelina rot in the sun, but I fold the page into eighths and put it in an envelope. My nephew in Los Angeles is a Davis fan; he'll get a kick out of it.

I scramble my eggs.

Back a few pages in section A, I find a story about a man killed yesterday in an unusual car accident, after running down three bicyclists. The paper has a black and white photo of the car under water.

I can't help wonder what he put in the Hamilton biography.

My trailer occupies a ten-acre plot off a chain of side roads that stem from Carefree Highway. The driveway crosses a hundred yards and I have to climb the hill behind my place to see my neighbors. Problem is, from the boulder on top I can see three million of them.

I pull a tarp from my bike, otherwise protected from the sun by a lean-to built of saguaro wood, corrugated sheet metal, and roofing nails.

Out here, there's no one to tell me I can't cook a steak on a campfire in the dead of a dry summer. I don't pull weeds. I moved here to get away from homeowners associations—clear, albeit anecdotal evidence American society has run amok. I blame the socialist instinct—a disease that threatens all democracies—but only infects them after people learn how easy stealing is if the government does it for them.

Soon enough, every citizen is a slave to an infinite number of meddling neighbors, and all are subject to the will of the Washington aristocracy. Fuck them all. I get worked up thinking about it. The answer, of course, is state's rights. Put government back into local hands, like Jefferson wanted from the get-go. People don't tolerate lousy government when politicians are close enough to hang.

I prefer coyotes and snakes for neighbors, quiet nights punctuated by the cries of long-extinct Hohokam Indians fending off Apache attacks. I've found seven hundred year old petroglyphs on the rocks in the desert by Cave Creek. Their specters whisper through arroyos, and some nights I can smell them cooking rabbit on juniper fires.

I don't get misty thinking about how pure a bunch of vanished people was, and I certainly don't wish I lived in their world. I don't admire their primitive ways. They used bows and arrows. I have a .50 cal sniper rifle, and can shoot the wings off a deer fly at five hundred yards. But I respect those early men. They were a hardy group displaced by a superior political power. They were atavisms, even in their day.

Like me.

I let the Triumph engine warm before climbing aboard. Have to let the oil circulate.

Silver Miner's bank in Cave Creek is a small institution named for a mine that never existed. "Silver" Miner was a man who started a bank on a lark, found he was making money, and passed it to his sons forty years later. A national chain bought the sons out a year ago. They fired the senior employees to improve their margins, and the new people are still learning to leave me alone.

"How are you today, Mr. Cinder?"

"Fine. Hot out. Like to cash a check."

"Sure. You know you can do all this online, now, at no cost?"

"Thanks."

"We can get you set up in no time."

"No thanks. I'm not on the grid."

The clerk counts out fifty one hundred dollar bills, projecting her doe voice like she's horny for a bull elk on the next ridge.

"If you had a debit card, you wouldn't need to carry all this cash. It wouldn't take but a few minutes to get you set up."

"Thought I told you 'no' the last time." I count the money.

"I see your balances are in cash. You qualify for our money market accounts, which are very safe, and would give you a much better interest rate."

"You mind letting me count?" I hold her eyes and she minds her tongue.

I start from the top. Done, I tuck the bills in my wallet and leave. The bike seat fries my ass but at fifty years of age, it's kind of nice. I head for the Desert Broom library a few miles out of town. Heat radiates from the pavement; in the distance, oncoming headlights shimmer like the road is wet.

The library parking lot has a couple of cars I've never seen. I note the colors, makes, and models as I cross the blacktop. The sliding doors part and the air conditioning hits me like a block of ice. Inside, from behind the desk, a young woman in an emerald green outfit speaks as I walk past. She's a freckled brunette like Gretchen, and she's new here.

"Do you need help finding anything?"

If she didn't remind me of Gretchen, I'd be a vulgar old man. "Know right where I'm going, thanks."

I find Hamilton tome and take it to the browsing area. Inside is a small slip of paper with flamboyant handwriting.

It's a Savage world.

I hold the paper to the light. Squint. Read the effeminate penmanship again. A sensitive man could have written it—maybe. I'm not sure. He may as well have decorated the corners with hearts and flowers. I leaf through the book pages. Nothing else.

Out the window, cars move through the parking lot of the grocery store opposite the library. Creosote leaves flutter in a tired breeze.

"It's a Savage world. The fuck?"

Amid the traffic on Cave Creek road, a black Jeep moves in the northbound lane. It has a winch. Muddy tires. Tinted glass. If I had a cell phone, I'd call the police. Or not.

Whatever Delp hid, he did it so the guy in the Jeep wouldn't get it, but I would.

"Savage world, savage world …" Bribes are savage. Politicians are savage. Indians … no, they changed that ….

Leaning close to the glass I get an angle on the Jeep, which sits in the left lane with its blinker on. After a U-turn at the light and fifty southbound yards, it'll be here.

I drop the Hamilton book on the end table and race to the bookshelves. Savage. Savage. There—a book by a talk radio guy. I yank it from the shelf. Another note. Same gay script. "The Time of my Life."

Preston Delp is shaping up to be a prick.

I drop to the bottom shelf where twenty Time Life coffee table books protrude and yank one after another, then stop to scan the top of all the books at once. There! Nineteen-eighty. Reagan's year. A gap in the pages gives up an envelope. I pull the volume and a white packet falls to the floor. I grab it and walk fast.

The restroom sits to the right of the exit. Three men in dark clothes step up the metal ramp to the library entrance. Their foot-steps ring like hammered iron, even inside. The front man limps, and has a bandage on his head, but I recognize him. The two in back have alert eyes and their heads swivel back and forth with their stride. I don't want to know these guys. They look so tough, it's like they walk in slow motion.

The glass doors slide open as I duck into the restroom. I watch around the corner.

The men fan to different corners. I mill about at the entrance beside a rack of IRS tax forms, tracking motions of all three men. The one with a bandage talks with the helpful girl in the green skirt; he gestures and she nods. A moment later she stands on her tiptoes and leers across the library floor.

I'm holding a 1040 EZ—sign here because we already own you—and she points at me. The man twitches with recognition. I bolt through the open doors.

"Hey! Stop!"

I bound across the mini-arroyo, scratch past creosote bushes to my Triumph at the corner of the lot.

The man with the bandage emerges from the glass doors and begins a hobbled run. The other two close the distance.

I goose the engine, turn the handlebars, lock the front brake, and pop the clutch. The tire peals and the bike whips in a half circle. Hot air blasts past me as I weave around cars and find the road.

I lean forward, adding weight to the front tire until my head hovers over the speedometer. Probably best I don't see it. I mash through the gears in seconds, swerving lane to lane around other vehicles. The bike accelerates so hard my legs want to flap in the wind.

I can't resist; I look down. One hundred and five. The bike has no faring; a collision with sparrow shit would feel like small arms fire. I pass cars so fast it's like they're in the oncoming lane. Oddly enough, the side mirrors don't vibrate—you notice the craziest shit at a hundred and five. Two miles down the road I back off the gas. The world drones around me, and my racing mind insists it is too slow, too slow.

Through the mirror, the black Jeep crests a hill and crosses lanes back and forth as it passes cars.

"Who are you?" I pat the heft of the envelope in my cargo pocket.

Deer Valley's on the right. I swerve and jockey the bike between potholes. Accelerate. The road takes three ninety-degree turns, ducks through a wash, and emerges to run parallel to a canal—where a crew mends a chain link fence.

This is where Preston Delp died, right after visiting the library, accosting me, and planting the envelope. The Triumph negotiates the turns with grace and eats the open stretch like a lion late for lunch.

"What's going on?" I rush the counter of the Circle K at the corner of Deer Valley and Nineteenth Avenue. Josh Golden frowns. He's been hitting the weights for football season and his skinny carriage is square with attitude.

"Took you long enough," he says.

"Been busy. You get some girl knocked up?"

"I shouldn't talk here."

"Look. I'm in a hurry, but I got your message."

Josh hesitates. He leans over the counter, fixes my eyes. "I think I killed a guy."

The words soak in. Fuckin-A interesting. "I guess I'm the one to call."

"He looked dead. I cracked him in the head with the butt of his gun."

"His gun?"

"I took it from him."

I nod. "Justified?"

"He sat on my Mustang."

"Can't allow that."

"You're one to talk."

Josh tells me the details. A woman enters the store and angles to the cooler for a drink.

"Where's the gun?"

"At the house."

I look out the window behind him.

"If you don't want to help, just get the hell out of here. I'll deal with it on my own."

Josh follows my glance to the black Jeep Cherokee pulling into the lot. I thought I'd shaken free but now I wonder if my shadow has resources. Connections. Or mere tenacity.

I lay an envelope on the counter. "The man who had this before me is dead. The one in the jeep is looking for it."

Josh narrows his brow. "So put it out in the open where he won't see it." He looks out the window. The man with a bandage on his face limps from the driver's side. "Oh, fuuuuck."

"That your guy?" I say.

"That's my guy."

"Good news. He ain't dead."

"He after me, or you?"

The bandaged man enters through the main door. He's in front of me and his limp is less pronounced. He's fronting, expecting violence.

Two men in dark suits come in through a second entrance off to the right side. Each wears a sidearm in a shoulder holster under his suit jacket. They circle the counter, moving with the smooth grace of a Marine Corps drill and ceremony squad—somber men prepared to deliver death with mechanical precision.

The woman in the back, browsing the potato chip aisle, slips around the side and exits.

The lead man faces us. "Both of you in one place," he says. "I'm walking between the fuckin raindrops today."

I recognize the phrase; the thug either reads Nietzsche or watches Oliver Stone movies.

"You should buy a Lotto ticket while you're here," Josh says.

The man lashes out with a mallet fist and crushes Josh's nose; Josh falls against the tobacco rack. Cans of Copenhagen and Skoal scatter to the floor. Blood spurts and Josh folds forward.

Why did I leave the trailer unarmed?

"Real tough kid, yeah? I was resting on your car. You're getting a good deal if that's all I do to you." He turns to me. I'm standing with feet spread and shoulders sideways.

"You want some of this?" he says.

If this was a hit, he wouldn't be making conversation. "Let's dance."

The other two step closer but the bandaged man lifts his hand. They halt. He stretches his open hand to me. I ignore it.

"I'm Joey Buffa. You and me? We got no trouble. You just had some bad luck and fell into something belongs to me."

I step sideways.

Buffa eyes the envelope on the counter. "What's that?"

"What's your interest?"

"I own it," he says.

I weigh each man in turn, thinking probabilities. "You own shit."

The bandaged man moves fast. His fist shoots stomach-level into my belly. I crumple; my lungs are flat and the muscle that opens them is peeling itself from my spine. The bandage man steps over me and swipes the envelope from the counter.

"You don't want trouble from me," he says. Bandage Head leaves and the others follow. The cowbell on the door clangs.

We don't have much time. I crouch on all fours, wobbly from the blow but satisfied by what I've learned. "We better get out of here. They'll be back in a minute or two."

Josh sits on the floor behind the counter. He finds a rag still sloshy from fountain soda and presses it to his nose.

"I'm surprised you didn't go apeshit on him." He sounds nasal. "You're the tough guy, right?"

"I learned what I wanted."

"What was in the envelope?"

"The sports page."

Bandage Head's crew enters their vehicle. There's a fourth inside. They drive west, into the sun.

"We don't have much time, son." I'm at the door.

"We?"

"You put the bandage on his face."

Josh slams the register, locks it, and darts outside.

A quarter mile up the road, the Jeep's taillights flash. The vehicle lurches through a three-point turn. Josh hurries his pace, still clamping the rag to his nose. A vertical streak of blood brightens his lime green shirt. He calls another uniformed attendant, smoking a cigarette around the corner.

"I gotta split dude." He tosses the store keys. "Register's locked."

Josh throws his leg over the seat. I swerve forward and crack the throttle. The front tire jumps a foot from the ground. Josh slides to the backrest, safe unless I flip the bike. The Jeep swerves into the lot. We rocket around the back of the store and across a vacant lot covered in gravel and glass.

Racing through residential streets, we provoke the only man we see to raise his fist and shake it. We zig-zag to Interstate 17, sprint three miles north to Happy Valley Road, and begin a series of rapid turns until the road stretches straight for two miles. I open the gas wide but only get up to fourth gear before turns force me to back off again. I'm ducking so low my chin is kissing the tachometer and still the wind wants to rip me from the machine.

We cross two miles of desert in a minute; I barely have time to brake before entering a new housing development. I follow a dirtbike trailhead to the right. I haven't been to my desert lair from this direction for a year—and never on a street bike—but the trail hasn't changed. I balance the heavy Triumph, but its smooth street tires slip as scattered rocks roll.

"Where are we going?"

"I've got a hideout. We'll be safe while we do some thinking."

I haven't seen the black Jeep since the wide open stretch, but this son of a bitch might have tools to find me. I didn't think to check the bike for a transmitter, but it doesn't make sense that he would've had the opportunity to place one. I look to the sky for a helicopter. Blue and clear.

One question leaps to mind: if Bandage Head is FBI, and he is chasing a guy on a bike that matches a description of a suspected accessory to murder, why is he satisfied taking an envelope and leaving the suspect?

I have no idea who follows me, or what I am involved in. But out here, surrounded by cholla and rocks, I'll take all comers.

We ascend an incline cut into the side of a steep hill. The bike shifts on the rocks. A steep drop to the right empties into a grove of purple barrel cactus and luminescent green cholla—nature's needles, hard as steel and sharp as razors. A heartbeat is enough to drive the needles deeper, and the barbs are so efficient at snagging passing animals, cholla has lost the ability to reproduce with seeds. It grows in impenetrable groves. Dumping the bike would mean hours with a Leatherman tool and more pain than a man would want to face sober.

I slip into a gulley and the oil pan scrapes a rock. I look back for a trail of black spillage and damn near dump the bike. Screw it; I'll know in a couple minutes if the engine seizes.

We crest the hill. The trail becomes sandy smooth and weaves between cacti and creosote. The flatter spaces look like dried mud and sand, but sharp, jagged rocks clothe the knolls that roll at the base of a prominent hill to my right.

Three brown cows and a bull wander amid the desert brush.

"This is pasture?"

"Thirty square miles of it. No fences, though."

"No wonder they're gaunt."

Josh points to the right to an unnatural slope with grey talus layered dark on the red hues of the surrounding terrain.

"What's that?"

"Mine shaft."

The bike hits a rut and bounces; Josh grips my midsection. A second later we crest a knoll and ahead is a house sized boulder beside a big juniper. The trail leads close and at the last moment, I steer over a rocky patch that won't leave a tread mark. I drive into a subterranean cave opening that's invisible from twenty feet away. The air is suddenly cool. I turn the machine off and Josh dismounts. The engine ticks.

"Unreal." Josh says. "You dig this out?"

"No, aliens."

"What, like illegals?"

I nod at the wall, where someone drew a Martian with charcoal.

"This is my desert lair," I say.

We're in a tunnel that extends forty feet and emerges on the other side of the rock. The ceiling is five feet high, the walls an equal width. After the steep sloping entrance, the floor is flat and dusty.

I've cached food, a jerry can of water, purification tablets, and a solar powered radio in a hollowed-out room halfway on the left. A nest of Chilean Mausers hides under a flat rock, wrapped in oil-cloth. A separate metal box contains enough ammo to hold off the Federales until the water runs out.

Josh walks toward the opposite end of the tunnel and peers into the dark cache room. I hear him tap a duffel bag of provisions. He returns.

"So, uh, what's going on?"

Rentier sat in a 1994 Bell *Jet Ranger* helicopter, picked up at auction last year for a cool quarter million. The Republicans pitched a fit but the executive had to be mobile, and the state police had complained they needed their helicopters to ferret out criminals.

The whine of the engine heightened; she unlaced her hiking boots. Even in Williams, just west of Flagstaff, it was hot enough to sweat. She rubbed her heel. The photo op had required a mile-long hike in unbroken boots, enough to coax a blister on her heel. The cool cabin air pasted her sleeves to her sweaty arms and a single cold bead darted from her armpit to her bra strap.

Sometimes the little things took too much time. She spent the morning at an outdoor award ceremony while homeless people wandered in search of a morsel for breakfast. Playing the bigger game was important, but her myopic side yearned to climb into a ring, take off the gloves.

Find a single enemy and kick his ass.

She slipped on loafers and tapped Patterson. Showed him her cell phone. "I'm stepping off the craft for a minute."

Patterson leaned to the pilot's cabin and said, "The governor's had a delay!"

She darted forward of the aircraft, fifty, then a hundred yards. The engine whine simmered lower and she pressed her cell phone to her ear.

"Jennifer—connect me to Speaker Ortega."

Rentier stood behind a giant hemlock and breathed the damp scent of pine needles and humus. The air smelled moist and cool. Maybe she should schedule—

"Governor. So nice of you to call."

"Marisol—I won't keep you long."

"That was quite a story in the Phoenix Times this morning. A person could almost think you sponsored Vallejo."

"Meg is a lovely reporter and I indulged her," Rentier said. "Now that you mention it, where is Vallejo?"

"I'll know in an hour. If I can't flip one of my own, I'll buy a Republican. Either way, I'll try to call the vote this week."

Rentier frowned. "You know the special interests will take it to court, one way or another. Every delay risks votes this fall. We need to be seen as having momentum with this."

"I'll try."

Rentier pressed her fingernails into her palm. "Of course you'll try, dear. How's the fall campaign shaping?"

"Well, they're spending bit to retake my seat. A woman Democrat Speaker—that's hard for the good ole boys to take."

"You should find a group of good ole girls. I'm about to get on the helicopter, but we need to talk about the future. Vallejo, the fall elections. Beyond. Let's get together at my retreat in Sedona."

Rentier re-boarded the helicopter. The rotors thwapped overhead. The pilot watched her enter and buckle her seatbelt. She nodded. Soon he would initiate take off and the noise would prohibit conversation without headsets.

Patterson closed his Blackberry and scowled. He leaned to her ear. "The AG won't budge on Theen."

The rotors thudded overhead and the seats vibrated.

"Tell me you didn't ask her to support my pardon of a death row inmate in a goddam email!"

Patterson stared, blank.

"Mick—where's your head? What did she say?"

"Theen's dangerous." He glanced to the pilot's cabin. "But we need him," he yelled.

"I'll talk to her."

"She won't do it, I'm telling you."

"You don't tell me anything. So where's Buffa?"

"He went to Delp's house last night. Security drove him off. He has other leads."

She grabbed her headset and gestured to his. He donned it.

"Do you see what's happening?" she said. "Vallejo will pass and I have to sign it quickly. But I can't until I have the photos under control. I don't want to have to talk to you about this tomorrow."

Josh watches me like I might be the enemy. He doesn't know anything except I showed up at the gas station two minutes before the guy that rearranged his nose. He kicks the dirt and waits for an answer.

But first I need to understand what happened to him last night.

"How do you know Bandage Head?" I say.

"I told you that."

His nose isn't broken, but his nasal passages are plugged and the bridge of his nose is blue. Dust sticks to the sugary film left by the cloth he used to apply pressure. He sounds whiny.

"Where did you see him last?"

"Last night. Parking by a warehouse on 35th."

"What happened?"

"I looked up from the back seat and he was sitting on my trunk."

"And you decked him?"

"That's right."

His voice has a cocky weight-lifter edge. He thinks he's the baddest son of a bitch in the city. He's my son and I love him but he's an idiot.

"He decked you back, huh?"

"Piss off."

"You ever see him before?"

"Never."

"Did he threaten you?"

"Didn't have a chance. I was all over him."

"So he's sitting on the trunk and you're in the back seat. Was he looking away?"

Josh turns. "I saw his shoulder holster."

I nod. "You preempted him. I would have too."

We fall silent.

Josh says, "So what's your story?"

I tell him about being at the library, Delp's death, and the envelope.

"How long do we have to stay here?"

"All day."

"Screw that! I'm going to see Merry tonight."

I say nothing.

"Where are we?"

"I know you're used to taking care of yourself, but I want you to think this through."

"You don't understand! She thinks she saw me kill a guy."

"She'll get over it."

"You're a piece of work. I don't know why I called you."

"Tell me about her."

Josh sits on a rock and leans against the cave wall. "What's in the envelope?"

"Haven't opened it."

"Open it. I want to see."

"Whatever it is, it has to be dirt. Enough to ruin somebody. Enough to kill somebody."

"They're already trying to kill us."

"No. You need to learn how to take a punch without getting your panties in a wad."

"Whatever. You're some tough guy. You just stood there and took it."

I charge him. He's surprised and slack-jawed. I cross my arms at his throat and shove him against the cave wall. "I could have killed all three of them by the time you hit the floor. I didn't. That should teach you something."

I release him and back away, expecting a flurry of angry-punches. Josh dusts his shorts. He steps from the cave into the sunlight.

"Don't go out into the open yet. That'd be a bad decision."

He charges back into the cave. "You ever wonder why you have such a fucked up life? You ever wonder why you live in a trailer on the edge of nowhere? Why you're nothing but a loser alcoholic?"

"I never wonder about that, Josh."

"I'll tell you. You make bad decisions."

"I do."

"You don't know about women."

"Never truer words..."

"Drink yourself into a sorry mess and treat people like trash! Then blame your shitty life on the rest of the world. You're a gem."

I nod, feeling heat flush my face. "I know it."

"So don't tell me about bad decisions!"

"I'm here because of right decisions."

"We're talking about you walking out on my mother after milking her soul dry, you egotistical prick."

I suspect this isn't the time to reveal our genetic link. Josh leans at the cave entrance, partially in the light. His silhouette pouts.

"You ought to call your girl." I say.

"I left my cell at the store."

"I guess you'll have to walk about four miles to find a pay phone." Josh glowers and leaves.

A minute later he stands at the entrance again. "Where are we?"

"Stick with me, and you won't have to ask questions like that."

He stares. I stare back.

"She'll understand when you tell her why. For now, let's just think this through."

"How do we think this through without knowing why he's after us? And how do we know that without knowing what's in that envelope?"

I remove it from my cargo pocket and throw it to Josh's feet. "You open that, there's no going back. You're in."

"I'm already in." Josh picks it up and rips the top.

Back at her office, Governor Virginia Rentier waited for Jennifer to place a call. The light blinked.

"The minority leader on line two," she said.

Rentier lifted the phone. "Hi Dick. That's terrible news about Preston. Terrible news."

"Well, it is," he said. "But it doesn't change anything between us, if that's why you're calling."

"You have my condolences. Of course I'll attend the funeral."

"You'll be as welcome as anybody. If there's nothing else, good day, Governor."

The line clicked. She smiled and opened the file Patterson gave her. Rudy Ging Theen. RGT on the forehead.

His eyes said one thing: Irredeemable.

She had to win elections to help people, and winning required she champion positions that didn't feel right. Sometimes the imperative lay with the quality of the statement—how well it could be synopsized and sound-byted into something that made sense in a ten-second television clip. A stand like this—releasing a rehabilitated death row inmate—boiled down to the right message. Government institutions can heal people, and here's the proof.

If people never got over their distrust of government, they'd never see all the wonderful things it could do for them.

I take the photos from Josh's hand. "Satisfied?"

"Who are these women?"

"The one with the big hooties is the governor."

"She's like the president of the state, right? What's her name?"

"Virginia Rentier. Yes, she's the chief of the state's executive branch of government. Don't they teach you anything in school?"

"Well, I have a home economics class and I can darn my socks. And I've learned to accept guys who think they're girls."

I study him.

He smiles.

"Another good reason to get government out of schools."

"These pictures don't tell us anything," he says.

"They tell a little."

"The governor gets her freak on with other women."

"Aside from that. We know the dead man—a Republican—was set to blackmail the governor—a Democrat—with sex photos. The photos tell us the guys with their noses up our bungholes ain't taxpayer funded. The governor isn't going to trust the police because she has to think about leading them after the dust settles. She wants to handle this without any dust—and that means contracted help."

Josh nods.

"The man in the Jeep isn't going to read your rights. He isn't FBI," I say.

"Why did you think he was FBI?"

"Never mind."

"So how do we get out of this?"

"I don't know yet. Maybe just give the governor her pictures back."

"Seems like the right thing. It's none of our business."

"True, but I need more information. And the whole hitman thing kind of grabs my balls."

The sky darkens and stars emerge. The moon breaks over the mountains, promising light to steer by. I step back inside and the silver glow of the tunnel entrance and exit bookends the darkness inside. I stand at the front of the motorcycle, tightening the headlamps. I've just disconnected the wires.

"You ready to get out of here?" Josh says.

"I'm hungry enough to eat the ass end out of a number two skunk."

"I could eat baked beans out of a dead cowboy's ass."

"You win."

"If we get moving, I'll still have time to see Merry."

I shake my head and start the bike. Josh climbs aboard and we emerge on the north side into the night air. I circle around the boulder and back the way we came. The pace is slow and the engine barely idles to keep us moving.

At the bottom of the grade the trail switches left and drops into an arroyo. I stop, ask Josh to dismount, and reconnect the headlamp wires. The light catches the outline of a coyote standing frozen with its green eyes peering into the dual headlamps. Fearless, it watches until Josh climbs back on.

"A thing of beauty," I say.

After another couple of minutes we find Norterra Parkway, then southbound Seventeen. I seek a black Grand Cherokee but in the dark the distinction is useless. Near the 101 interchange the streetlamps light the road in an amber purple hue. We exit at Peoria Avenue and turn into the Metro Center, a mall with a circular parking lot and ancillary businesses on the rim. One is the Xavier Hotel, a favorite of businessmen and prostitutes. I park in the back beside a trash dumpster. The hedge on the corner will block anyone from seeing the bike. I feel safe for the night—enough to get a drink.

We get a nonsmoking room with two queen beds.

"I'm gonna grab a shower and use the phone," Josh says.

"The phone is where they get you."

I walk across the street to Whataburger and buy six of the greasiest burgers they make, loaded with bacon, cheese, and jalapeños, and grab a couple quarts of soda. Circle K sells Jack Daniel's and I buy two pints.

Approaching the hotel door with a greasy sack in one hand and an open bottle in the other, I slow. The hair stands on my neck. I climb the steps and look at the crack of light around the curtain. The door is locked but my sixth sense clangs. I slip the plastic key in the slot. The room smells of humidity and soap—the shower has been used.

"I have three of the baddest burgers in the west for each us." I look for moving shadows, a ninja hanging from the roof, but the room is empty. The bathroom is empty.

Josh is gone.

There's no sign of struggle. He took off to see Merry, I tell myself. He's reckless, but what sixteen-year-old isn't? I grab a burger and toss the sack on the end table. Take a bite. "What a burger," I say, and spread the photos on the bed with my clean hand.

"So this is how a gynecologist feels."

The photos are of the governor with three women—so explicit I can pert near smell 'em. Artistic at times, as if taken by a connoisseur. Passion flows from the ferocity of their snarls, ecstasy from the arches of their backs. I recognize none of the other women, but their eyes belie their poses. All three women share the same hollowness. They make business, not love.

Chapter Five

The noise of the helicopter rotors penetrated the insulated cabin but with the special noise-reducing headsets, the ride was quiet. Speaker of the House Marisol Ortega watched Sedona's red rocks through the window, enjoying a view quite different from the one obtained in a car or hiking trails.

Rentier patted Marisol's skirted knee and smiled.

"This is the part I love!" Rentier said, "Going down!"

Marisol gave a half smile. She'd heard the rumors, of course, but could Rentier truly be this forward? Could the Governor have the Speaker in her sights?

The house was secluded in the woods a few miles from touristy Main Street Sedona. As the helicopter descended to tree level the red rocks stood proud of the sky and the setting sun washed them in a deep ocher hue.

The helicopter landed with a subtle jar and after a moment the engine's whine lessened.

"You are free to disembark, Governor, Speaker. Hope you enjoyed the flight."

The rotors chopped the air as they exited; Marisol leaned forward and strode toward the front of the craft, and then to the side after emerging from the blade radius. The sprinklers had been on and the cool air smelled of water.

Marisol observed a ranch-style cabin with a wide, roofed deck extending the entire front and side. Behind the house, ponderosa pine filled a thin cove and obscured the base of a five-hundred-foot rock precipice that, with elevation, changed from red to white.

The governor led across a manicured lawn surrounded by an orchard. Smaller cabins, all part of the main estate, littered the tree line.

"Is this a getaway or Camp David?"

"Both."

They crossed the rough-timber deck and entered a great hall with stone fireplaces at either end, a bull elk head mounted above one mantle and a snarling wild boar over the other. Their footsteps echoed under the twenty-foot vaulted ceiling.

"Who decorated?"

"I did. Like it?"

"I can see knights drinking honeyed mead, telling stories about dragons and virgins."

"I see cowboys telling lies. They drink whiskey, and they're surrounded by whores." The governor laughed. "This is my boardroom when I need to recharge but have to work. Follow me. It's a little more comfortable out back."

She led through a large kitchen, with copper pots and pans hanging from a roof rack over a cutting board island that smelled of walnut oil. A servant waited at the door.

They stepped into a glass-enclosed patio and Virginia motioned to a teak chase lounge with brass fittings. "Have a seat. Relax."

Through the windows, high above them, the sky turned grey and the red rocks glowed with the last rays of sunlight. Below the shadow line, the rock walls were forbidding and dark.

"Don't you worry about people out there? Looking in?"

"Security patrols outside, and frankly, you get used to people watching you." She turned to the man. "Rafael, I've been thinking of your prickly pear margaritas all day. Care to join me, Marisol?"

"Make that two, please." She slid into the lounge and kicked off her heels. She crinkled her toes, pressed her back firm against the lounge until vertebra popped.

"Rafael is a man of many talents. He fixes the best margaritas in town, and he is a masseuse. You should have him work on your back."

"Mmmm."

Rafael poured Cuervo into a shaker. "I will make you feel like a million dollars," he said.

"You don't have an accent. Tu hablo?"

"Yes. But it is not permitted."

"I'm doing them a favor," Virginia said. "Our culture is full of bigots who will prevent them from rising to their true stature if they sound different. I hold a strict line: no Hispanic culture in this house. No language, no food, no holidays."

Marisol nodded, eyebrows arched.

"Sal?" Rafael held the glass up and winked.

"Please."

"I heard that," Rentier said. "If his hands weren't so magnificent, I'd fire him."

A moment later he brought their drinks and stationed himself at the door.

Rentier sipped. She leveled her head at Marisol. "Where is Vallejo?"

"One vote short. Clyman's fighting tooth and nail. He's used procedural tricks I've never heard of."

"You're the majority. Who's the turncoat?"

"Mulrooney."

"Throw him off committees. Threaten to support someone else in the primary. Crack the whip."

"I try to lead by building consensus."

"Mumbo jumbo. There's that word again, *try*. Consensus is just agreement. Leadership is how you get it. Until you dominate the math they use to calculate their political survival, they will ignore you. Someone else will dominate them."

"I've been firm."

"Threaten Mulrooney's chair in Ways and Means. He'll fold when he sees a woman about to give him a public flogging." Rentier drank again and her words formed around the upended glass. "Then he'll be your bitch."

Marisol giggled.

"Good. I can expect the bill on my desk by Monday, then?"

Marisol drank; the alcohol was strong. She placed the glass on the tray. "You've been very proactive on this bill…"

Rentier nodded. "This legislation will have consequences. Most of the time, it's hard to tell if we're helping or hurting. Government gets gummed up. That's why Bill Clinton was effective—he cut through."

"A great president."

Virginia rubbed her scar absentmindedly. "I said effective. Government doesn't need to be big and expensive. It just has to work. It amuses me; the right-wingers say 'we will always have our poor.' And we progressives say, 'maybe not, if we just try.' What's the harm in trying?"

Marisol nodded.

"The key is getting people to look beyond their selfish interests. Sometimes you have to do it with force. Then you have progress—like Vallejo. Lives improve. Wealth moves from the top to the bottom, and things begin to change. Your people see that."

"My people?"

"Hispanics vote Democratic—and it's a damn good thing. We're losing the elderly and aborting a million white and black Democrats a year. Your people are going to save us."

"You don't believe that?"

"Come on."

Marisol shook her head. "Hispanics want government that works."

"Hispanics reproduce," Rentier said. "The elderly don't. Hispanics follow opportunity into Republican held territory. Old people just drive back and forth between Pennsylvania and Florida. It isn't all roses, though. Hispanics haven't embraced sexual liberation. Still a little uptight."

"We're Catholic," Marisol said, her mind elsewhere. Pennsylvania? Florida?

"And as they earn higher incomes, they begin to vote against us. We have a fight on our hands."

"But only if they earn higher incomes. The migrants…"

Marisol stared. The pieces fit. She triangulated, worked moves, weighed risks, absorbed potentials. Behind the simple calculus lay a more sophisticated equation of political strategery. The Vallejo bill would enable large numbers of a migrant society to identify with Rentier as they moved across the country, upsetting the electoral balance wherever they stayed—and they had a propensity for drifting into Republican strongholds.

Rentier was laying the groundwork for a presidential run.

"What year will you run?" Marisol said.

"Sixteen." She shrugged. "Twenty."

Marisol nodded. This Sedona visit was anything but innocent or accidental. It worked on three levels so far and the conversation seemed a personal invitation to earn Rentier's trust. Or was it staged to earn Marisol's?

It all came down to the House of Representatives, and Marisol Ortega was in charge. "You'll get Vallejo on Monday if I have to kill somebody."

"You may prove yourself indispensable."

"I just want to keep doing the people's work. They need us. Some of these people—you wonder how they get along without us."

"They can't. That's the point. But we can't do their work if they don't vote for us."

Virginia held her drink to Marisol in a toast. "To a new vision." They touched glasses and Virginia finished hers.

Marisol took another sip. It was better this time. She drained the glass in a long swallow.

"Well, sweetheart, let's put on our robes," Virginia said. "Rafael is waiting."

The kid worked at a gas station. Buffa staked it out from a Kentucky Fried Chicken, Pizza Hut, and Taco Bell parking lot. He sat alone with the windows open until the breeze kicked back the rancid odor of his sweat. Billy Idol wailed about a rebellious woman who saw him to bed, he said. Or did she give him head? Buffa tapped the steering wheel.

He got out of the jeep and winced when his foot hit the concrete. He labored across the lot, scratching the skin next to the bandage on his cheek.

The kid had a Mustang convertible. Not too much chrome. It looked stock, but clean, and the wax job reflected light like polished onyx.

Buffa removed his keys from his pocket and gouged a streak from the rear taillight to the front fender. Cut paint rolled up against his fingers and forced him to look around in case the scraping sound attracted attention.

Buffa bought a cup of coffee at the gas station. Walking back, he checked his handiwork with a sideways glance. Nice.

His cell phone rang. He read the number. Patterson.

"Yeah?"

"I didn't hear from you."

"Good news, bad news, yeah? I have a good lead on who got the photos. I'm just waiting to pick them up."

"That easy, huh?"

"Fuck no. I'm gonna raise the price if it keeps up like this. I got expenses."

"Our client is restless. I'm restless."

"Your client don't push me, got it? Now I'm gonna do a job here, and do it right, and this bullshit ain't gonna make me do it different. Yeah?"

"I need results yesterday."

"You'll have 'em tomorrow."

Josh took a bus and walked a block to reach the gas station where he'd left the Mustang, never feeling quite so exposed as crossing the bridge over the wash. If a Jeep jumped the sidewalk he'd have nowhere to go except over the side, with a thirty-foot fall to the rocks below. He quickened his pace, but couldn't jog. A blood clot blocked his nasal passage.

The security light above his Mustang lit a squiggly bare metal pinstripe from front to back. He saw it from thirty feet. The air left his lungs; his face grew hot. He turned a circle, no black Jeep. Bandage Head hadn't stuck around. Josh trotted to the car and, on his knees, ran his finger over the gouge, cut to bare metal.

He scanned the lot again, looked at the people inside the quick mart, then the folks eating at the neighboring fast food joint. He fought the rising temptation to kick his Mustang.

The roof latched to the windshield frame on both sides. He unclasped each lever and hit the switch. The night sky opened above him and a chill ran down his spine.

He pulled from the side lot to the front, left the engine running, and jogged inside for his cell phone.

"Hey cheese nuts, you're in trouble," his buddy Ron said.

"Yeah."

"Boss man heard you took off."

"A customer busted me in the nose. Look at this. I had to get it checked out. Why didn't you cover for me?" Josh grabbed a handful of beef jerky and a Lunchable from the cooler.

"I didn't see nothing."

"I'll handle him later."

He paid.

First he'd go home and ditch his stinking clothes. Then he'd shower.

Back in the car, he pressed Merry's speed dial.

"I want to see you."

She looked better than ever: a skirt that revealed where her thighs narrowed to join her rear and a top that made him want to grab in the middle and pull. She hopped into the passenger seat and gave him a peck on the cheek, but her eyes held his longer than usual, and she sat with her legs angled away.

"How do you feel?"

"Fine. What do you mean?"

"You know. Are you okay?"

"Fine."

Josh drove; the wind picked up and he turned the stereo on loud. He could feel her studying his nose; he turned and found her eyes wet. He hadn't noticed the jittery look.

She feared him.

"Could you put the windows up so we can talk?"

Josh did, and tapped the stereo off. He took a deep breath. "The guy from last night isn't dead, and the situation is a lot more complicated than I thought."

"How?"

"I called Nat before work this morning—the ex Army guy my mother dated. Just to get him to call me back so I could ask him some questions. You know—he's an old G.I. Joe, or some shit. I thought he might know what to do ..."

"So this guy is still after you? How do you know he isn't following you right now?"

"I've been careful."

They drove on Scottsdale Road, headed north. Josh slowed and turned into a scenic nature drive, a dirt road twisting through the desert, passing cacti and juniper, creosote here and there, aloe and Spanish Yucca with pointed bayonet leaves sharp enough to impale a man. He stopped where a thicket shielded the car from the road, fifty yards distant, and turned the engine off.

"It's creepy out here." She looked straight ahead.

"We always come here."

"We don't always have some Bandage Head trying to kill us."

"It's not like that."

"And we still have to talk about what you said last night."

"I also said I loved you."

She smiled and kissed his nose. Her scent was like Christmas. "It's still creepy out here. I guess I don't like being in a car with the top down."

"Want me to put the roof up?"

"Then we won't be able to see around us."

"Maybe if we were in the back seat, and I sat up, you know, to keep my eye on things—maybe then you'd feel safer if you hunkered down, sort of lower …"

She punched his arm and giggled. "Mmm. If you put a Coke can on the back of my head again, I'll bite."

Still in the hotel room, waiting for Josh, I study the photos and down a pint of Jack gulp by gulp. The governor looks good in the buff; all naked women are vulnerable and this one is no different. The Neanderthal who hides behind my cerebral cortex and handles a good deal of my thinking interprets the naked governor as a woman in danger, and his protective instinct is aroused.

I reject using these photos of her most private moments to bend her to my will. Whoever took these photos is her inferior.

If not for the men who killed Preston Delp, I'd send her the envelope and tell her where the pictures came from.

Pounding on the door startles me. I roll from the side of the bed, conscious of the squeaking mattress, and slip to the side of the window where the curtain gaps from the wall. Josh stands outside, grinning like a girl burped his clown. Below him in the lot a dark vehicle pulls in. Its headlights point toward Josh and I can't place the make.

The headlamps turn off. There's a winch. Bandage Head gets out and favors his right leg.

I unlock the door and swing it open.

"They followed you, son. Close the door, now!" I sprint across the room and tuck the envelope of photos into my pocket. Pull my boots on and yell, "Get inside, lock the door, and come on!"

I put a half-full bottle of Jack Daniel's into my right cargo pocket and slide the balcony glass door open.

"What are you talking about?"

"Lock the door and come on!" I swing my leg over the rail.

"That's three stories."

"Follow me."

Pounding erupts from the door like fifty Saxons with a battering ram. I lower myself from the rail, climb down to the concrete slab. I release my clutch, swinging forward, and land on the next patio. A man sits on a lawn chair in his bathrobe, smoking a cigarette.

"Sorry buddy. Come on down, Josh. All right, swing forward."

I steady Josh when he lands.

"That shit will kill you." Josh points to the cigarette. The man stubs it out.

"One more time." I throw my leg over the rail and Josh follows.

"From here, keep your knees bent and roll, arms over your head. Watch me, and follow quick."

I jump, my landing a smooth transition from vertical to horizontal motion. The bottle tucked in my pocket shatters. A thick shard of glass punctures my thigh and the alcohol burns like a blowtorch. It's deep. From the dimensions of the pain, half a bottle is inside my leg.

 I pick myself up in time to see the Josh execute a perfect roll; he leaps back onto his feet in a stance that says he's ready to dodge a bullet.

"You been watching war movies. Nice job."

I limp to the bike.

"I should get my car."

"They know your car."

"They know your bike."

"We need to stay together."

"I left the top down."

"Priorities, son."

"Holy shit, look at you. You okay?"

I glance at the red swell on my pant leg. "Never better."

"Once we get on the highway, pull that glass out of my leg."

I lean forward and accelerate, careful not to let the rear tire slip.

The bike leaps onto Peoria Avenue. I pass a car and get in the northbound turning lane for Interstate Seventeen. The light is red and the car in the oncoming lane is moving fast. I goose the gas and flash across the road with a couple yards to spare. The wind yanks my hair and with each click of the gear shifter, I feel a chunk of glass the size of a snuff can sawing leg muscle. Through the side view mirror, the Jeep Grand Cherokee tails us.

Yellow lamps illuminate the next few miles with a moonlit glow; the empty road seems paler than in daylight. Bandage Head is easy to track by his headlamps. Smooth as silk I'm going ninety; the engine growls like a caged bear. I check the tach. There's a lot of room from here to the red band.

I want to be torqued at Josh but I remember the thrill of being sixteen. I envy him for wanting a woman that bad.

My leg jabs and I look down. Josh clasps the shard of whiskey bottle. I loosen my leg muscles, anticipating the sudden tear that will follow.

"You want this out?"

"Take it out!"

A slow pressure builds, like he's pulling a bristle bore cleaner through meat. I kick and have to swerve the bike to keep my balance.

"Pull that fucking thing out!"

Blood soaks my pant leg. The wind catches it and sprays an atomized mist onto Josh the way a high-end paint sprayer would.

"At least the cut is sterile!" Josh yells.

"Pull it!"

One more sudden jab of pain and it's over. Josh holds the glass in the air, fighting to keep his arm projected into the wind, long enough for me to see. It is three inches long and has a fishhook curve.

"You want to keep it?" he yells.

I shake my head and he whips it to the side of the highway.

"You're going to have to put pressure on it till it clots!"

Josh inserts his thumb into my leg. I feel a pinch. More glass is at the bottom of the wound. He pulls his thumb out and presses the puncture with his palm.

We approach the merge lane coming from Greenway Road. Out of nowhere a black full-sized van paces us, a nose ahead. It's three lanes over but crosses one lane line and then another. A six-foot concrete highway divider blocks my left. The glass in my leg tears the shit out of something and I'm starting to think in terms of Smith & Wesson arbitration.

I ease off the gas. Bandage Head closes from behind. We're going eighty. I drop back another five. The Jeep edges closer to my bumper. I swerve to the second lane, lock my elbows, and crush the brakes. The fat tire squeals and I smell burning rubber.

My mind works faster than time flows around me. Everything is acute. Josh leans off-center and I compensate by putting the bike in a side slide. The jeep surges beside me. I turn the front tire and the bike corrects, snapping the ass end into place like a bowstring finding center. The Jeep screeches and its nose dives. Bandage Head is behind me again. I goose it and open some distance.

The van rushes ahead; the driver sees me and crosses toward the right lane. He's positioned himself to prevent me from taking the right exit.

"They're just trying to scare us! They need that envelope," I yell over the wind.

"It's in your pocket!"

"They don't know that!"

The van jockeys back and forth in front.

"They're going to rein us in until the Jeep catches us." Josh looks back. "He's closing."

The wind whips our clothes and Josh ducks tight and clings to me.

"Hang on."

I downshift to fourth and the bike motor jumps an octave; I curl back my wrist. The front wheel lifts an inch from the pavement and the machine rumbles like I've flicked a Bic under a Saturn V moon launcher. My mouth flaps like I'm in a wind tunnel. I fight to lean forward. The front tire finds the road and we blast through a hundred ten in a second.

The van swerves across the road and cuts me off. I hit the brake and lurch forward.

I back off, then accelerate again to the opposite side of the highway. The van adjusts, I feint left. The van stays in front.

A sign passes overhead. Pinnacle Peak in a half mile. "All right, you son of a bitch."

"The Jeep is right on us!" Josh yells.

The glare of headlights has grown in my side mirrors. The highway converges into a split four-lane. The van eases, and the Jeep charges from behind. I push left, then right. The Jeep matches me from behind. I follow through to the off ramp. I've lost the van, but the Jeep follows. I accelerate up the slope toward the intersection.

The traffic light at Pinnacle Peak is red. I feel like a camera duct taped to a missile.

I know this road. No headlights come from either direction.

I hit the intersection doing ninety; we float over the road and land on the down sloping onramp. Approaching the highway again, I snap my head back for a quick glance. The van driver dropped back when I took the exit and he's lost two hundred yards. The jeep crosses the intersection. I got him by a hundred yards.

Back on the highway now. The potholes come quick. This is a roadwork area; the lanes detour across blacktopped berms, each ridge wobbles my tires. A hundred and ten in a construction area: the definition of hairy.

The bike is heavy but gyroscope stable. The engine cranks six thousand revolutions per minute; halogen lamps stun the road and the bike consumes it. It seems to affect the flow of time. Or maybe it's the adrenaline-whiskey cocktail in my veins.

Long as I lead, I'm safe. I don't worry about helicopters anymore because this pursuit isn't legitimate. What kind of irony—this bad guy has me calling the FBI legit.

When there are no lights in my side mirrors I back off the gas until I can sit erect. The wind whips me but it's good to flex my back. My pulse slows and the pain in my leg climbs to the top of my mind.

When I shift my foot I feel the glass in my thigh. Even at this speed, I smell the Jack Daniel's soaked in my pants. Josh must be drunk on fumes.

We're past Black Canyon City, coming on New River. I exit and slow until I reach the cross road, and stop.

The engine idles; without wind, the machine is a giant heat radiator. I balance the bike between my thighs to stretch my wounded leg. The puncture throbs and the chunk of glass inside saws against muscle. Behind on the exit, a nondescript black shape consolidates into a Jeep. Farther still, a set of headlights emerges from around a corner. It pulls into an area covered by street lamps.

"That guy in the Jeep is crazier than I am. He's been running at a hundred without any headlights, trying to sneak up on us."

"They'll kill us if they can."

"I know it."

We're on the highway again whistling through the hot summer air. My options are thin. I could cut across to Prescott or Sedona, but my connections are in Flagstaff.

Josh doesn't know the FBI wants me for murder. I could deceive him and allow him to think they are just more of the governor's goons, but the last twenty-four hours have shown me the snowballing effect of bad decisions.

The liar knows no love; his love is deceit and rings false like two plus two is five. The person loved this way is not loved at all, and knows it. When we get to Flagstaff, I'm going to pour Josh a shot of Jack and give him the straight poop.

"We're going to spend the night in Flag, son. I'm not letting off the gas until we get there."

"Who are these people?" he says.

"Shit if I know."

I haven't spoken to Liz since yesterday morning. I don't know if she's locked in an interrogation room, shivering, staring at a mirrored wall, or if she is in bed alone. Or with another man. We are not exclusive, and the way I left her — *can't I ride with you?* — I wouldn't be surprised if she throws the next mug of coffee in my face.

Liz is one of those gals. The first kiss says there's more where that came from, but the aftertaste—well, seconds are rare.

Rosie has an older-sister relationship with Liz and projects herself into every drama. Sometimes she's a big-hearted woman; others, the devil's sister. Her eyes are warm like flowers in Death Valley.

Right now, this pair is my best option.

I push the bike hard ascending the ridge at Bumble Bee, leaning through harsh mountain turns and exploding forward on the straight stretches. We reach the summit moving a hundred and forty and the tires leave the ground. My body conforms to the gas tank and Josh presses tight to my back. We land with a smooth chirrup of rubber and road. My knees press as close to the engine as I can stand. I feel the heat even as the wind fans it away.

Prescott. Camp Verde. Sedona. Mund's Park. I cut back to a hundred and twenty, then ninety. The guardrail posts creep by like I'm out for an evening jog. Entering Flagstaff, I coast to forty-five, the speed limit. My heart pounds and I sit upright into the cold air. I could walk this fast.

"Any one behind us?"

"All clear," Josh says.

It is one a.m. Flagstaff is at eight thousand feet and with the climb, the temperature has dropped forty degrees in the last hour. I press my legs close to the engine manifold and thaw my hand by the bottom of the gas tank. The moon blots the dimmer stars but the crisp air and the stillness comfort my ears after a screaming climb up the mountain.

Josh clings to my back.

I turn off the main drag and begin a series of rapid turns; in five minutes I'm at Liz's place. There's a lamp in the window and a television flickers behind it. A junky Dodge Charger sits in the driveway and an ancient gold Subaru Brat decorates the lawn. I navigate between them, pulling around the house and parking on the back patio. It smells musty. The headlamp lights a stack of cardboard boxes, Parker Brothers games, a clear trash bag filled with clothes or rags, a rusted grill, a baby carriage.

I cut the engine. The silence rings like church bells. Josh rubs his arms and shivers; I lean close to the engine rubbing my hands by the block.

"Whose place is this?" Josh says, jumping up and down to warm himself.

I point to a yellow flag in the back window. It has a coiled snake and the words, "Don't tread on me."

"Friends?"

"I hope."

Footsteps sound inside and the porch light comes on.

"One thing, Josh. They don't know my name is Nat Cinder. Here, I'm Tom Davis. Got it?"

His eyes narrow but he nods. "Yeah, Tom."

Rafael's oiled hands and prickly pear margaritas combined to create a new level of intoxication for Marisol. When he finished, it was just her and Virginia Rentier in their robes, feeling tingly—who would have thought being with a woman could be so exquisite?

The helicopter landed on the roof of the Executive Tower. It was late. Virginia led Marisol into an elevator. It hummed in harmony with Marisol's relaxed mind.

Politicians have always sought to deepen their alliances with other powerful politicians, Marisol thought. In the widest view, one of the best ways to add tensile strength to a relationship was to climb into bed. Eros. Of the kinds of physical love, what but the misunderstood and maligned homoerotic love can forge people together upon pain of the highest social reproof? Here the bond is not merely affection, or the ability to ask intimate favors. It is the secrecy of forbidden meetings.

"That was a lovely escape," Marisol said. "I've got to get up early."

The elevator door opened at the garage level. Virginia pecked her cheek and let her hand pass slowly through Marisol's as they parted.

Marisol sought her eyes. "This... tonight... Was this?"

"It's our secret."

"Fuck! Fuck! Fuck!" Buffa slammed his palms on the steering wheel. The Jeep wobbled and the tires peeled, still moving at ninety-five miles an hour. The bike had disappeared again.

"No more chances!" His voice was raspy.

He retrieved his cell phone from his pocket, flipped it open, closed it. He pulled the Jeep to the side of the road, got out, and paced in the cool mountain air.

"Fuck!" His voice trailed off into his own echo.

Philly was where you could get the best steak sammiches in the whole world.

The van that had been trailing him pulled over as well.

"How'd you lose him?" Buffa said.

"Did you see that bike?"

"Why didn't you take him out on the onramp? He was right there."

"He braked."

"You missed."

Johnny smiled. "So let's find him."

"How ya dumb fuck? Call the cops?"

"Nah, we go street by street. We got his plate."

"Why you so happy? What the hell's wrong with you? Like he parked on the street. He might be twenty miles closer to Albuquerque by now. Or L.A. But we have the plate number. Genius."

"What do you want, boss?" That same dumb grin.

Buffa punched his Jeep and busted a blood vessel in his index finger. He held the digit to his lips and paced.

"You say we got his plate?"

I'm about to tap the door when it opens. Rosie fills the door-frame. I step back. Her girth blocks my sight. She sees Josh and her neutral frown shifts to a smile that forces a blush to her cheeks. She steps to the patio in her tube socks and flannel nightgown and gives me a mechanical hug.

Her heavy breasts wobble out of sync, and Josh gives them a sly glance. Rosie pulls me by the shoulders and kisses me on the cheek. I look beyond her into the darkness, trying to coalesce a human shape out of a breeze-driven shadow in the trees.

Rosie studies Josh.

"This is my, uh, Josh," I say.

She sizes him with a broad smile. "A fine looking young man. I know the girls go crazy for him."

Josh looks at the floor.

"This is Rosie." I say.

"Hi."

"Oh! What happened to your leg?" She pads closer to Josh.

"It's his blood. He's still got a chunk of glass in him."

Now she turns to me. "Let me see."

Liz appears in the doorway wearing a long T-shirt for a night-gown. She crosses her arms and shivers. "What'd you do, Tom? You smell like the distillery."

She smells of cigarettes from four feet away, but she doesn't have a deck of smokes smashed two inches deep in her thigh to explain it. She yawns and pads onto the porch.

A car pulls into a driveway a few houses down and a light breeze catches the leaves of the oaks that divide this property from the next.

"Maybe we should go inside, girls?"

Josh watches Liz. She's younger than Rosie by a few years and built to opposite specs. Her upper arms are as thin as her forearms and her thighs widen at the knee. Her voice is like a crunching beer can and her face is pretty the way some paintings are, before you get close. She wears black bras but prefers not to.

I met her at a pub two years ago. I'd held the pool table eleven racks when Liz slid up wearing cut-off shorts and a halter. Legs that start at the bottom and go to the top. I put her out of my mind and figured the angle on an eight-ball bank shot. She leaned over the table while she slapped a pair of quarters on the edge. I looked up from the tip of my cue to see two clouds of opal white flesh rimmed in black lace, with the trace of an areola insinuating its way to freedom.

I scratched and she played the chump I'd just run the table on.

It all comes back while I look at her on the porch, and vanishes when she jumps and says, "Oh shit I came out without any drawers! Uh-huh." She stretches her T-shirt to cover her panties and darts into the hallway.

"That's Liz." I say.

Josh smirks.

"Let's get you in the bathroom and take off your pants." Rosie says.

"Mind if I grab the couch?" Josh says.

"Make yourself at home. There's milk in the fridge and that bologna is Oscar Meyer—the good stuff. It's got a little bite 'cause I opened it last week, but it won't hurt you."

She pushes me to the hall. We enter the bathroom and Liz, wearing sweatpants, joins us.

"You've still got broken glass in your pocket!" Liz says.

"What happened yesterday morning when I left?"

Liz sits on the commode and lights a Marlboro. "Nothing."

"What does that mean? Did the FBI stop here?"

She nods. Rosie assembles tweezers, isopropyl alcohol, and a washcloth on the sink. I catch her reading me.

"What?" Liz's face is distorted and her voice high. "They hauled us to the station. They took our fingerprints and asked us about a murder the other day. Nothing."

"A murder?"

"Nothing!"

She's flighty, I tell myself. A couple bricks shy. If she sounded rational, I'd be suspicious; but this is vintage Liz. A year ago, I was with her on San Francisco Street and we saw a young woman with a tattoo over her ass. I said it might as well spell TRAILER TRASH. Liz got a tat that day with those words in a giant gothic font. She's Jim Morrison's wild child.

Rosie kneels before me, unbuckles my belt, and draws my pants to my knees with telling efficiency. She smirks, expecting me to comment. Liz sucks a deep drag from her cigarette.

The hair on my neck rises. It's nothing specific like a brick smashes through the window. It's the peripheral things, a shadow, a vocal flutter, a smell.

"I don't like this," I say. I pull my pants high enough to walk and leave the girls in the bathroom. Josh snores on the couch. The light's off and I peek through the blinds. There's no one outside—lamps light the street well enough to be sure—but I'm nervous. I lift the phone from the cradle and hear a dial tone.

The living room is attached to the kitchen by a divider that functions like a bar. Through the window, shadows sway in a breeze. I cross for a better view and rub my eyes. Just shadows.

It's like hearing a plausible story that backs up a lie.

Liz startles me, holding a Mickey Mouse glass half full of liquor. I sniff it. V.O. It tastes nothing like Lynchburg's finest, but I gulp half. Liz drags on her cigarette and leads me by my arm to the bathroom, stopping at the hallway junction while I take another gulp of booze.

Liz steers me to the toilet and shifts me to face the shower; she takes my shoulders and pushes me to the seat.

Rosie sits on the ledge of the tub with a dripping washcloth. "This'll burn," she says, and wipes the blood from the hole in my leg. I look at the pulpy wound and it stings like someone else's.

Liz watches my eyes through the mirror. She stands behind me and massages my neck. Her prodding fingers feel good; muscles roll under her touch. Her hands are calloused like she works with a shovel or an axe for a living. She might. I've never asked where she gets her money. My mind swims.

Rosie fishes inside my leg with tweezers and Liz whispers a promise about a blowjob to end all blowjobs. I can't see her, but Rosie watches her with steady eyes. I turn and Liz's mouth is pursed, mid-phrase.

It takes me back to the night I met her.

The bartender announced last call as I dropped quarters into the table and pushed the lever. She shot good stick, but I didn't have the ego to let her clean up on me all night. I racked the balls and she stood at the end of the table, tits almost falling out; when she reared back it was like a stallion on its hind legs; her mane flowed and her jugs were bulked up and magnificent. She heaved and balls spattered and bounced like she'd fired the cue from a cannon.

Not a single ball dropped. I ran the table.

When I nailed the eight ball, I noticed Rosie at the bar across the room, sitting with the stool turned a hundred and eighty degrees, watching. It was the first time I saw her, and she looked like she was grokking a math problem. Brows furrowed, eyes cold. She held my look for a second and then her face melted into charm and grace. Liz cussed and followed my eyes, and something passed between her and Rosie.

A half hour later I was drinking Jack at their house. They were roommates. That explains that, I thought, and never thought of it again, until now.

Nothing disconcerts like two silent women.

Rosie triumphantly holds the tweezers aloft, clamping a shard the size of a nickel. She souses my wound with alcohol, dries it, slathers Mercurochrome around the edges, and wraps my thigh in gauze.

She stands and clasps her hands. "I'll toss your pants in the washer." She drapes my fatigues over her arm and leaves me alone with Liz.

I snap free of the spell and clutch my pants, remove the envelope. I toss them back to her. "You should get Josh's too." I say.

"What's that?" Liz nods at the packet.

"A long story for another day."

I hear the ratchet-sounding dial on the washing machine.

"You hurt my feelings," Liz says.

"Didn't know you had any."

She punches my arm and her bony fist catches a nerve. Her eyes twinkle like December road ice and she takes me by the hand to the bedroom.

"Let me get on your computer. I need to look up a couple of things."

She inserts my index finger into her mouth.

"Honey, you don't know where that finger's been." I extract myself and jiggle the mouse to take the computer out of hibernation.

"Looks like you got whiskey leg when I need whiskey dick," she says.

"Just a few minutes, Liz. I got to find out who's trying to kill me."

It's strange neither she nor Rosie asked how I wound up with a whiskey bottle stuck in my leg, or who I'm running from. She creeps behind me and I imagine a raised cleaver or a snub thirty-eight, but I turn and she has a petulant face that says deny me again, lose me forever.

If she gargled Listerine for thirty seconds I'd nail her. As it is, I turn back to the computer screen.

If I'm being watched right now, I have finite time and freedom. I don't know if Liz and Rosie are part of the set up. Perhaps Liz's straightforward approach tonight is meant to get me talking, my words recorded by some hidden device? This is not the place to spend the night, but while the FBI waits for me to incriminate myself, I have a chance to find the information I need on the Internet.

I sit in her thirty-dollar Walmart office chair and roll up to the Ikea desk. The I-Mac rests on a stack of phone books. I open a browser window and go to Google. What did Bandage Head say his name was?

"Hey, what?"

Liz has thrown a pillow below the desk, and now on all fours, crawls past my leg into the cubbyhole. She stations herself on the pillow and pulls me out of my boxers.

"You, uh, hmmm." I shift forward. Not bad at all. "Joey Buffa." I say.

"Whgght?"

"The guy who's trying to run me down said his name was Joey Buffa. You just keep on doing your thing. I feel positively presidential."

I'm caught in an exquisite paradox. I suspect there's a van outside with suit clad men listening to the sounds she makes while I tickle her throat. I'm like a fox dangling my foot in a trap, with the furrier around the bend.

I Google "Joey Buffa" and pull two news stories from Philadelphia that tie Buffa to a mob boss. Buffa was indicted for murder but it fell apart when a witness disappeared under police watch. The district attorney promised the investigation would continue. The victim pushed drugs; now he pushed daisies. No harm, no foul. The second story says Buffa was named a person of interest in the macabre death of Jeremy Rummans, a man killed in a trap he'd apparently set for Buffa.

"You're doing real good down there, baby."

She starts something sideways that scores points for originality.

"Wow. Shit."

She makes it hard to think. Preston Delp. Back to Google. Delp is still listed on Minority Leader Clyman's website.

I pour a shot from the bottle and gulp it. Seventeen years. After my discharge from the 5th Ranger Battalion, I married Dick Clyman's daughter. In fifteen months I was a father to be. In sixteen I was alone again. I pour another shot, drink it, and shake the memories loose. Seventeen years.

I lean back and watch Liz's head bob.

Someone took pictures of the governor and the photos wind up in enemies' hands in the legislative branch. On the surface, it looks like the exercise of extra-Constitutional power.

So the governor is being blackmailed. Why?

I search the state House website; check the calendar of pending legislation. A bill called Vallejo is scheduled for floor debate tomorrow, and a bill to limit the use of Mexican consular cards as a valid form of identification is scheduled the next day. Vallejo sounds familiar. I've read about it on a libertarian website. What the hell is Vallejo?

I find the bill on the House's web site.

Liz, Liz, Liz. I look at the computer and at my shaft. IF the FBI's outside, this blowjob could put me in jail.

"After you get done, I need to talk to you about what happened the other day. I have a confession to make."

Let the FBI stew on that. I pull Liz out from below the desk and push her toward the bed.

Chapter Six

Josh awoke with a start in a dark house he didn't recognize to the smell of a foreign blanket and couch. His neck ached but his overriding thought was that Bandage Head knew where Merry lived.

"What?" His pants were gone. A washing machine was running.

Josh stretched his neck. He slipped on his shoes and crept toward a light under the door at the end of the hall. Standing outside, he heard tapping on a keyboard.

"Nat!" He whispered.

A chair rolled. The door opened. Nat sat in his underwear and socks with a blanket draped over his shoulders. Liz was in the bed, snoring. She mumbled.

"Bandage Head knows where Merry lives."

Nat's eyes were unimpressed, glued to the monitor.

"Call her."

"He can track her down. She's next."

Nat nodded. "Warn her. We can't do much else."

Beside the keyboard, partially hidden by the base of the monitor, a whiskey glass sat half full. An empty Seagram's bottle lay beside it. A legal pad to the right held scribbled notes.

"You're a piece of work." Josh went back to the living room couch. He flipped his cell phone open and sent a text message to Merry.

KEEP EYES OPEN BANDAGE HEAD MAY KNOW WHERE YOU LIVE

The cell phone glowed pale blue and vibrated on the night table. Merry blinked to clear her eyes. It was Josh. She flipped it open.

BANDAGE HEAD IS COMING TO KILL YOU

Adrenaline shot through her limbs. She jumped from bed, pulled the drawn curtain aside and looked below. A street lamp lit the back yard but shadows hid large spaces by the block fence. At least she could see no one was in the tree.

Merry propped her pillow against the headboard and sat. She read the message again. She'd misread. She pressed the keys.

HOW

HE FLLWD ME

SHLD I CL COPS

NO NO NO

"Screw this." She dialed his number. "What do you mean 'no'? This guy's going to kill me."

"Merry, listen. Since Nat and I got away, he'll be looking for ways to pick up our trail again. He'll probably watch you and wait for me to come see you. So just keep your eyes open."

"This is crazy."

"You'll be fine."

"I'm mad at you. And I have a stomach ache."

"I'm sorry."

"I'm going back to bed."

She stared into darkness and wondered if the call ended badly. Her father would want to know something like this. She should tell him.

Men were animals. When they were young, all they wanted was to fight and get laid, and when they got older, all they wanted was to fight and get laid. For a woman, those enthusiasms could sometimes combine in a threatening way. Even the weakest man wanted to be lord over somebody.

Fortunately, God provided women tools to counter men's brute force. Women possessed superior intelligence, adaptable to running multibillion-dollar businesses, sewing shirts, or contorting men into paroxysms of horniness. She had recently discovered the full power of this tool—how to cultivate the desire for release, and then withhold it.

Women could be ruthlessness. While boys scampered about the fringes of the dance floor, girls plotted how to murder adversaries with curling irons. Nature required a woman to act, sometimes in cold blood, and had constructed her heart to be capable of it.

The secret to survival lay in recognizing her strengths and leveraging them against a man's weakness. She remembered Bandage Head on the trunk of Josh's car. He wouldn't be quite as clever as she.

Older men looked at her with hungry eyes. This one would be no different. She knew the art of subtle invitations; inviting a man to conquer her would make him vulnerable. If she did it right, he wouldn't be able to resist. And she would crush his nuts and drive a pair of scissors into his neck.

She snuggled under the sheets and closed her eyes, bringing visions. A faceless man attacked her and she kneed him in the groin and crushed her fist into his nose, driving cartilage into the brain. He collapsed, a surprised snarl frozen on his dead face. A second attacker rushed in and she gouged a fingernail deep in his eye. He shrieked. She turned to a third, who had slipped on blood, and crushed his temple with the spike of her heels.

She slept.

I'm slumped at the computer. I fell asleep to Liz's snoring; now she's talking to someone, behind a wall or a door. She's in the bathroom.

I'm not sober, not drunk. The digital clock reads three a.m. I haven't slept more than a few minutes. I step to the bathroom door, careful with my heels on the wood floor.

"He just dozed off without saying anything … I know … How much longer?"

She waits for a response. Then says, "I don't feel safe … What do you mean more? That's your job … Do it *now*."

I grab my shirt. My pants are down the hall in the laundry room, my boots in the bathroom.

The FBI watches the house from outside. My son, who thinks he has no father, sleeps on the couch. The woman whose dried juice cakes my pubic hair betrays me this very moment. My mind bounds like an antelope, scarcely touching down. Take Liz and Rosie hostage? Bolt out the front? Sneak somewhere alone?

"Liz," I say.

She hushes, then, "I'm in the bathroom. What?"

"I can't sleep. I have to tell you about the other night. I think I'm in trouble."

"Hunh?"

"Never mind," I say. "I'm going to the gas station for a bottle."

"I'll go with you."

"I'll be right back, then I'll tell you everything."

I grab the envelope of photos and my notes from the desk and step into the hallway, closing the bedroom door behind me. I pad down the hall in my socks and press Josh's shoulder, keeping my eyes on the lookout for Rosie.

"Liz and Rosie are on the other team," I whisper.

"Gross."

"No, not that team. They're hooked up with the FBI."

He snaps from the couch, eyes comprehending.

I get our pants from the dryer and my boots from the bathroom. We're dressed.

I cup my hands around Josh's ear and whisper.

"I don't know where Rosie is. Liz is in the bathroom talking to the FBI right now. They've bugged the place, and they think I'm going out for a bottle of booze. If we both leave right now, they'll be all over us. So this is what we do…"

I tell him the best plan I can think of in thirty seconds.

Outside, I back the Triumph off the back porch. My pulse races and my eyes dance after every shadow. These guys—wherever they are—can end my life. They can stick me in a cell until I rot, or they can shoot me where I sit and make something up. They are the central police. They answer to themselves. Laws are not barriers to their power, but tools to extend it.

I drive to Circle K and fill my gas tank, ensuring two hundred twenty miles of freedom, and cajole the hag behind the counter to sell me a pint of Jack Daniel's. I take a swig for the sheer good taste of it.

A block from Liz's house, I pull the clutch, let the bike idle, and coast parallel to the curb.

A dark figure rushes toward me from across the street. Even expecting Josh, my heart pounds. He runs with ease of a man with good knees. He straddles the bike and we pull off. I drive nice and easy.

"I think we're going to have trouble," Josh says, close to my ear. "Your friend Rosie followed me downstairs and held a gun on me."

I try to look at him but can't; I slow to pull over.

"Keep going," he says.

"You aren't shot are you?"

"No. I surprised her. She's got so much junk in her basement, I threw a board game at her and clubbed her with a stuffed animal. That didn't work so I fed her a forearm."

Liz and Rosie will be calling the FBI in minutes, if they haven't already. I don't see a tail, but they might have a helicopter so high in the sky I can't hear it. The first time I made it out of Flagstaff, I wasn't their true target; they weren't prepared.

Josh has the right to make his own decisions. I've been using the urgency of the situation to continue a lie of omission, and the deceit rests on my shoulders with all the other sins I've committed. For the moment, we have our freedom. That might end in thirty seconds, or not at all. Either way, Josh needs to know the truth.

Ironically, we're on the road where I picked up Yellow Horse running from these same folks. The sun will rise in two and a half hours.

I have a cache nearby—a couple miles through the woods as the crow flies—but I don't need guns and food right now. I need to get back to Phoenix where I have a different identity, and resources.

Forest Road Twenty-Eight passes on my left. I hit the brake and circle back to it; drive a hundred yards on ruts. I hit a twenty-foot mud puddle and almost upset the bike, but goose it, pop out, and pull onto the grass.

"See if you can find a flat rock for the kickstand," I tell Josh.

He jumps off and places a stone where it will support the bike. I turn off the engine and the darkness under the trees snaps up around us. The moon's set for the night, and after the wind in my ears, the engine, the tires, silence intimidates.

I lead him a few feet away and every footstep in the tall grass whispers our presence. I take a seat at a fallen log and Josh sits beside me. I listen for a helicopter, or anything else.

We're alone. I swallow.

"I guess something funny is going on?" he says.

"What do you mean?"

"Why would the feds be interested in those photographs?"

"They're not. I pulled over so I could level with you."

He says nothing.

"I was a mid-level manager for Honeywell in 1989. Your mother was my assistant."

"You're my father," he says.

I nod, but he can't see me. "You don't sound surprised."

"I figured it out three years ago. When you dated Mom."

"How?"

"I've never slept very well. I heard things. And come on—you look like me."

"Does Cyndi know you know?"

"I don't think."

My stomach curls with the anger of anticlimax. He knew the whole time. When I took him to watch Diamondback games, when I bought him a CD player and he said it was old fashioned and iPods were cool, and I bought him one of those, when—he knew the whole time. He judged every act with the same innocence as God, and with all the weight. My eyes rim.

"I'm ashamed," I say.

"I'm not angry."

"I haven't given you the things I should have. You have to be angry."

"The world is shit. You dealt the hand. I'm playing it."

He's built his identity without a father, and he's satisfied with the product.

"I haven't done right by you."

"Then level with me. This FBI thing in Flagstaff isn't related to Bandage Head. Why are they chasing you up here?"

"I'll get to that. But first I want you to know that you can go to whatever college you want. I'll pay for it."

"I don't want your money."

"I've been investing in a college account for you for twelve years. Besides, I've got more than I need."

He snickers. "How much?"

"About five million."

He's quiet. "You live in a trailer."

"If money could buy what I want, I'd be worth a hundred million. It can't."

"Okay. I want to go to Michigan."

"Football?"

"Best program on the planet."

"I know some boys in Nebraska that would argue. But you sure you want to pick a school on the merit of its football program? You could go to Harvard."

"I know. They're pussies." He pauses. "What's going on with the FBI?"

"Two nights ago, I witnessed a murder of an FBI agent. The Bureau wants to talk."

"So tell them what you saw."

I shake my head. "I helped bury the body."

"You did it under duress. The guy was going to kill you too."

"No, Josh, I could have stopped it, maybe. I didn't think fast enough. And the killer is a friend. I helped him get away."

"Is this connected to the photographs?"

"I don't know how it could be."

"How come Liz and Rosie don't know your name?"

"That's a long story. After Gretchen died I traded options for a living. Made a lot of money. I was depressed. I stayed in, read books. It was about the time the House impeached Clinton."

"You know, I'll bet he'd be a cool ex-prez to hang with. Chicks. Drugs."

"Set that aside. I studied politics. Washington D.C. The Constitution. History. The Articles of Confederation. The Supreme Court, you name it. I figured out what's wrong."

"That's easy. The corporations—"

"Josh—hold on. The problem is the federal government. Period. Not declining morals. Not race problems. Not corporations. Not global warming. Everything goes back to the central government."

"What's this have to do with not using your name?"

"I wanted to do something about it, not just talk. But this country has a habit of stamping out little folks who stand up to the Machine. You've heard of them, but not the truth. Ruby Ridge, Waco? I took a different name and started fishing for people with the same ideas."

"Thomas Jefferson Davis is a rebel?"

"A secessionist. And the agent my friend killed was trying to put us under arrest. For sedition, of all things. Sedition. You ever look that up?"

"It's spying."

"Not hardly. It means talking against the state. It's a law against free speech—you know, your First Amendment right."

"Did you kill him?"

"No. I watched it."

"Did you order it?"

"No, but it doesn't matter."

"So Liz and Rosie are working for the FBI?"

"I guess the Bureau hauled them in and made them inform on us. I bought time to escape by telling Liz I'd confess everything once I got a bottle of booze."

"And now they know my name."

"Your first name."

"Shit."

"Well, I wanted you to know. You've got your own decisions to make."

"Getting ready to dump me in the woods?"

I shake my head. "I guess I deserve that. No, I'll do whatever I can to get you out of this mess. You're not involved with the FBI. But this Bandage Head fellow has your number, just like mine. We've got to deal with that."

"Can't we just give him the photos?"

"Then the governor gets away with murder. We have to figure out how to get out of here."

"I can get us out of town. You got cash?"

"I always have cash."

"Serious cash? I'm not talking twenty bucks."

"Of course."

"I have a friend from football that just moved here from Phoenix. Lives outside of town on the north side. He's a senior; he's cool. We buy his car and haul ass."

Buffa crossed the hundred miles down the mountain to Cave Creek in the same time it took to climb it. He didn't slow for the drop into the Phoenix basin, with its hairpin turns, squealing tires, and seven-degree grade. De Roulet followed too close. If he'd followed the bike that tight, Buffa would have a stack of nudie pics on his front seat and he'd be collecting pay in the morning.

Johnny De Roulet. What the hell was the Boss thinking, sending this punk to Phoenix to "help?"

"You've got the license plate," he'd said. That was true, and though the dumb ass planned to drive up one street and down another looking for it, he'd given Buffa an idea. He called an old friend, Jimmy Guigli, of the Phoenix police department. Guigli had the night beat.

"Jimmy. How you doon? Buffa. Need to run a plate."

"How you doon? Yeah. I gotta minit."

It was easy to remember, "TREAD."

A moment later he had Cinder's name and address. "You know anything 'bout him?" Buffa said.

"Nathan Cinder? This guy's nobody. Not even a parking ticket. Lives way out. You gotto turn off Quick Draw Road and follow 'bout tree miles. Then right on Yancey Road. You follow that and watch for a driveway. There's only one."

"You stayin outta trouble?"

"Puttin' bad guys away."

"Yeah. Stay the fuck away from me."

Buffa shared a laugh and closed the phone. In a few miles he would reach the Carefree exit. The LED clock flipped to three a.m. He needed gas. It was a hell of a pull going up to Flagstaff and back. He pressed a button on the dash three times and read the result: sixteen point three miles per gallon. He had enough gas to get to the twenty-four hour service station right off the exit, and he could use a cup of coffee. De Roulet could go home.

Three minutes later Buffa stopped at a pump. De Roulet pulled alongside and jumped out. Buffa started the pump and saw his bright eyes.

"Need some gas?" De Roulet said.

"You figger that out yourself?"

"Ha!" De Roulet pointed and laughed. "That's really good."

Buffa paused.

"Look me in the eyes and answer straight. You on dope?"

"Nah!"

"You coked up little bitch!" Buffa swatted but De Roulet jumped away. Buffa lurched and caught him by the arm.

"How long you been coked up?" He grabbed his ear and led him against the van, hidden from passing cars and the station attendant. He had to be careful. De Roulet was somebody or else De Luca wouldn't have sent him. But nobody was going to blow his operation. Buffa smacked him three times.

"You gotta understand something. Look at me." He grabbed his chin and forced eye contact. "You hear me, you little prick? I don't care who you are. You use that shit when you're working for me, you die in the desert. Capice? Nod 'yes'."

Buffa moved Johnny's head up and down for him.

"Ca-*fucking*-pice?" He knocked his head against the van.

De Roulet smiled.

Buffa hadn't left Philly on the best terms, but Dante De Luca was a shrewd man who could make a buck off another man no matter where his ambitions led. Buffa had always known that Philly was in his blood, and walking away from his past was impossible.

As a personal favor to De Luca, Buffa had agreed to let Johnny De Roulet tag with him. De Luca needed someone he could trust to teach the boy some sense and get him off the streets in Philly where he was building a reputation too fast. It was either a sign of trust, or a lack of it. In this business, there was no way to know. Trust was never real. Respect was never honest. It all drew from force and fear.

"Go home, you doped up fuck. I'll call if I need you. I see you like this again—I put you out your misery."

The gas pump clicked and Buffa returned to his vehicle. He kept his eyes toward Johnny and took his receipt from the machine. Coffee, he reminded himself. He'd been awake for twenty hours and he hadn't slept well the night before.

Inside the store he sniffed the coffee pot. It was fresh.

Johnny drove away while Buffa paid.

The attendant was a freak. Goth, was what they called it these days. Take a punk like that, beat his ass, give him responsibility and the promise of a severe pounding if he fucked up. That's how to handle it. Buffa sipped coffee and burned his mouth. He took another taste and caffeine hit his brain. He had to get to Cinder's place. Had to find the photos, or something to show Patterson. Couldn't let De Roulet divert his focus.

He let his windows down and opened the sunroof. More coffee. He'd driven Carefree Highway a few times but didn't know where Quick Draw Road turned. Plus it was dark. He'd be at Cave Creek in five miles.

He found his turn. Everything was cowboy. Dead Horse Gulch. Horse Thief Basin. The pavement ended and he rolled on a rutted dirt and rock road. A coyote darted in front of him, followed by another. Two of them. God, he needed a woman. Just for a little while. Not more than a fucking day. Finally he found Yancey and turned. He bounced along for fifteen minutes until the road merged back onto Quick Draw. He'd missed the driveway. He turned around.

There—he turned left. He'd missed it because it was a narrow cow path twisting between cholla and saguaro. Needles screeched his paint like a hundred fingernails on a chalkboard. The driveway went on, and ahead, in the high-beam glow, he saw the glint of a window and the outline of a trailer against the mountain behind it.

Buffa finished his coffee and pulled a flashlight from the glove box. Drew his nine-millimeter, left his headlights on and stepped out of the Jeep. His ankle clicked with each step. It hadn't been doing that earlier. He urinated on a purple barrel cactus and watched the trailer. There were no lights on, no dogs tied to the step or the rickety shed to the side.

Nat Cinder, apparently, was a neat man. A garden hose was coiled on a rack attached to a post in the ground. Buffa stepped on stairs built of railroad ties and twisted the doorknob. The door pushed open. He stepped inside.

"I shoulda had Johnny go inside first."

He flashed the light. The floor creaked under his step. It was orderly, but the layout was unusual. National, state, and city maps were thumbtacked to the walls. Printed Internet news stories filled the gaps. A computer desk spanned a twelve-foot wall with a makeshift bookshelf the length of the desktop, supporting a couple hundred books. The computer had a vibrating string screen saver.

To his right he recognized an ancient Zenith floor model television. His mother had the same model. It had to be thirty, maybe forty years old. The nappy gold carpet, worn thin in the walkways, was also just like Mom's. Creepy as hell.

He stood at the shelf reading the titles of political texts, history, even fiction. This guy was the real deal—one of those sorts who could tell you what Ben Franklin had for breakfast on May 3, 1772.

"Come on, Cinder. Where's the flag?" Buffa flashed the light to the wall and circled around the room.

"I knew it."

Six feet long, hanging behind him, Old Glory. Below it, the famous "Don't Tread on Me" coiled snake flag.

Buffa opened desk drawers and ran his fingers across the folders, reading tabs: "Johnson/JFK assassination," "Oklahoma City," "Ruby Ridge," "Waco," "Reno," "Foster," "TWA 800," "Second Amendment," "Federal Reserve," "Interstate Commerce Clause," "Jekyll Island."

He pulled each file, flipped through the documents, and dumped them on the floor. No naked women.

He heard a noise outside and turned the flashlight off. Stupid, he thought. The Jeep's headlights were still on. He pulled his nine and stepped outside.

"Who's here?" He called.

Nothing. He walked to the Jeep, turned off the headlights, and waited for his eyes to adjust to the darkness. The sound didn't repeat. Probably a cow that hadn't come home, still rustling through the brush.

Back inside the trailer he rifled through the remaining file drawer, then opened and closed every cabinet door on the top end of the desk. More books and papers, but nothing glossy and nude.

Beyond the kitchen a short hallway opened into a Spartan bedroom. A single bed with no headboard but a wool Army blanket, a bureau that was stripped to bare wood, and a towering gun cabinet with, he counted, twelve rifles and shotguns, with a pistol propped in the back corner. He pulled the knob. Locked. He held a pillow from the bed against the glass and gave it a quick jab. The pane crashed inside the cabinet and shards fell to the floor. He withdrew the handgun and held it under the flashlight.

"Ain't you a beaut?"

He looked at the shiny barrel. A date stamp read 1917, and the breech said "Erfurt." Other symbols littered the frame, one resembled a crown, another an eagle with outstretched wings. He'd only ever seen one firearm where the action toggled up and back. It was a Luger, and dating back to 1917, it had probably been picked up from a corpse in one of the World Wars. The serial number stamp on the barrel and frame matched. This thing was worth some money. He checked the chamber and threaded his belt through the holster.

He looked over the other firearms, since they were free, but he wasn't much of a rifle man.

Buffa surveyed the room. Cinder made his bed like an Army recruit, the blanket tucked tight enough to bounce a quarter. He lifted the mattress: nothing. He tossed it aside and ransacked a bureau, flinging rolled underwear and T-shirts to the floor. Nothing.

At the opposite end of the trailer, he glanced in the bathroom, entered a small bedroom.

"Fuck."

There were bookshelves from floor to ceiling, free-standing shelves in the center, each stuffed with books.

"Must be five thousand books in here."

He pulled one from the shelf. *Presidential Leadership*. He threw it to the floor. Another: *For Whom the Bell Tolls*. He pitched it. *Scalia*

Dissents. Bushwhacked. Human Action. Natural Right and History. The Monkey Wrench Gang.

"Who the fuck are you?"

Buffa grabbed a rack as high as he could reach and pulled, but bolts fixed it to the ceiling. He swiped the closest shelf, sending a few dozen volumes flapping to the floor.

"Where's the pictures, Nathan?" He cleaned off another shelf, and kicked the books on the floor into a stack of mangled covers and folded pages. Buffa slammed the door and went to the last bedroom.

It was locked. He pounded the door with the side of his fist and it reverberated like concrete bearing up to a sledge hammer. The hinges on the inside had been fitted so tight he couldn't slip a credit card between the door and jamb. He stepped back and kicked it with the bottom of his good foot. It didn't budge, but his bad ankle cracked and gave under his weight. He landed on his tailbone and water filled his eyes.

Chapter Seven

Attorney General Jane Lynwood slid a file across the desk. Opposite her, a brash prosecutor with a family name and a gold-paved destiny waited. She'd called him a minute ago. Earnest Whetton, Junior, was in for a surprise.

"I want you to evaluate this for me," she said.

Earnest caught the sliding file before it fell from her desk. "Theen? Rudy Theen? To what end?"

"The governor is considering releasing him and wants the AG's recommendation."

"A pardon?"

"Commutation, pardon; it's undecided."

"Same thing. Theen's a murderer. What could possibly mitigate that?"

"He's a pastor now. Writes motivational books for boys."

"Doesn't that strike you as convenient?"

"He's reformed."

"He should have reformed before he murdered someone. It was a clean trial. My father put him away."

"Don't allow loyalty to your dead father get in the way of your future."

Earnest closed the file and dropped it on Lynwood's desk. "The governor has the authority to pardon him on her own. Why involve the AG? Why involve me?" He leaned against the armrest. "Ahh. My father put him away, so if his son says he's healed, it must be so. When he kills again, the governor points at you, and you point at me. Nice, Jane."

Lynwood held his eye and remembered the words the governor had used on her a few minutes earlier that morning.

"Sometimes, to get the things we want, we have to give others what they want. Especially the people who can destroy us."

"Did you put up a fight? Or just roll over?"

"This isn't a negotiation. Take the folder. And I want you to think very hard about the recommendation you give me."

"First gear slips, so don't use it if you don't have to. Don't turn the heat on either, 'cuz the heater's broke and it'll blow anti-freeze inside. The spicy smell is from plugging the radiator with black pepper. It works—kinda."

Josh's friend, Nobel Tyrone, is a shade tree mechanic who has earned a full ticket ride at Ohio State as a quarterback. He takes the wad of bills from my hand and gives me the keys. His shoulder muscles ripple without provocation.

I look at the car I just spent a grand to borrow, a Ford Tempo with a rust-amputated trunk, and I'm reminded of a capitalist principle. In this case, supply is low and demand is willing. Exploitation is mutual and both parties are happy for the deal.

"I appreciate the help. I'll bring her back in one piece."

"I'll enjoy taking your bike to school."

"No. The bike stays parked in the garage. I was clear on that. You can take a bus for a grand."

He lifts his chin with a good-buddy snicker. Says something about bling, whatever the fuck that is.

"Let's get on, then," I say.

I start the four-cylinder engine and grind the stick into reverse. The sun has risen but the overcast sky hides it. Cool air helps wake me. Josh leans his head against the seat and I back out of the driveway. It's going to be a long drive and I'll need his eyes to scout danger, and his conversation to keep me alert.

I pull a cassette out of the tape deck. Tupac. I toss it to Josh.

"That's one of his best."

"How can you tell?"

"Well, you aren't going to find George Thorogood in this car. I'm surprised you're not checking the AM dial. You know, Rush Limbaugh."

"He isn't on yet. I like Rush, but Rush don't like me."

"Why's that?"

"I don't vote Republican. There's no such thing as the lesser of two evils, Josh."

He looks out the window but I see his shit-eating grin in the glass.

"Let me give you a scenario," I say, pulling onto the main drag. "You're a five-year-old kid. A man busts into your classroom with a gun and ties you to a chair. He points at one girl's head, and then another. He says, 'I'm going to kill one of them. You choose.'"

"What's that got to do with anything?"

"It's the same as picking a Republican or a Democrat."

"That's not even close."

"Why? Either choice is bad—and the gunman doesn't give you a third. His gun in your face makes a third choice impossible. They've held the threat of force against us for generations now, saying pick this or pick that. Then they justify the shit they did to fuck is, saying 'we're the people you elected.' The gunman may as well kill the girl he wants. Why force you to choose—unless to blame you? They take our money before we even see it. You fight it, a man with a gun shows up on your doorstep. They spy on us at home, saying some caveman on a camel is a threat to our way of life. They take a man's house so their buddy can put in a mall and pay higher taxes. All with a gun to our head. Pick this or pick that. You elected us, now do as we say. And what they say is go to war. Fort Sumter, Pearl Harbor, Gulf of Tonkin, 911. All staged to get us into war, to keep our eyes looking out instead of in. Someone comes along every now and again that wants to end it, like Jack Kennedy. The Machine stomps him like a fucking bug. Another thing. Why you think they say the battle against terrorism will '*last a lifetime?*' You think the US couldn't crush every single middle eastern country, inside of a week, if ending the war was the goal? Nah, they want war and all the goodies they get with it. You better pay the fuck attention, because in two years you're eligible to be cannon fodder."

Josh says, "What's any of this got to do with the situation we're in right now?"

"Nothing, and everything. I got to pull over for breakfast. My stomach's raw."

"Surprise, surprise."

I swerve into New Frontiers, a health food store. "You want anything?"

"Sure. You're buying," Josh says.

A few minutes later I have a bag of breakfast and a jug of green juice. We get on the road again, turning onto 89A, the scenic route through Sedona.

"Anyone ever say you come across bitter?" he says.

I shift to fourth and let the little motor struggle. It doesn't have the horsepower and I drop to third. So that's how it is. Speak the truth and you're bitter. How can I condense everything I know, a cohesive, systematic understanding of the world—driving a Ford fucking Tempo with a slippy clutch?

"What this has to do with the situation we're in is this: Government accumulates power by controlling money—the more regulated the markets, the more oversight, the more tax code—the more fingers the government has on your wallet, and the more leverage to yank it out of your pocket. They control the wealth because they use it to do two things. Buy votes from the takers, and start wars to scare the shit out of the doers. The lie of democracy is that since we get to vote, and we elect the sonsabitches, this God

damn leech called government is true-blue American, and represents
the will of the people. Truth is, the same old tyranny is back. We have
two choices in Washington, and they never change. Pick this, Josh, or
pick that."

"How's that fit with the governor being a lesbian?"

"I don't give a rat's ass about her being a dyke, except someone
thinks he can blackmail her with it. If she had pictures of the minority
leader with a cock in his mouth, she'd use it too. What's important is
why she's being blackmailed."

"Which is…"

"Power, don't you get it yet? That's how these people operate!
She's pushing legislation that changes everything. Traditional culture
disappears. Individuals and self-reliance disappears. The state expands
because people vote for the liar that promises to give 'em the most.
That's how James Madison predicted the Republic would fall. And
it's happening before our eyes.

"This Republic started with thirteen states that wanted to keep
power close to the people. They'd just thrown the Brits out. The last
thing they wanted was a strong central government. But they made
one because the Articles of Confederation didn't give them a way to
deal with foreign governments. France was about to go to war with us
over debt, and the French weren't total pussies back then. So the
Founding Fathers built a federal system. The states ceded limited
powers to the central government, and retained the rest for
themselves."

"Help me tie this to the Governor."

"Every war has expanded the power of the central government. Our first standing army was in 1791, to fight Indian wars. The income tax, and the expansion of the Treasury, has roots in the Civil War. World War One gave us nationalized railroads and the precursor to the FDA, and they took over the food business. The FBI grew. Then the CIA came from World War Two. You get huge companies dealing with trillions of dollars of war income, Lyndon's buddies, and the Vietnam War keeps them in cash. The Patriot Act comes from 9-11. The Shadow Government. Every time, politicians promised that taking our rights away was a temporary thing, but they stuck, and the central government holds powers today that would have George Washington recruiting a new army. Politicians don't want to deconstruct the central government. They're devoted to accumulating power, not destroying it. Virginia Rentier is after the presidency, and she'll do anything to get it."

"What is she doing?"

"The bill is called Vallejo, and it's going to make it so anyone can vote. Anyone."

"What's wrong with that?"

"You assume everyone living here has this country's best interests at heart. But not with the welfare state. Think about it. Originally, only landowners could vote. Why? Because they had property to lose—and could be trusted to reign in the government. You let everybody vote, people with no stake, and it don't take long until they vote themselves a raise. People used to want the government to stay out their way while they built a castle. Now they want the government to build the castle and make the payments. Vallejo's gonna import people who've fucked up their own governments for the last three hundred years, so they can come fuck up ours. There's something special about this country, but we're a cunt hair from losing it, Josh."

He's grinning at me.

"You ever see a cunt hair, Josh?"

"Yeah."

"Then you know how close we are."

"I don't get why the governor would want that."

"She's buying votes. Power, Josh. They live for it."

"Isn't that democracy?"

"No, that's democracy with no morals, no cultural pride, no individualism, and more important than anything, no accountability. That's democracy when the lazy half reaches the tipping point."

"Who investigates the governor? What about checks and balances?"

"That's interesting. Who has the power to investigate the government? Used to be that the citizen was the watchdog. The Founding Fathers intended that the population would be vigilant—"

"Nat! What was that green shit you drank? Who investigates the governor?"

"The attorney general. Jane Lynwood."

"Let's take the pictures to her."

"Well, there's one little catch."

"What?"

"She's in the pictures. You show her those black and whites, she'll investigate you."

"Then who was blackmailing the governor?"

"The guy in the canal was the Minority Leader's chief of staff."

"So give the pictures to the Minority Leader. Done."

"I like your thinking. Machiavellian, at that. But you're not understanding. I don't want the legislation to go through, but I don't want to hop in the den with them."

"Is it that, or is it him being your ex father in law?"

"No."

"How'd she die?"

"Leave it alone, Josh."

"What? In a car with you?"

I'm silent.

"While you were driving?"

"You're pressing my buttons."

"Drunk? Think maybe it's that, and not that he wants to rule the world?"

"I learned from that. I got a code, now. No grey areas."

"The governor's unchecked," he says. "You're going to have to pick this or pick that."

Rentier sipped cappuccino and read a draft of her speech for the first annual Global Warming Economic Conference. If she'd had any sense, she would have hired an assistant with a mind as fit as her legs. Patterson—another problem. Couldn't fire them all at once like Jimmy Carter did. People get concerned. Well, the misery index didn't help, either. But after the election—heads would roll.

Jennifer paged.

"What?"

"A prosecutor is here from the AG's office with paperwork. Earnest Whetton."

Rentier leaned, but couldn't gain the vantage to spot him through the doorway. "Tell him to leave it with you."

"He said he has a message for you. Only you."

"I don't have time for this."

"Governor—this is Earnest Whetton."

Did he take the handset from Jennifer? Rentier stepped three feet from her desk and met Whetton's eyes. He stood with square shoulders that suggested breeding and idealism.

"I have to see you about Rudy Ging Theen," he said.

She heard him in both ears. "Put Jennifer on the line."

"Governor?" Jennifer said.

"Send him in." She turned. "And get security now."

Whetton strode into Rentier's office. He placed a file on her desk.

"You have a message from Jane?"

"No, it's from me."

"I thought I recognized you. Your father tried Theen."

"That's right. Rudy Ging Theen killed a man in cold blood for drug money. It would be unconscionable to release him and put others in harm's way. I didn't sign this, and I'm advising against a pardon. As firmly and vehemently as possible."

"What does Lynwood say?"

"She's smart enough to hand it off, like you. There's no political gain for you—"

"Excuse me?"

"The fact that you're willing to try makes you lower than whale shit. But you know that. Good day, Governor."

He closed the door and Virginia stood at her desk. Blood pressured her eyes and heat flushed her cheeks. She cupped her hands and held her head.

"Governor?" The door swung open and Jennifer said, "Security is here."

"I don't need them."

"Dick Clyman's holding on line one. Do you want to talk to him?"

"Just a minute." Rentier rolled her neck side to side and took a deep breath. She spun, looked out the window at her city, counted to five.

"Dick, how are you holding up?"

"I'm dandy, Governor. I just wanted to give you a shout. There's going to be big news on Drudge if Vallejo goes to vote."

"What kind of big news, Dick?"

"I think you know what we're talking about here."

"You know this line is recorded."

"And you know the country will be interested."

"Be careful."

Rentier closed the line and took a deep breath.

When she first ran for Congress, one reporter gave her problems. Times were changing, but most Arizonans still viewed people like her an aberration.

The most vehement on the right wing called her something worse, a name that hurt the way sticks and stones couldn't. Physical pain heightened the sense of existence. Descartes could have just as easily said, *I hurt, therefore I am.* Or even, *therefore I have a right to exist.* But these right wingers who thumped their Old Testaments—the same book that had the Chosen People ripping pregnant women's bellies open, and crushing babies' skulls at a river bank—these people used a term far more insidious than aberration.

They called her *abomination.* Something so evil it is forever banned from the sight of God.

Her father quoted fire and brimstone by day and snuck into her bedroom at night. She brushed her hair in her room. Her mother was away, playing bridge or whatever excuse she used to give the old man free reign after dark. He opened the door; a cigarette dangled from his jaw and he wore a white T-shirt with armpit stains.

For weeks he'd been touching her and using her hand to touch him, and at first, his attention was narcotic like the first time she'd touched herself. But it wasn't affection, she learned; it was service. She didn't earn special-girl status. He just left her room until the next time. It was her fault he wanted her; and now that she'd gotten him started, she didn't know how to make him stop.

Virginia brushed her hair. Eleven years old. The first nubs of breasts forming. Freckles on her face. Thin hair down there… But her face was pretty. Everyone looked at her and beamed. Smiling, she could imagine her face could take her to Hollywood. It helped her forget she was what they called the Mexican girls, a slut.

He stood behind her while she dragged the brush through her hair, pulling it out, stretching it. Her eyes welled with water and her heart trembled with fear.

"You think you're too pretty?" he said.

"No, daddy."

He held his cigarette close to her cheek and she flinched.

"You feel how hot that is? You remember that."

Virginia Rentier, Governor, stood from her desk and brushed wetness from her eyes and fought her rolling stomach. He tried to take everything from her. Everything. Just like you take the life of a cow when you want a steak. Livestock. Chattel. Daughter. He dropped a sharp hook inside her and dragged for her soul.

"But I was a good girl!" She pressed her hand to her face. "But I was good!" The pain was like fire on eleven-year-old skin.

Yeah. She got hard. You're fucking damn right. But she made something of herself. She met a mean world and said, *I'm meaner.*

Through college, boys were an extension of her father's predatory will. When suitors called she always had to study for a test or write a paper. Her father paid her admission. She placed herself under his thumb. How could she be with a man?

After college she paid her own way and breathed free air. Her father wasted under the divinely judicial pain of lung cancer, soon to meet his fire-breathing God. He lay in bed, Auschwitz skinny, nothing but strands of flesh draped in sallow skin. A hospice worker left and her mother waited in another room.

Mother always had been thoughtful about leaving them alone.

"How are you?" Virginia said.

"I need… cigarette."

Her gaze traced the outline of a plastic tube from her father's nose to an oxygen tank a few feet away. She pulled a pack of Camels from her purse.

"You don't smoke," he whispered.

She shook her head.

"No filters," he said. Was that approval?

She lit one and placed it in his mouth, half hoping to witness a sudden orange flare and an explosion worthy of his evil. His lips closed and the cherry glowed. He exhaled a cloud that smelled like a slice of murder, just enough to know she'd finally done something.

She tossed the deck of Camels on his chest and put the lighter in his hand, and never returned.

He died three days later, but she'd said her goodbye with a pack of Camels, and if he didn't get the message, fuck him.

After the crucible, only Virginia Rentier remained. She took an undergraduate degree in political science and applied to a dozen of the best law schools, Harvard, Yale, Virginia, Cornell. Each informed her by polite letter that the year's applicant pool was very strong and they appreciated her thinking of them.

When the last of the rejections came in the mail, she rewrote her essay. She had been molested by her father and had a personal commitment to helping other girls and women fight back. She was either going to serve the law, or break it.

Arizona State University's College of Law accepted her. It proved providential. She blossomed. A cold and rigid law professor saw inside her, recognized her unique potential, and lured her into bed. The affair planted the seed of her future modus operandi. The professor had been on the admissions board and had read her essay, and the older woman's gift helped define Virginia. Sex could be a pleasurable tool to wield.

At twenty-five her appetite exploded. She counted lovers with four vertical hash marks and a horizontal marking the fifth. The tenth. The fifteenth.

But though she seduced women and took her pleasure from them, she never relaxed; she climaxed like an animal and was done with it. She chose women because a man violated her, but she didn't give herself to them. Women were unforgiven as well. It was her mother who smelled sex on her father night after night, and did nothing.

Sex was biological. Its release didn't calm the rage.

When she entered the political arena she had no Ivy League pedigree or wealthy patrons, just her looks and wits. She volunteered for Brownward's 1988 presidential campaign and made contacts, learned the mechanics of power from the inside. How to gain it with promises and conviction, spend it to get results, and replenish with goodwill.

She met a wealthy insurance agency owner who seemed as impressed with her looks as her political skill. He wanted her, and even better, so did his wife. Her eyes reserved secrets but her body and dress gave signals. The touch on her arm lasted too long. She held her eyes too steady; her nipples stiffened with a casual brush—and the fact she wore a blouse thin enough to let Virginia feel them—these were messages. They seduced each other, and later Virginia found the wife controlled the checkbook.

Many women had pasts they could never forget, but would not remember; women whose childhoods compelled adult success. Some nabbed men with worldly power, and dominated them at home. These women thirsted for her. Others found strength and position through years of absolute dedication to careers because there was nothing waiting at home except a fuzzy white cat. These women craved her. One by one, she showed them something between their legs save guilt and loathing, and added a stanch devotee to her network.

Finally, when she ran for congress, she learned a corollary lesson. Some women would hate her.

The one who taught her that was a reporter.

Cars crash on the hill after Bumble Bee. Hairpin turns zigzag down a steep grade for miles, daring Civic-driving punks to test their immortality. I'm tempting Darwin myself, driving this Tempo. The brakes shudder and wobble; the rings are shot and the engine burns oil. I downshift to brake and the exhaust farts white clouds—but I get great gas mileage.

I remind myself to buy puts on Ford.

"I got to take a leak," Josh says.

"There's an exit coming up."

A few miles down the road I pull onto a dirt stretch that leads upslope to a nest of shrubs. We have a bird's eye view at the crest. Paper plates, in the middle of the desert. A tire. A clock-radio. A sheet of plastic, twenty feet long, snared in the brush. How did this obscenity get here? I don't ask Josh. He'll tell me it's the corporations.

Josh splatters a golden braid against a shrub and I may as well let loose, while we're here. I whiz a few yards away, and listening, compare my slow trickle to Josh's fire hose. Josh looks over his shoulder at me.

"That's all right," I say. "After this much use, signs of wear are normal."

The sun is warm and we've already dropped to three thousand feet. Another grand and we'll be in desert.

Josh reaches in the Tempo to the radio. He finds an AM station on a newsbreak. I recognize the timbre of the announcer's Hispanic voice, but can't hear the words.

"What was that bill you were talking about?" Josh says.

"Vallejo."

"Radio says they're voting on it today. It'll be a law."

"Did the radio say that last part, or did you add it?"

"It'll be a law, right?"

"Not quite. Is the House voting, or the Senate? Has it come out of conference? Has the governor signed it?"

"I don't know. I go to a public school, remember?"

"That don't mean you have to be ignorant."

"Quit playing with your pecker and come listen yourself."

"Well, what was it? The House is voting?"

"I think. Listen." He turns the volume.

"...this bill is a travesty, an absolute travesty. The people of Arizona don't want it and this Congress simply refuses to listen..."

A reporterette continues, *"That was House Minority Leader Clyman, who opposes the bill. The Senate is scheduled to vote later this afternoon, without amendment, in a rare show of unity with the house. This is Lupita Guitierrez, reporting live at the Capitol."*

I take a quick look around the highway, the dirt road, the sky, and get in the Tempo. "You ever hear of the Rubicon?"

"Yeah. It's a badass Jeep," Josh says.

I shake my head. "It's also a river, and in the days of Julius Caesar, it was the border between the Roman Empire and Gaul. The Roman Senate—a group of back-stabbing pussies, like ours—ordered Caesar not to attack Pompeii, on the other side of the river. Caesar crossed the Rubicon. He took irrevocable action."

Josh nods. "Vallejo is the Rubicon..."

"When this bill passes, there's no going back. The Democrats have a bare majority right now, but passing Vallejo will turn three hundred thousand socialists who can't vote into Democrats who can. It'll never be undone; the people who would undo it'll never hold a majority again."

"Can't we go to court or something? Wouldn't someone stand in the way?"

I shake my head. "We have two options. Blackmail the governor, like the others were, or expose her as a murderer and have her removed before she signs the bill. They got the gun to the head, Josh. Pick this or pick that."

I don't tell him about the third option.

Rudy Ging Theen squinted in the sunlight. Eighteen years, one hundred and ninety-three days had passed since he'd last stood outside a penitentiary. The prison's façade was ghostly white like an ancient Catholic mission, and the weathered wood trim completed the illusion. He studied the building for a moment; he'd never dreamed he'd step outside of it. The dirt was the same and the air was just as stifling outside as in. But the façade was something you couldn't see from the inside. He cupped his hand over his eyes.

"Well, Rudy, I figured they'd send someone here to meet you," the guard named Blanco said. "You can wait inside if you like."

"Jorge, I believe I'm going to get a little ways down the street before the governor changes her mind."

"Sure, yeah," Blanco said. "It ain't gonna be the same around here. Good luck to you."

"Thank you, Jorge."

"There's a bus stop a couple blocks that way. Oh, here." Blanco took his sunglasses from his front pocket and gave them to Theen. "You'll need them if you're going to be outside today."

Jorge shook Theen's hand. Theen took the first step and the next. He turned. "Each one makes me feel a little closer to being a free man."

"Praise God."

Theen smiled. "Praise the Lord."

His wallet held three hundred dollars and he carried a notebook with a few addresses of pen pals.

He'd expected to be greeted by the family of the man he'd slain. Protestors with placards demanding justice. The chaplain he'd studied with. A sniper in a corner window. The governor's point man, Patterson. Anything but no one.

Theen stepped toward the street. Sober and old was different than young and flush. His rickety knees popped and he felt like he hadn't stood up straight for years.

The diesel exhaust of a passing truck combined with a wisp of morning humidity to create a smell that took him back to a Luv's Truck Stop, with gravel underfoot and Copenhagen pressed to the corners of his eyes to keep him awake. A revolver stuffed in his pants. Those days were long gone.

Sweat stood on his brow when he reached a bus stop by a gas station. A small girl with red hair and a pink bow waited in the shade. Theen read the bus schedule.

"Hi there, sweetie. Do you know what time it is?"

"Fourteen minutes after nine," she said, and shifted away.

He looked at the schedule again. He had a few minutes.

He walked to the gas station.

"I want a can of Copenhagen," he said. "Been twenty-two years since I had a rub of Cope."

He sat on the bus stop bench and cut the paper snuff can sidewall with his thumbnail. The pungent odor reached him at the break of the seal. He pinched a wad and pressed it in his lip. The red-haired girl wrinkled her nose.

The bus swerved and stopped with a screech of brakes. The girl shuffled aboard and he stepped on behind her, watching her smooth tiny legs. He dropped into the empty seat adjacent hers, and looking ahead, caught the driver's eyes in the mirror. He looked away.

Marisol Ortega, Speaker of the House of Representatives of the State of Arizona, sat on a leather chair behind an acre-sized desktop. Behind her, a credenza with a bookshelf towered to the raised ceiling, both built by her uncle Jesus in Mexico. He'd recommended verdecillo, a ruddy Mexican hardwood, with hand-carved stiles and floral painted glass. Jesus had taken half of her first term in the House to build it, and then the shipping company took over a month to transport it through winding mountain roads, jungle and desert.

Marisol was an anchor baby, born in the U.S. to parents who had crossed the border illegally. Her parents never risked going home to Mexico, but after graduating from high school, Marisol longed to know her history, and visited the extended family she knew only through stories.

Uncle Jesus welcomed her. She helped in his wood shop, and he taught her that honorable work was indispensable to honorable character. She chided him that the Savior was also a carpenter, and he took umbrage. He was not a proud man; just a decent one.

"Marisol?"

It was Mike Schwartz, an intern who ate rice with chop sticks and always ordered squid.

"Yes?"

He passed her a single page with an Excel spreadsheet. "The vote count."

She pulled the center drawer open for a pen and saw a plastic bag of green powder. She smiled.

"Thank you." She glanced down the list. "Oh, Mike? Tell Mulrooney I want to see him. Right away."

She rolled the Ziploc bag of powder in her fingers and thought of the first time she had seen it. The shippers had just unloaded the desk and she checked it for damage before signing the papers. The bag was in the center drawer, looking like lime Kool-Aid, or worse, some drug a smuggler forgot to remove. She tasted it. It was wood. Later Jesus told her it was rare for red verdecillo to produce green sawdust. He'd bagged it and sent it for good luck.

She opened it a year later when Jesus died. The musty scent was something a man might wear as cologne.

Jesus would have made a great American.

She folded her arms and counted the 'nays,' then jumped at a sudden thud on the door. Mike Schwartz popped his head around the corner.

"Mulrooney?" she said.

Mike nodded.

"Send him in." She kept her seat.

Mulrooney strode three steps and stood hands to hips. "I'm not gonna budge on Vallejo. Anything else, or can I get back to work?"

"Have a seat."

"I'll stand."

She sat in an imperial leather chair and he stood with his back to the door.

Marisol gazed at the spreadsheet, aware of her pulse, her breathing, the sweat on her neck. After a moment she looked up to him.

He smiled. He'd bested her, and the rest of the drama would follow footsteps laid in advance—he justifies his stand, she attempts to buy him, he blocks her with the threat of further undermining her power—which she only derives from consensus. She excuses him, and he crows about how he's beaten her again.

And, she thought, it was all because she humored him in the first place, tried to gain his allegiance by making him the chair of the most powerful committee.

His face reflected wide on her desktop, polished like glass by a poor Mexican man. She stood and met his eyes.

"I'm calling a vote on Vallejo in two hours. I expect your enthusiastic support. If the bill fails, whether you vote for it or not, I'll put someone loyal in Ways and Means. I'll move your office to the adjunct building. And then I'll personally recruit a candidate to unseat you in your primary, and see to it that not one dime of PAC money gets to your campaign."

His nostrils flared and his eyes thinned.

"One last thing," she said. "You may also find that the AG has an interest in a couple of your land deals in Buckeye, and that her sense of timing is catastrophic. Go think about Vallejo."

Chapter Eight

I've been driving the speed limit and once we get close enough to the city to ride the access road along Interstate Seventeen, I take it. I'd rather sit at a dozen stoplights with low visibility than up on the highway where the bad guys might already be on the lookout for a Ford Tempo with a trunk about to fall off.

"I'll enjoy getting out of this car," I say.

"We can switch to the Mustang."

"We'll pick it up, but this one's going to my place. I'm not trading a Triumph Rocket for a Tempo." I pull into the mall parking lot, a few hundred yards from the hotel where Bandage Head surprised us last night. From this distance, everything looks normal. It's getting hot enough no one wants to be outside.

"So what are we going to do with the pictures?"

"They lead to a dead man on one end and a corrupt governor on the other. In a shit storm, the only way to stay clean is to get out the wind."

"We ought to stick together," Josh says.

I nod. "When you get to your car, I want you to look it over before you climb inside. Check the undercarriage."

"For what?"

I shrug. "Anything that doesn't have dirt on it. Then we'll go to my place. You can get some sleep while I research a few things." I punch his arm and point at the Mustang.

"If you thought Bandage Head put a bomb under my car, you'd look for me," he says. "Right?"

"Check under the car."

Josh walks to the Mustang and lays on his side at the rear bumper, tinkers under the vehicle, and repeats the motions at each side. His posture says he thinks it's cloak and dagger bullshit.

He hops inside and the taillights flash.

Drab walls held the smell of countless visitors' armpits and asses. The narrow hallway led to a barred door, and before it, on the left, Mick Patterson stood at an opening similar to a ticket sales booth at a movie theater. A long scratch stretched across the Plexiglas, and on the other side, a guard hunched over a form. Patterson read his name tag.

"Hey uh, Blanco. I'm here for Theen."

"Cut him loose this morning. Wasn't after nine." He kept his eyes on the form, diligent civil servant.

Patterson slammed his fist to the ledge and a mint dish bounced. "This morning? I spoke to you clowns yesterday. His release was at eleven!"

Blanco peered from under brows like a shelf of rock. "Warden cut him loose. Ole Rudy Ging Theen's a free man."

"Where is he?"

"We give him his things and pointed him to the bus stop."

"Just brilliant."

"You want to talk to the warden?"

"Oh, piss off." Patterson left.

"Rough night?" Luigi hulked behind the bar like a bulldog on his hind legs, chest bulging as he polished a glass.

"Crown," Johnny La Rue said.

Luigi glanced at a clock.

"Yeah, at eleven. Whaddayou care?"

Luigi lifted his hands, his face plaintive, jovial. "You do what you need to do, Johnny. I'm just sayin'."

"Right. No problem. Just gimme a shot, aright?"

Luigi popped the shot glass on the bar and poured.

"Hold on." La Rue downed it and said, "Another."

Luigi filled it again. "You all right, Johnny?"

"Mexican been around lookin for me?"

"Nah." Luigi picked up his rag and rubbed the same glass. "You sure you wanna be messin with that crew?"

"Whaddayou, my father now?" La Rue drank the second shot and slid a hundred-dollar bill across the bar.

Luigi glanced down. "Business good?"

"Real good. Gimme a bottle a Coors."

La Rue took the bottle to a table at the back of the bar. He sat in shadows. Watched the entrance. Lit a cigarette.

"You keep rubbin that glass like the fuckin Queen's gonna drink out it."

Luigi shook his head. La Rue glanced at his watch and reached to a television mounted on the wall. He checked his watch again, then flashed through the channels, settling on a *Dirty Harry* marathon. He sat.

The door opened and a swarthy figure stepped through the bright light. La Rue turned from the television. The man walked to the bar. His ponytail draped over his muscle shirt and a black tattoo of the sun radiated over the ball of his shoulder. The man looked at Luigi, said "Water," and turned back to Johnny.

"You La Rue?"

"That's right."

The man took a glass from Luigi and drank from it as he walked to the table. La Rue studied the gold on his neck and fingers.

"We gonna make a deal, or what?" La Rue said.

The Mexican was silent. His sober brows sloped over frowning eyes.

"Fuckin say something," La Rue said.

"How much?"

"Two keys."

"Mi madre moves two keys. You said business."

"Two to start. Then I talk to my boss."

The Mexican lifted a single finger. "One time, one exception."

"And I want a sample. Right now."

The Mexican glanced to Luigi at the bar.

"He's aright," La Rue said.

The Mexican pulled a folded piece of paper from his pocket. "This is pure. No Borax. You never have nothin like it."

La Rue unfolded the paper, wet his finger and tasted the powder, then took a straw from the salt and pepper tray, cut it, and snorted the line.

His nostril burned with a familiar flare. "We'll see," he said. "How much can you get?"

"You know … this territory … "

"We'll be moving it northeast."

"I move as much shit as I want, to the high bidder."

"My boss is the high bidder."

"You run back to your Boss and call me."

"Two keys?"

"Tomorrow night. Meet me here at ten, and we go for a ride."

The Mexican left. A cool, distant rush swelled in Johnny's brain. He felt like shooting pool; it would be a can't-miss day. This was good shit. Really good shit. He finished his beer.

"Hey!" Luigi said.

"Yeah?"

Luigi frowned, shook his head sideways.

La Rue laughed and stepped out of the bar. Sunlight blinded him. He cupped his hand over his eyes while fishing his sunglasses from his pocket. A pair of Latinos in denim and wife-beaters sat across the street on cement steps leading into a laundromat. One saw him and nudged the other's leg.

His shoulder collided with a passing man. La Rue spun, his arms ready to brawl, but the black-haired man kept walking. The two across the street walked parallel with him, ignoring him. La Rue angled across the street.

"Hey!"

The two ignored him. They wore sneakers and gold, one with a sideways ball cap, both with baggy jeans.

"Hey, you Mexican motherfuckers!"

They stopped.

"What's up?" La Rue said. "You workin me?"

They were short and stood with slumped shoulders, wavering back and forth, perpetually ready to attack. The smaller man had a scar across his right eye socket and the eyeball didn't move. He tilted his head. "Loco," he said to his friend. They kept walking.

La Rue watched them go. A dozen yards away, the short one turned and said, "We are everywhere, gringo."

The van sat around the corner and Johnny jumped inside and locked the doors. He opened his cell phone and pressed the buttons while he pulled onto the road.

"Johnny in Phoenix."

"Hey, kid. You on a cell?"

"Yeah. I'll have two, tomorrow night. I'm thinkin I'll be home in five days."

"Good," De Luca said. "Why you takin so long with Buffa?"

"I'm close. I gotta real good reason to wait. Real good. I'll make you the J. Edgar Hoover of Philly. I'll call later."

"You do good with this, Johnny, you're my man in Phoenix."

"Thanks, Boss. Later."

He turned at his apartment, a four-level joint with a pool and covered parking. Girls sunned on lounges but he couldn't see through the fence and shrubs. He'd have to look from his kitchen window. He bounded up the steps and his neighbor, an old bastard with rotten teeth, had left his trash on the doorstep. He did it every week and it always reeked of tuna. Johnny pounded his door with the side of his fist as he ran past.

Upstairs, he lifted his mattress and retrieved a ziplock bag of cocaine. La Rue lay a picture frame on its back, cut a line on the glass with a razor, and snorted it.

He shaved a few days' stubble and showered. Slapped on cologne and his cell phone bleated. It was Buffa.

"Johnny, you straight?"

"I'm good."

"Am I gonna have a problem with you?"

"No. No problem. Did you call the Boss? I swear I'm straight."

"No. This is your second chance. You don't get a third, so you better keep your shit clean. I need you and the boys this afternoon. Pick me up at two in the van. Nah, make that one forty-five. Bring a piece. That a problem?"

"No problem."

"Johnny?"

"Yeah."

"You be straight, you hear?"

"I'm straight. You think you get the pictures today?"

The line was dead.

Lindsay scampered to Merry's locker and began retelling a sexcapade about Eric, all-star everything. She twisted her hair, a signal Merry recognized.

Lindsay lied.

Merry looked past her for Jenny, who'd promised to walk home with her.

"…on the hood of his car…" Lindsay said. "Isn't that crazy?"

"You're such a whore," Merry said, smiling.

Jenny rounded the corner and waved. Merry bolted.

"Are you ready?" Merry asked Jenny.

"I'm so excited! Corey's driving me home. Want me to see if you can come with us?"

"You're going home with him?"

"He can take you too." Her smile faltered. "I'm sorry."

"Never mind. I'll be okay. I only asked because Josh was so worried about me."

"Are you sure?"

They parted; Merry stored the betrayal carefully in a mental file. She turned the corner at the school and walked to the main road. Three blocks, a turn, and a final block to her house.

Her skin grew hot under the bright sun and the heat made her drowsy. Summer school was formatted like normal school days, only with alternating study and class periods, so she ended up going through a week's assignments and readings every day. She'd angered her chemistry teacher, and now she listened to him five hours a day.

Or maybe the pervert just liked looking at her knees. He did enough of it.

She yawned and noticed a Coca Cola vending machine across the street at a gas station. The sugar would go straight to her butt and the guy in the van by the machine wore a look she recognized. It said, *'my wife doesn't care where I get my appetite.'*

She'd be home soon, and she'd make espresso.

Her arm reddened—she'd forgotten her sun block that morning. Her face was hot and she remembered the last time she'd gotten a raccoon burn. Her friends—the bitches—would bray and point. She dropped her shades in her purse. None of this would have happened if her father had bought her a car.

She stood in the shade of a tree for a moment and sent a text message to Josh.

SO FAR SO GOOD

Ahead, a man in a black pair of pants and a black T-shirt sat at a bus stop. She squinted. He slumped with his feet stretched across the sidewalk, his back low on the rest. What a bummer to be on this side of the road, in the sunlight, when the bus stops on the other side of the road were catching shade right now. Her skin was clammy. The humidity must be rising.

As she approached, the man at the bus stop sat up. Guys always changed their behavior when she neared. Like she didn't see them before, when their bellies were hanging out and their shoulders hung slack. There's no way to make a soft body look hard, but that never stopped them from trying. This one—wearing black when the temperature was a hundred and fifteen, would be here a while. The next bus didn't come for a half hour. He turned away but watched her with peripheral vision. Guys always pulled tricks like that.

Houses lined the opposite side of the road and on the same side, a two-foot hedgerow extended about fifty yards along a dusty vacant lot that had a "sold" sign. If this guy wanted something, he'd have to take it in the open. She was safe.

Ahead, a hundred yards away, two boys sailed across the street on skateboards. The muted sound of roller skate wheels drifted in the heat.

The man on the bench shifted forward with his elbows on his knees.

I trail Josh by two car-lengths and a black Ford Taurus paces me on the right. He followed Josh out of the mall exit, right onto Peoria, and into the left turn lane to pick up Interstate Seventeen. Now, on the highway, the two young men in suits and dark glasses cruise without conversation and keep their eyes on the Mustang. Their haircuts look like month-old high and tights—crisp, but long enough to blend into the business community. The driver snaps a glance my direction. He says something to his partner.

I drift with the flow of traffic, back and then in front of the Taurus. Josh hangs back a little when the gap between us grows to a hundred yards. The Taurus varies his following distance. Josh never completely pulls away before the Taurus passes a car and gets back into spitting distance, but I haven't had any doubt since I read the government license plate.

I miss my Triumph; on it, speed is a decision. The Tempo is weak. I downshift and press the pedal; the engine thrums in a slow crescendo until I pass the FBI boys. I feel their looks press my temple.

Side by side with Josh, our eyes meet. I pull ahead, retake his lane, and stomp the brake into the floor. The Tempo's rotors are warped and the car shudders like I hit rumble strips at eighty miles an hour; the peal of locked tires on cement sounds like an Arab calling sheep.

The Mustang smashes into my trunk, crushing me into the seat. The brakes are still locked and my forehead catches the top of the steering wheel. Josh rams me again and his horn sounds a steady blare. I swerve to the side and Josh pulls over behind me. His face is crazy with rage in my rearview. He jumps out of the car and his horn is still screaming. It's stuck.

The FBI agents pass and pull over. Their reverse lights come on and the Taurus races back to us. I only have a moment. I storm back to Josh waving my arms like a crazy man.

"Play along. You don't know me. These guys are FBI."

"What the fuck! My horn!"

The Mustang isn't crumpled but Josh studies the nicks in his bumper. The FBI agents are a dozen feet away.

"Turn your horn off! That pickup cut me off! Which you would have seen if you didn't have your grill three feet from my bumper!"

"Get the fuck out of my space, old man." Josh brushes past my shoulder and opens the driver door. He fiddles under the console and

pulls a fuse panel off. A moment later the horn stops. The Mustang
idles.

"Hey!" one of the FBI men shouts. I turn and the one in the lead
looks like the Brawny paper towel guy in a suit.

"You saw it, right?" I say. "He was following so close he couldn't
stop if he wanted to."

The smaller agent wears a Harvard ring. He's the junior of the two,
but neither has seen his twenty-sixth birthday, I'd guess. Harvard
looks at the other, waiting.

"Don't they have driver's ed any more? Look what you've done to
my bumper! My trunk is collapsed."

Josh smirks.

Brawny flips open his ID. "I am special agent Henry Wilson with
the Federal Bureau of Investigation. This is special agent Joel
Burnside. Can I see some identification, please?"

"My name is Professor Doyle McIntyre. I am a law professor at
Arizona State University, Sandra Day O'Connor School of Law. This
is a traffic accident, and for the record, you have no jurisdiction. What
do you want?" I say.

The chance that one of them is a lawyer is pretty good, though the
Bureau dropped its requirement that agents be attorneys in the sixties.
They had recruiting problems because everyone figured out they were
fascists. If they're lawyers, I can spout the mumbo jumbo for a few
minutes. Then I'm toast.

Harvard looks at the tear in my pants. The bloodstain washed out,
but the tear didn't. I'm wearing a ratty T-shirt and work boots. Driving

a Tempo that was manufactured when these guys were shitting diapers green. I'm not what they think a law professor looks like.

"You can either work with us here, or we take you to the field office for questioning."

"Of course I am happy to assist any way I can. However, without a crime—I fail to see where this is anything other than, at best, a fishing expedition. At worst, this is harassment. Let me see your identification again."

I reach inside the Tempo and grab a notepad, and copy their badge numbers.

"So, gentlemen, please explain how I can help you?"

Harvard glances at Brawny.

Brawny spreads his arms and guides us away from the traffic. On the dirt he says, "We're investigating a homicide. You match the description of a suspect. You were involved in an accident with a person who is known to have been with the suspect as recently as last night. I need to see your identification."

"In that case…" I open my wallet and give the agent an ID that matches the name Doyle McIntyre.

Harvard takes my license back to the car and makes a cell phone call. Brawny stands beside me, watching.

"What subjects do you teach?" he says.

"I am on sabbatical right now. However, when I return it will be first year Constitutional law, and a third-year Second Amendment elective."

"Second Amendment. Are you carrying?"

"Oh, no. I'm not one of those guys. I actually head a small organization that is trying to repeal the second amendment. We no longer need it. We have a military and police—why keep the minutemen around?"

He leads me away from Josh, who sits on his bumper.

"You ever see this kid before?" Brawny says.

"I have not. These punks—the way they drive. I ought to start a lobby to change the driving age to thirty." I laugh. He grimaces. "Or twenty something. How old are you, agent?"

"Never mind, sir."

"Well, we could have an exception for law enforcement."

"Thanks."

"Why are you after the kid? Did he kill someone?"

"He was seen last night with a person of interest."

"Person of interest?"

"A witness."

These agents weren't in Flagstaff. They're local boys following instructions to tail a car. The only connection is the Mustang.

Harvard returns with my identification. The identity is secure, but I don't know if someone in Flagstaff took a picture of me as Tom Davis. If so, I own the face they're looking for. It's a pick this or pick that situation.

"Mister McIntyre—"

"Professor—Special Agent."

"Of course, Professor. Were you in Flagstaff recently?"

"This morning. I have a brother. We are not on good terms. Frankly, he is unstable; I only meet him in public places. I saw him this morning for coffee. We're handling an estate matter—our mother has passed."

"What is your brother's name?"

"Half brother. Tom Davis. We each took our fathers' names."

Harvard tries not to smile but he knows he just got important in FBI-Land. "Are you aware that your brother is a material witness to a homicide?" Harvard keeps his gaze on Josh.

"No—but that would certainly explain his erratic behavior. He seemed nervous."

"We're going to need you to come with us," Brawny says.

"It seems my needs and yours are different. I can't leave without the punk's insurance information. If he has any."

A Harvard man should see through my story, but he's excited to have located the fugitive's brother. If he thinks, he'll wonder why I'm in an accident with the kid they're tailing. FBI men don't believe in coincidence. I thought I was bold, but I'm digging a hole. One thing I know: if I go to the station, I'm going to prison.

"I need you to come with us," Brawny says.

"Gentlemen, I am at your disposal. I will, of course, need to consult with my attorney. As I said, I am involved in estate matters and I have to tread lightly—my cooperation with you could prove financially beneficial to me. I'm afraid I must avoid the appearance of impropriety. I'm sure you understand. I should be able to meet with you as early as this evening."

I turn. "I'm going to get this kid's insurance information. Anything else, right this moment?"

Brawny shakes his head, deep in thought. Harvard waits.

"Just a minute, Professor," Brawny says.

I halt, my back to him. I look at Josh to see if his eyes register a threat. I turn. "Special Agent?"

"I'm afraid I don't have time to wait. Where does your brother live?"

"Is there some reason you don't want me to talk to this young man about his insurance company? What the hell is going on, here?"

Brawny deflects my parry with upraised hands. "Go ahead."

"Thank you. My brother's official address is in Waco, but it is a post office box. I suspect he wanders a bit. When I need to reach him, I use his cell phone number."

I give him the first number that pops into my mind, and when he reads it back I realize it is Charlie Yellow Horse's. "I can bring correspondence showing Tom's post office box, if that will help, tonight at the field office."

Brawny isn't convinced he is done with me, but I am. I pivot before everything unravels. Josh still sits on the driver-side fender of his Mustang. We're a few feet away and I keep my voice low.

"You have to trust me."

"Why'd you wreck me?"

"We only have a second. Do you trust me?"

He nods. Barely.

"I want you to punch me in the nose, hard enough to bust a vessel. Then I want you to get out of here. I'll slow them down. Take the next exit. Don't try to outrun them; ditch the car. Leave the cell phone. They can ping it. Take a bus and report the car stolen from the hotel."

"They're coming this way."

"Come by tonight and we'll get everything square."

"Are you shitting me?"

"Do it now. Now!"

I read confusion and panic. Then his fist fires like a gunship howitzer, shoulder high. I see a flash and hear the boom.

I wake up gagging on blood, my nose swollen so big it parts my vision. I spit blood. Harvard kneels beside me; Brawny is gone. A thirty-foot skid mark records Josh's escape. Harvard steps away to answer his cell phone.

I struggle to my feet and take a nasty Corona beach towel from the back seat. Corona—I'd rather be on the beach sucking one down. I wipe my nose and press the towel to my face. Both airways are clogged and I'm dizzy. I clean my face in the side mirror, wetting dried blood with spit and rubbing it away with the towel.

Harvard flips his cell phone closed.

"Did your friend get him?" I say.

"Not yet. The kid took the exit, turned into Walmart, and we lost him there."

"But your guy is on him, right? Right?"

He looks like I caught him with his pecker in a goat. "Agent Wilson gave you assistance, and then went after the kid."

"I can't believe this." I get into the Tempo. "I'm going to come see you tonight. You make it your business to have that kid under arrest."

I drive away, leaving the agent on the side of the road.

I'm not a lesbian, Marisol thought, and took a drink of water. But Virginia Rentier's mouth was on her mind. If she could formulate an equation that combined every aspect of her being, her history, her hopes, her character, her vitality and passion, it would spit out last night as the single inevitable solution.

Last night was their little secret, Virginia said. Marisol wished she could go back to that moment and relive the connection that tied them. The night wasn't just her first experience with another woman. Since winning election to the House, it was her first experience at all. A tantalizing future waited.

She'd broken free of sexual mediocrity, workaholic days and lonely nights. Virginia Rentier touched the axis of two poles, and her touch was electric. No more of the middle for Marisol; she was a sensual bitch. She had a woman for a lover. Exciting as her first kiss at thirteen.

A man cleared his throat and she blinked. Mulrooney glowered at her from his seat. Marisol smacked the gavel.

"The House is in order. If there are no objections or matters of procedure at hand, the vote is called for HR Bill 39457, commonly referred to as the 'Vallejo' bill, sponsored by myself, Marisol Ortega, and cosponsored by Jared Shoskovich."

The floor was quiet.

"The vote will be by show of hands. All in favor?"

Those seated on left side of the chamber raised their hands, except Mulrooney. One wary hand lifted on the right. She had the majority. She stared at Mulrooney. He stared back, arms crossed at his breast, head back, arrogant. A moment passed.

"Mister Mulrooney, your vote is unclear. Is your hand up, or not?"

His hand drifted higher and his head tilted forward.

"By a vote of thirty-two to twenty-eight, HR Bill 394572 passes."

Josh sat at a table at the Bajio Grill in the Lowe's complex, watching the parking lot through wide panes of glass. He'd bought a chicken enchilada and found a seat by the time the FBI agent located his car. The agent parked behind the Mustang, wrote on a notepad, made a cell phone call, then, still on the phone, looked inside the Mustang.

"Josh! What happened to your nose?"

He jumped. It was Melinda "Trashy" Sabachi. He'd dated Emily, Mel's younger sister, but would have gladly dropped her for a night with her older sister. He'd known Mel's reputation before she graduated, and since then it had only garnered endorsements.

"Hey, Mel. Long story. It's not as bad as it looks. What's up?"

"I'm taking a break. Got a new job at Trustycuts. I got my license."

"What kind of license?"

"Beautician's. I can cut hair now."

"You need a license to cut hair?"

"Of course!"

"Shit. Nat's right."

"What?"

"That's great."

He watched outside. A second Taurus pulled behind the first and the agent conferred with its driver.

"I'm gonna get lunch. Be here in a minute?"

"Uh—sure."

She flashed a fuck-me smile and spun to the line. In the lot, a third agent emerged from the passenger side of the second Taurus, carrying a smallish black case. He rested it on the hood of the Mustang, putting tiny scratches into the finish, no doubt. The agent peered at the driver's side door and window, then removed an instrument from the black box and waved it at the door handle. Fingerprints.

Trashy Sabachi plopped into a chair beside him. She reached for a bottle of hot sauce, exposing a rose tattoo on her right breast.

"Like it?"

"I can't see all of it."

"Here." She pulled her top below the nipple.

"Pretty neat rose," he said. "I can't quite smell it from here."

She beamed. "I couldn't believe it. They said it wouldn't hurt, but it did. I had to put ice on it."

"Yeah. Hey—where's Trustycuts?"

"Two doors down."

"I need a favor."

"We'd have more privacy someplace else."

Josh watched the men outside. "I need a haircut."

"Really? Because I'm still building my clientele. It takes awhile. You know, there's girls in there that are booked for the next two months? What are you looking at?" She glanced out the window.

"You see those three guys in suits? They just came tearing up a few minutes ago. I think they're FBI or something."

She stared. "Really? Wow." Her eyes narrowed. "You're teasing me!"

"No, they are. Look—they're spreading out. They're looking for something."

"No kidding! Right here in Phoenix."

"Hey, can you cut my hair or what?"

"You mean a favor? Free? They told us never—"

"I'll pay you. I just meant today. No appointment."

"Oh, you'll pay." She dropped her brow. "You'll pay."

Josh took his last bite of enchilada. The first FBI agent angled toward Lowe's. The second walked back and forth in the parking lot, looking between vehicles. The third remained at the car taking fingerprints.

"You gonna eat?" Josh said.

"I am." She lifted the burrito to her mouth and teased the end of it with her tongue, then slipped it into her mouth and tore the end off. Her eyes got big and she laughed with a mouthful of rice and beans until she choked and reached for water.

"I'm in a hurry," Josh said. "I'll get one of the other girls to do it."

"No! Just a minute." She took another bite and chewed faster, then another. "I'm done. Let's go."

They left their trays. On the sidewalk, Josh walked between Melinda and the wall and in ten seconds they stepped inside the chemical-smelling salon. She led him to a styling chair and leaned his head into a sink. Josh saw the bottom half of the entrance in the mirrored ceiling.

"I want you to cut it short and dye it black. Real short, real black."

"Like, Army or something?"

"Almost."

"You're hair is so pretty. Such a shame."

"Pretty? Cut it all."

She splashed warm water onto his head and applied shampoo, moving her hands foreplay-slow, and Josh closed his eyes.

"That's nice."

Mel leaned close. Her hip pressed his arm and her palm brushed his cheek. Patchouli tickled his nose.

"Look, your FBI guy is here."

Josh opened his eyes to patent leather shoes and a grey suit. Everything was upside down in the ceiling mirror and soap ran in his left eye. Mel looked at him, back to the FBI agent; her jaw parted and she switched sides to block his body from view.

"What's he doing?" Josh said, hushed.

Melinda looked at a wall mirror. "He's checking out everyone's feet. He hasn't come in yet. Hold on… Okay. He just left."

Josh loosed a deep breath.

Melinda leaned to his ear and whispered, "Did you rob a bank or something?"

"I decked my father to give him cover and I ran here."

"Oh," she said. "Did he rob a bank?"

"I can't talk about it. Can we just get this done?"

"Danger excites me," she said.

A half hour later his hair was short, black, and tousled at the top. She shaved his lower lip.

"What are you doing?"

"I have an idea. Hold on." She opened a package of false eyelashes. "I'm gonna stick about ten of these on you. Stacked up like an Imperial beard." She pressed them in place, one by one, then spun the chair to face the wall mirror.

The lashes formed a straight black beard, eyeball wide, under his lip. "I need a beret," he said. "I won't look like a complete pussy until I have one."

"I'll bet it tickles," she said.

"No, it doesn't feel bad." Josh read her randy face. "Oh—yeah sure, down there. Does this place have a back door?"

"You owe me thirty dollars."

He gave her two twenties.

"There's a special fee for getting out the back. Come on."

She led past other beauticians, through a curtained door and into a back room with stacks of Paul Mitchell products and a bookkeeping desk. She steered him to its corner and pushed him seated; standing close, she pulled her top to her neck.

"Bite my nipple. That's the only way you're getting out of here."

"What if someone comes back here?"

"No one will."

Josh put his mouth on her breast and sucked her nipple.

"Bite, dammit."

He clamped with his teeth and she moaned. She pressed close to him; her pelvis ground the corner of the desktop. Her breathing became husky and her core jittered under his mouth.

"Harder!"

He squeezed her other breast in his hand and bit until he tasted salt. She convulsed and after fifteen seconds of spasms, pulled away from him.

"That?" he said. "That did it for you?"

She beamed. "The door is over here—if you have to go."

Chapter Nine

Buffa opened his eyes to a bleating phone. He'd been dreaming of a woman and hated to give her up. The phone stopped ringing ... then started again. Buffa rolled. He shook his head—he was still in his clothes. Too much coffee mixed with too little sleep. He lifted the cell phone from the bedside table.

"Yeah."

"Yeah? What the hell's going on? Where's the photos, right now?"

It was Patterson. Buffa said, "I dunno. Who's this?"

"Who the royal fuck do you think it is? Tell me you're not napping, for chrissake."

"Oh, Patterson. I was up all night." He looked at the clock. "And I'm going out again in a couple hours."

"You have the photos, right?"

"I chased the sonuvabitch all the way to Flag, and lost him. But I know where he lives. I checked out his place. This guy is out there. Way out there."

"Do you have the photos?"

"He's militia. Guns, Flags, books. You know."

"Do you have the fucking photos?"

"No."

"You're off the deal. Done." The line was dead.

The words woke him. Buffa hurled the cell against his pillow. He paced behind the couch, shouting short jabs of profanity, then picked up the phone.

"Listen to me, you Nazi son of a bitch. I'm going freelance, and I'll have those photos tomorrow. You decide whether you want to pay my regular fee, or a freelance rate."

Buffa waited by the picture window and pulled aside the slats every few seconds. He checked his watch. De Roulet had two minutes. If he didn't show on time, Buffa'd halt the operation long enough to drive him fifty miles on Interstate 10 and put a bullet in his head. He wasn't in the redemption business.

The van pulled onto the driveway. Buffa exhaled, but tension kept his back stiff and his eyes beaded. He went outside, ankle clicking with each step. He'd forgotten to ice it but at least he'd cleaned the cut on his face. He'd left the bandage off his head so the cut would dry. The gash would make a hell of a scar, and in his line of work, it was like an all-caps credential after his name.

He jumped into the passenger side and nodded to Tony and Frankie, in the back seat. Buffa held their eyes and saw their empty hands. He turned. "Johnny?"

The kid faced him. Buffa peered. "You straight?"

"I'm straight." He rolled his shoulders and bobbed his head like a street fighter getting loose.

The two in the back—Tony Ianolio and Frankie Maghen—were solid operators. Buffa used them for almost all his nongovernment work. If the Boss planned a move against him, one of these three would likely deliver it. Maybe, Buffa thought, he'd have an opportunity to leave all three in the desert.

"Get on the 101 east," he said.

"Sure." De Roulet backed out the drive.

When they merged on the freeway Buffa explained the operation.

They exited to Seventeen south, drove down Olive, turned onto Kachina, and dropped Frankie off at a bus stop.

"Watch your timing," Buffa said.

Frankie grinned. "No problem."

Johnny turned around and parked at a gas station where the field of view included the girl's walk from school to the turn that led to her house. He hopped out and bought a bottle of Coca Cola from a machine.

Buffa smirked. Kid had to have his coke. Asshole.

There were a dozen things that could go wrong with an operation like this. Doing it on the street in the broad daylight was a gutsy operation. On the other hand, witnesses didn't know what the hell they saw and always contradicted each other.

She appeared in the distance. "That's our girl," Buffa said. He watched her walk. Closer, she stopped, looked at the van, and continued with a quickened step.

"She might have us," Buffa said.

"That's a good lookin' girl," Tony said.

"Ain't that a shame."

The girl turned the corner and walked on along Kachina. Frankie, at the bus stop, sat up. The girl looked back again.

"She's nervous," Buffa said.

"She ain't seen nothing yet," Tony said.

"All right, Johnny. Let's go. Nice and easy. Tony, get by the door. We gotta time this right."

Johnny waited on traffic, then crossed the intersection. The girl walked ahead, only a few feet from the bus stop.

"Pick it up."

The girl approached the stop. Frankie sat poised. The van neared to twenty feet, then ten. The girl turned to look and her face was childlike blank. Inside the van, Tony yanked the sliding door. Frankie lunged from the sidewalk bench, pushed her across the curb as the van skidded to a halt. The door slammed open.

The girl raised her arms and bounced from the door. Frankie's face hit the glass.

The moment froze. Frankie shook his head and Buffa looked through the closed door at the girl and Frankie, both barely on their feet, swooning. Frankie fell straight back on his ass and sat there. Buffa opened his door as the girl turned to run, and Tony swung the side door open again.

"C'mon, C'mon, C'mon!" Johnny hit the steering wheel with each burst.

Frankie grabbed the girl's ankle. She fell on the sidewalk and screamed.

Buffa winced. It was the kind of scream that would send men running to help her. She grazed his thigh with a kick. He swiped at her foot, sending her tennis shoe flying.

Frankie stood opposite him; they shuffled her to the van and tossed her against the far side. Buffa lost his step as his shin hit the bottom of the door. He rolled inside and Frankie jumped in over him. Buffa pressed against the girl, who slumped in a quivering daze on the cargo-hauling carpet.

"C'mon! C'mon! C'mon!" Johnny yelled from the driver's seat. Buffa realized he'd been yelling that the whole time. Frankie pulled his legs in. Tony slammed the door and the van lurched forward.

Josh pushed the back door open. A row of palm trees lined the middle entrance to the Walmart complex, and behind, the backs of businesses. A gold Subaru Brat from the early eighties squeaked toward him. After it passed, he stepped into the sunlight.

He kept his eyes straight and approximated a careless gate. The place crawled with FBI and from the feel of it, a dozen pairs of eyes watched the back of his head. He adjusted his hardon through his pocket so it wasn't quite as obvious as Trashy Sabachi left it. He'd never told a girl no before. It didn't feel right.

He stepped through the Walmart entrance like it was a finish line. A grey-haired greeter took a step toward him but didn't welcome him to Walmart. A beefy kid slammed a stack of carts to the right. Josh veered to the menswear section and grabbed psychedelic green running shorts, a baseball cap, a new pair of sunglasses, and from the luggage area, a daypack. In groceries he grabbed three one-liter bottles of Gatorade.

Josh flipped through the cards in his wallet. He'd sent his last payment in to Visa, but he was at his credit limit. He passed the card to the smiley-faced cashier and ignored the butterflies in his stomach. Her face was flat, no read there. Behind her, a suited man strode through the entrance, pulling his sunglasses off as he stepped past the greeter. It wasn't one of the agents who'd joined the task force at Lowe's. This guy was at the accident. He'd know Josh's face.

"Sign here." She pointed to the swipe device.

He scribbled his name. The entrance with the agent was closest, and he looked this way. Josh slipped the cap on his bare head, took his bag, and crossed to the restroom. He took a stall at the end and removed his pants.

Leather-on-tile footsteps echoed around him. Josh peeked through the gap; the agent stood at a urinal.

Josh flushed and masked by the noise, pulled on the running shorts. He'd hide himself in plain view, like the Purloined Letter; thank you Mrs. Sprague. He stuffed his pants in the backpack and listened. Urine tinkled on porcelain. He took a deep breath, steadied his nerves, and pushed the stall door open. The agent turned his head as Josh walked behind, and found his eyes in the mirror. Josh looked through him.

Josh crossed the store to the exit. The grey haired greeter stepped toward him. "May I see your receipt, sir?"

Josh searched his pockets.

"What's in the pack?"

"I bought the pack. It has my jeans in it. Just a minute."

"You pay for everything?"

"Here." Josh handed him the receipt. "I'm in a hurry."

"I'm not." The man traced the numbers with his pudgy index finger.

A stream of customers strolled by, averting their eyes. Josh stood light on his heels, ready to sprint.

"I'd like to check your backpack."

"Too fucking bad." Josh moved. The old man grabbed his arm. Josh shoved him into a row of grocery carts and leapt toward the exit. A burly man-child with Amish side-whiskers and an energy-saver brain stood to the side in a Walmart blue smock. Josh saw his leg too late. He tripped and clocked his head on the glass doorframe. The fat kid sat on his legs and the grey-haired man handcuffed him.

"Any reason you don't want me to look in your backpack?"

"Yeah. I have some fucking rights in this country." He felt the eyelash beard flap as he spoke and pressed his face into his shoulder to reseat the glue. When he lifted his face, the FBI agent studied him from the entrance.

"Hey mister—you look like the law and order type. Tell this rentacop he can't search me without probable cause."

"Check his bag," the agent said.

The grey-hair took Josh's pack from the floor and rooted inside. He checked the outside pockets, removed the Gatorade bottles and tossed the pack to the floor.

"Compare the receipt, asshole."

"Looks like you stole a pair of distressed jeans, to me."

"I wore them in. I'm wearing the shorts that are on the receipt."

The FBI man shook his head. "You better cut him loose."

"He's a thief. I seen him before!"

"But you didn't get him this time."

The grey-haired guard removed the cuffs. "I'm gonna search you every time you come here, you thieving bastard."

Josh swiped his pack and filled it. "The next time you touch me, you'll be flat on your back, choking on teeth."

Josh stepped into sunlight. His adrenaline coursed high but time ran slow and he felt a displaced sense of calm as he strode across the parking lot.

Nat had said a lot of things and some of them came back. Did it make sense that a national police force was chasing him right now? Would the crime have occurred at all if a national police force didn't exist?

The bus stop was metal mesh over three-inch pipe, angled overhead to provide spotty shade. He read the bus schedule. Ten minutes to wait. Josh pulled his cell phone from the new pack; he'd forgotten to remove the price tag. He broke it off and dialed Merry. The phone rang four times and dumped into voicemail. Josh listened to the message to hear her voice and snapped the phone closed when the prompt came.

Merry wasn't a girl to miss a phone call.

A bus rolled to a stop and he entered. He sat in the back and scrunched into a seat with his knees on the back of the seat before him. The bus pulled forward and passed the Lowe's parking lot. The same two cars were parked behind his Mustang, but that didn't mean other agents weren't scouring the area.

Nat had said to call the police from the hotel and report the car stolen. It was like he was in a ten-foot hole, and Nat said to dig deeper to get out.

The air in the bus was stagnant. Head resting against the seat, Josh closed his eyes. Light patterns swirled on his eyelids and morphed as the bus passed in and out of shade.

Josh slept.

The sound of air brakes and discs on rotors squealing wakened him with a vague sense of time lost, but no approximation of how much. He lifted his lidded eyes and saw he was deep in Phoenix, at Washington and 3rd Street.

"Pardon, is this seat taken?"

Josh turned. A frowning young man in a suit stood in the aisle. He had patent leather shoes and clean-cut hair.

Virginia Rentier rode in the back of a sporty hybrid SUV, rented for the day, to the Phoenix Civic Center for the first annual Global Warming Economic Conference. She delivered speeches from typed index cards, and made last-minute changes in red. The driver took a rear VIP entrance, bounced up the ramp, and squealed tires reaching the back entry. Her pen jumped across the page. She gritted her teeth.

Her state police security detail led in another vehicle, and was already patrolling her path to the conference.

Two days had passed in a whirlwind. The Senate would move today or tomorrow to pass Vallejo. She'd hold the signing at the Cesar Chavez center to underline her solidarity with Hispanics.

If she had the photos. If.

Virginia strode into a garage elevator and braced herself. The booth lifted; her stomach rolled, and the doors slid open. She flinched; elevator doors did that to her. Her men stepped out and she followed. She stood in a secure area but in the distance, late-arriving conference attendees waited in the check-in line.

Any minute she'd hear news that would affect their lives, news that would solidify into the first rung on a ladder that leaned against the national stage. Her people had already spoken to 60 Minutes and Charlie Rose. If she could steal the headlines from the bureaucrats in Washington four or five times a year on issues of national significance, the top fundraising talent would see her as viable.

The conference organizer, Faisal Noor, took her hand in both of his. A generous smile split his face.

"You have just a few minutes before we introduce you, Governor Rentier. You'll be following the gentleman from Toyota, who is speaking now."

Virginia nodded. Destruction lay in those photographs. If Clyman timed their release to the launch of her national presence, right wing zealots from across the country would combine and bankroll Arizonans to remove her from office. With close-ups of her pleasure-twisted face on Drudge, it wasn't like she could look square into the camera and say, "I did not have sex with those women."

An aide named Helen, a straight girl with promise, placed an update in her hand and she glanced at it and gave it back.

"About five minutes, Governor," Faisal said.

"Helen, let me see your mirror." She checked her blush and mascara. Her eyes caught her scar. It was invisible, but she stared at the spot and it throbbed.

"Governor, it's time to step inside."

Josh turned from the window and spoke the young man in the suit. "What line of work are you in?"

"I'm an attorney." The man spoke with calm eyes.

"You ride the bus?"

"It's better in town. No parking to worry about."

"You defend people?"

"I lock them up."

"FBI?"

"DA's office." He opened a brief case and pulled a file, angling the manila to block Josh's view. He studied the text with an affected frown.

"Had any good cases? Kidnappings? Murders?"

The attorney kept reading. "No, but I put away a guy who stole a prescription pad from his doctor and forged a Vicodin scrip. Got two years out of that one."

"Cool."

"Yeah. If you don't mind—"

"Sure, no problem."

Josh sat up. The bus stopped and swapped old passengers for new.

"Sure is hot in here," Josh said.

"Uh-huh."

"Who's the best defense attorney you've ever seen?"

The folder closed and Josh looked up to see the attorney's eyes fixed on his. "That would depend on what kind of trouble you are in."

"It's not me."

The attorney nodded. "O.K. What are we talking about?"

"I'm doing a report for school and have to interview an attorney. Part of a career path project. That's all."

"Right. Well, I don't know. Murder, I'd probably say Oscar Thornton. I don't think he'd sit down with you, though. He charges seven hundred an hour."

"What if a person, say, knew about a murder? Would he be in trouble?"

"Could be. The state believes citizens are obligated to report capital crimes. If you think about it, there isn't much difference between participating in murder and helping a murderer avoid the law."

"What if my friend knows a person who saw a killing? Is my friend in trouble?"

"Then the moral obligation exists, and whether you'd be prosecuted or not is a matter of the DA's mood." He put the folder away and closed the case. "You're too young for this kind of trouble. What's going on?"

Josh looked out the window. "Why don't you give me one of your cards?"

The attorney opened a small leather cardholder and passed one to Josh.

"Pleased to meet you, Earnest."

"You're too young to know this, so I'll tell you and hope you're smart. Legal problems grow when they are ignored. Call me. I'll connect you to the right attorney."

Rentier crossed to the podium and glanced at her notes. A spotlight splashed her in a bluish white light, even as she recognized individual faces under the bright house lamps. She cleared her throat and sipped from a bottle of Arrowhead water, then leaned to the microphone. Stage heat tickled her scar. She grasped the podium, then released it and spoke.

"In 1966, a NASA team working for the Apollo mission took astronauts to the Navajo Reservation because the terrain resembled the surface of the moon. Two astronauts, in silver space suits, tested equipment.

"Nearby, an old Navajo man and his son watched. The NASA team noticed them and explained that the men in the silver suits were preparing to go to the moon. The old man said, 'Can I send a message with them?'

"The NASA men thought this interesting, and recorded the old man's voice. 'What did he say?' they asked the son. The boy wouldn't tell, so they took the recording to the village. Finally, with cash in hand, they found a Navajo who would translate.

"'Watch out. These guys will steal your land.'

"Sometimes I get blank stares when I tell that—but I thought it was appropriate today. The old Navajo man might agree with what I am about to say.

"This will come as no surprise to you, but we are not separate from our planet.

"Although 'conservation' and 'nature appreciation' are in vogue, oil companies sponsor PBS programs and promote their ethanol businesses with chic phrases like 'reducing our carbon footprint,' both conservationists and nature lovers share a flawed understanding of our relationship with our environment.

"It may seem a minor difference. Those meddling environmentalists, you know? But its ramifications reach far beyond our collective comfort zone. Both movements assume the laws of involvement and interconnectivity are null, and we can work, manufacture, and pollute, and the only product we reap is the one we have designed, and the only ill consequence, the one we are equipped to negate.

"Exxon Valdez spills eleven million gallons of crude oil. The cleanup costs two billion dollars. Government imposes a five billion dollar fine. Problem solved. Right?

"Eleven thousand Alaska residents volunteer to help clean the mess, and twenty-six thousand gallons of oil are still in sand. Local fishing and clam industries collapse. Prince William Sound is no longer pristine.

"The same catastrophe occurs every day—death by a thousand cuts. We spew ash and smog into the air and install scrubbers on industrial chimneys. We drive gas guzzling SUVs, and pass legislation to mandate higher mile-per-gallon vehicles.

"In the coming green economy, this paradigm will fall by the wayside, and we will understand we are not separate, but are *part of.* We don't stand aside and act upon our environment; our environment engulfs us, absorbs the cost of the actions of which we are aware, but also those of which we are not.

"Earth accepts we have spilled a million barrels of oil. It watches us spend two billion dollars on cleanup. But unseen by us, She keeps a ledger of a trillion more slights and infractions we are not equipped to comprehend. She tracks the damage to Her crust from a million oil wells, the damage to Her arctic from a pipeline, the damage to Her air from burning oil—in short, everything.

"Why is our western, capitalistic society so destructive? This is an aside, sort of, but why do we rush to war? Hasn't every historian on the planet agreed that we fight wars over resources? Oil? Land?

"The common mindset of the conservation crowd is combat. The conservationist recognizes a chasm between humanity and nature; human concerns are destructive and nature must be shielded from them.

"This is convenient for big business, because it allows companies to buy white-coated environmentalists, who measure specific outputs, combat them with specific measures, and supply a steady stream of conscience-laden quotes to a PR firm. These big companies take what they want from the earth, and as long as they tie a nice bow on their box of environmental concerns, we consumers buy the paradigm that the environment is over there, separate, and we can tweak our impact upon it. Lucky us, we've got that pesky environment taken care of. Everything in its place, nice and tidy.

"The reality is that we cannot put the environment in a box. It can, however, put us in a box.

"We desert people understand in our bones how tenuous our clutch on our world is, how disproportionate our size versus our impact. All our actions, from the cars we drive to work, the lights we casually flip on, the humming computers, the natural resources our industries consume—the entire web of wealth we call economy—is part of the earth. In the desert, we are not separate from the environment; we are the environment.

"Phoenix is home to a group of corporate leaders who realize our interconnectedness. Phoenix companies are taking the lead with this new green understanding. My very good friend, Barbara Parsons, the CEO of Xansol, is here today. And on my right, over here, I see Oliver Lulla, CEO of TetraChem. Thank you, yes, they deserve applause. These two know better than most what kind of opportunity Phoenix represents for the green future. Their companies, Xansol and TetraChem, have added over six hundred jobs to our economy in the last two years, in fields that didn't exist before we began paying serious attention to green economics. I'm proud of Barbara and Oliver, because through them and others like them, Phoenix is leading the way in developing the technologies that will save planet Earth.

"At Xansol, they're making solar panels that fit on baseball caps. They've built panels that look like desert rocks, to hide behind your house while they power your refrigerator. Xansol's logo may be a hippy in the sun, but they're light years ahead of where the industry stood just a decade ago.

"And at TetraChem, they're making advanced, zero-outgas polymers, sustainable fertilizers, environmentally safe adhesives, and a host of other products that lead the business world by example. In the best sense, Xansol and TetraChem have formed a partnership not just with the people of Arizona, but also the Earth, Herself. Their businesses thrive not just because the green movement has come of age, but because a zero-impact business is an efficient business.

"We hold the future in our hands in so many ways, but must change our collective paradigm. We must begin to consider the full consequences of our actions.

"I am an optimist. Society is a partnership between the people, their government, and industry. Together, we can steer ourselves to a brighter future. Thank you."

On the brief ride back to the Executive Tower, Virginia checked her blackberry.

"Vallejo vote is in."

It was from Jennifer. Virginia dialed her. "Did it pass?"

"By two."

"Next time don't tell me the vote is in. Tell me it passed by two. Now, get me Patterson. I want to see him in ten minutes."

"He drove out to see Carlos Raul to schedule the signing party."

"Fine. As soon as he gets back."

"You'll probably be at the funeral for that police officer the other day."

"Well, Mick can come early and I'll be late. I need to see him immediately. Call him."

Merry Paradise lay on an oily carpet with a thin trickle of blood connecting the corner of her eye to a cut on her scalp. She fought the temptation to wipe it away. They hadn't bound her wrists, and she sensed the longer she lasted without attracting comment, the longer she lived.

The one sitting across from her wanted her. He sat with legs crossed and leaned against the side of the van, his head lolling with the roll of the vehicle. She'd seen that look before, although never on a man who wore it with such brute honesty. He stared at what he wanted, and she refused to meet his eye.

Before it was over, this one was going to take her.

The man in the front passenger seat was the one Josh tackled. His face was gashed open where Josh hit him; the swollen flesh glistened like it had a fresh coat of lacquer. What kind of an animal would leave it uncovered?

They had taken several turns before she realized she might pay attention and guess her location.

"Here, Johnny." The man pointed left.

She glanced at the mention of a first name.

"That's right, girl. My name is Frankie. What does that tell you?" the one staring at her pelvis said.

"Leave her alone."

This voice came from farther back in the bed of the van. She couldn't see him and had forgotten there were four of them.

He was probably looking up her skirt right now. Maybe he hoped to take her out after it was all over, buy her cheap earrings. She had to stop this smart aleck thinking. They meant to kill her. And at least one of them was spending his idle moments arranging the details of a rape scene.

Why her? Why Josh?

Because Josh tackled Bandage Head for sitting on his car. She remembered Josh exploding from the back seat, all butt and legs, kicking and driving until he followed Bandage Head over the side of the car. When Josh had him on the ground, he took the gun and smashed his ugly face with it. He crossed a line into violence. She remembered the glazed look in his eyes when it was over.

Her chances wouldn't be as good, but this wasn't going to be a physical contest. She had to use her brain. And the other tools God had given her.

She separated her legs just a bit for the protective one in the back—a small reward, a hint of promise—and shifted her weight until her blouse was askew for Frankie. Not too much. Not too obvious. Each bump wobbled her knees farther apart. She kept her eyes lidded and out of focus.

The van slowed. Gravity tugged her forward then pressed her against the wall as the vehicle turned right. The wheels bumped over a curb. They'd entered a driveway. A garage door clanged open and the van eased inside. Her pulse quickened.

This is where they would do whatever they'd planned.

The walls were bare. No racks with boxes. No black marks. The house was new; maybe they only used it for things like this.

The garage door descended, sealing the stalls in a gloomy, sixty-watt yellow light. She lay on her numb arm, waiting.

Bandage Head looked back and motioned to Frankie, then opened his door and stepped out.

Frankie nudged her. He pushed her exposed knee instead of her hip, then looked with steady black eyes at the other man in the back of the van, and she imagined the other met his glare.

Johnny the driver slammed his door. Merry lay motionless. Frankie touched her again, this time extending the moment, pressing her thigh, moving his hand toward her panties, slipped underneath. She stared at the roof of the van. He pressed harder; through the corner of her eye she saw him watching her face.

The one in back crawled forward and shoved Frankie closer to the door. "We don't got all day."

He turned to her. "You alright to move around?"

She met his eyes and nodded as if he had asked her to marry him.

"Then get up," he said, and crawled past her.

She obeyed, seeking his eye as she rose. It was good to cleave to this one and not the other. A loose bolt gouged her knee but she withheld a whimper. Should she be pathetic? To arouse the protective instinct of the one, at the risk of stimulating the predatory instinct in the other? Or should she be tough, make each aware she would resist, while enticing them to combat one another?

She exited feet first. Frankie smacked her behind. The other was ahead; she appealed to his eyes. They were blank. She crawled out.

Bandage Head clasped her arm as if afraid she would bolt in the closed garage.

"You don't have to squeeze so hard."

He pushed her away. "Go inside." He pointed to the door Johnny had taken a moment before.

Merry walked lopsided, missing a shoe.

"Tony—take her to the living room. Put her in a chair and watch her," Bandage Head said.

She registered the name. Tony. The one who might protect her.

"Come on," he said.

Tony led with a sideways gait, watching both her and the hallway ahead. The tile was cold underfoot. She looked in an open bedroom. The windows had blinds, but no curtains, and a pair of folded cots lay crisscross on the beige carpet. The bathroom on the right was empty save a plastic bottle of hair gel. They passed an empty bedroom and a master bedroom with a futon and a junky dresser, with flaked white paint on wood, then turned a corner.

The living area resembled every other new home she'd seen, with vaulted ceilings and a lot of open space. An island separated the carpeted dining area from the tiled kitchen. A red upholstered chair with coffee stains sat opposite a television on a wicker stand, with three metal folding chairs scattered around it. Throughout the house, she smelled decay, as if someone had forgotten to take the garbage out or left an open can of clam chowder in the shade.

Tony pushed her ahead, not rough, but not friendly. She crossed the room to a leather sofa and sat on the edge, scrutinizing the men as they streamed into the room. She tucked her legs under her thighs to one side; her calves bulged.

Tony turned on the television. Frankie opened the refrigerator and tossed a can of beer to Johnny as he rounded the corner from the hallway. Johnny saw it at the last second, and swatted it aside.

"Asshole," Johnny said.

The can smashed on the ceramic tile; it bounced and mid-stride, Johnny caught it with his foot and kicked it onto the cream carpet. It rolled to a stop, shooting a fine mist of Coors two feet into the air.

Merry wiggled aside and wiped the beer from her leg. Frankie leered. Tony watched the television. Johnny continued through the kitchen to the great room.

"That's going to taste real good," Frankie said.

Merry's eyes shot to Tony.

"Why you lookin' at him? Tony—what'd you do to get the love? Show me the love, bitch."

Tony turned the television volume higher.

"I like the silent type," Merry said, looking at Tony.

Tony turned from the television. His face was flat, indistinguishable from any other. His features weren't grotesque, but they didn't add up to an attractive man. She understood. Tony wasn't gay, he just didn't know what to do. He was watching Oprah, for heaven's sake. He probably thought he should cry with her after it was all over.

"What's your name?" she said. "Tony? Is that right?"

He nodded.

"You don't have what he's looking for," Frankie said. "Tony's a bone smoker. You wait 'til tonight—"

Tony lunged across the room at Frankie and launched a punch from his right side that connected with Frankie's chin and sent him sprawling against the kitchen wall. He followed with a mid-level punch to Frankie's stomach. Frankie doubled over. They grunted and cussed.

Merry looked to the front door; getting there would mean passing Johnny. He arrived between the kitchen and great room and leaned against the wall, watching Frankie and Tony roll on the floor, pummeling each other without really connecting. He seemed an outlier, not quite part of the group.

Bandage Head appeared at the entrance to the master bed and stepped across the tile. Leaning forward to lift Tony off Frankie, he looked at the circle of Coors foam and a wider arc of wet carpet. He cuffed Tony's head.

"Get the fuck up. Clean this up."

Tony stood and waited for Frankie to rise. He looked at Merry and she smiled at him. His lips budged into a grin.

Bandage Head watched the exchange. He opened his mouth but before the words came out, Frankie picked up the can of Coors and held it over Tony's head. "Faggot."

Tony batted the Coors can away and it flashed past Merry's head to the window behind her, cracking blinds and shattering glass. Bandage Head stepped between Tony and Frankie.

"You idiots. Fuckin' girl's playin' you." His nostrils flared.

He pointed to the carpet and said to Frankie, "Clean that up."

He turned to Tony. "There's towels in the guest bathroom."

Bandage Head jerked Merry from the couch; his fingernails dug into her arm as he heaved her across the room. Her sock hit the wet rug and she slipped on the tile. Bandage Head held her, wrenching her shoulder.

He shoved her into the master bedroom and slammed the door. She shrunk in a corner by a bureau.

"You think you're smart? Pit one dumb dago against another, right?" He shook his head and stalked at the foot of the futon. "They weren't fighting over screwing you or not."

He backhanded her. The sting burned her skin, but it was deeper; he'd connected bone to skull and white stars flashed in her mind. She crashed to the mattress and rolled supine, brought her knees high and kicked herself backward. He swiped her foot and pulled her.

"They were fighting over who would go first." His hand went to his belt. "The answer? Neither."

Chapter Ten

Patterson opened the door, glanced inside, and stepped to the center of the room.

"Have a seat," Rentier said. She read his face. "You don't have good news for me about our little matter."

"Good and bad. We know where the photos are. However, Buffa has failed to acquire them on several occasions, and has resorted to more … rigorous … methods." He paused. "We are to the point that you shouldn't know what is being done on your behalf."

"Why do ex-military people always want to manage up?"

"No, that would imply you are incompetent. This is protection. This is what I'm good at. Society doesn't understand that leaders sometimes must use consummate force."

"And you're willing to fall on your sword for me?"

"My service is nothing without my willingness to do whatever it takes."

"Ah, whatever it takes. I've heard that a lot, lately. Usually right after nothing has happened. You're saying the matter is settled as far as I am concerned?"

"Almost. I'll let you know when it's over."

"I appreciate your fealty." She faced him. "But I'm not brimming with confidence. Details. Now."

Patterson looked at the backs of his hands. "Joey Buffa has learned that Delp hid the photos at the Cave Creek library. A local found them, and Buffa has not been able to obtain the photos."

"Knock on his door and take them."

"It isn't that easy. The local's been elusive. Buffa claims the guy is some kind of survivalist holdover from the seventies, or something. Lots of books, lots of guns. Our own Eric Rudolph."

She nodded.

"I've begun a preliminary investigation. His name is Nathan Cinder. He's unemployed—do you know him?"

"No...'

"You look, uh... Nothing. He's unemployed, but worth, near as I can tell, about two million. His assets are scattered across a dozen institutions, and he likely has real estate holdings I haven't found. I wouldn't be surprised if he has gold coins in mason jars."

"So what is Buffa doing about it?"

Patterson raised his hand as if the other rested on a bible. "Cinder has no connections to anybody that we can find. He was an only child, parents long dead. Family tree is a two by four. But three things are interesting. He has a young friend, the son of a former woman-friend, who is somehow involved in all of this, and he was married... get this... to minority leader Clyman's daughter."

"Was married?" Rentier said.

"She died."

Rentier nodded, and her gaze drifted to the floor.

"How?" Rentier said.

"He was driving. She was the passenger. He ran a red light and a bread truck crushed her. He was banged around, hospitalized for a few weeks."

"I guess he could afford the best attorneys."

"This was pre-M.A.D.D. He paid a fine and kept driving. His money came later. I haven't studied his assets in detail, but his tax returns suggest he's a sophisticated investor."

"He made two million in ten years?"

"About that."

"When this is over, put him on our mailing list."

"Well, he doesn't make political contributions, unless you count Sierra and the Birchers."

"Both?"

"Yep."

She lifted her coffee mug and studied the black fluid. "So you're telling me he's insane?"

"Close. The third interesting thing about Mr. Cinder is his resume. He was a Harvard grad—1978—with a bachelor's in history. He served four years in the Army Rangers, then earned an MBA from Wharton in 1985."

"You said *Rangers* like it impressed you."

"Rangers are trained to be shock troops. They take missions regardless of odds. They don't fuck around. They don't quit. They don't fear. If a person goes up against a Ranger and isn't impressed, he's an idiot. A dead idiot. Anyway, after the service, Cinder worked at Honeywell, married, and remained there until his wife died. Then he dropped out. There are no sources of public information that include him, other than property records."

"And this guy just happened to find the photos in the library?"

"Right."

"And he just happens to be the son-in-law of the man who is blackmailing me with those same photos?"

"Ex-son in law, I suppose. I don't know how that works."

"Bullshit." Rentier stared at the floor. "Well, when you say *whatever it takes* you better fucking mean it."

I drive close to my trailer but come in from the back and hike the last half-mile to the top of the mountain. I haven't had water in a while, but Jack Daniel's slakes thirst just as well, with the added benefit of caloric nourishment.

Just below the hillcrest I sit on a pocketed black outcrop. Though it's hard as iron, I come here to think. The jagged edges massage my skin and keep me awake. The shadows of the summit hide me from the valley floor.

Two arroyos shoot down the hillside like wheel spokes, formed over the years by heavy runoff. The rocky flats between them are colored like crumbled Oreos. The arroyos divide around my trailer, and by the time they reach the road, two hundred yards of desert separate them.

My back presses a bare, flat shelf and my feet hang. My heart pulses in my leg wound. The antibacterial ointment is two days old now and the last thing I want is an infection. I had cellulites in Ranger school and damn near lost my hand.

The climb has me breathing heavy for a while, partly because of the blood clot blocking my nose. I should have told Josh to hit my jaw. I settle back and close my eyes. The sun catches me from my right side and I'd like to dial the temperature back to the nineties.

I wake with pinpoints of pain on my scalp from the rock. Below, a person prowls about my trailer. He has short, black hair and a backpack. He goes inside, turns on the light, and comes back outside. From his gait, I bet it's Josh.

He's waiting on the step when I climb down. His face is ashen. "What's with the hair cut?"

"I had to get it cut to escape. How'd you get away?"

"I drove. You look sore."

"I haven't been able to reach Merry all day."

"Thought I said to dump your cell phone."

"This is my mother's, and she got it from a boyfriend. She pays the bills, but it's in his name. No way in hell the FBI gets this number."

"Okay."

"You, uh, might want to go inside. Unless you keep a nasty house, someone's been here."

I flip the light switch. It looks like someone parked my trailer inside a Boeing wind tunnel. Papers litter the floor; files in disarray. I open the top right drawer and check in the back, then go to my bedroom.

"Fuck a goat."

"What?"

"He took my Luger. Fuck." I step through glass to the cabinet and count barrels. "That's all he took."

I lift a holster from the foot of the cabinet and weave my belt through it, then fill it with a .38 revolver. I've been unarmed too long.

A safe hides in the back of my closet, built into the wall. I push clothes to the side. "You mind turning your back a second?"

"No problem. Dad."

Josh goes back to the office and I open the safe. Under a stack of papers on the right corner is Gretchen's safe deposit key—the sole relic I have of her work as an aspiring journalist. I don't know the institution that houses the box, but I assume it holds secrets I'm afraid to see. In the weeks before she died, she behaved like a hunter on the trail of a prizewinning beast, but secretive; and her face carried a lingering flush—the kind that comes from a good lay. I can't imagine she carried my baby and slept with another man, yet I'm afraid to pursue the safe deposit box.

The safe in my closet is in order.

In the kitchen, I polish off the regular Jack Daniel's and refill my flask with Gentleman Jack from the freezer. Mixing them would be bad form.

"You drink a lot," Josh says from the office, nebbing in my shit.

"Doesn't look like he took anything but my Luger. Just a couple more things to check."

Down the hall, the door to the bedroom on the left hangs open. A knee-high stack of books lay haphazard on the floor, knocked from shelves. Spines are broken and pages crumpled. My eyes flit to a copy of *A Farewell to Arms*, still on the back shelf. It's unmolested.

"You read all these?" Josh says.

"I thought something was wrong coming down the hill. My books cried out to me."

I lift one and another, flatten bent covers, unfold pages, and place them on the shelves. "It takes a special kind of evil to dick with a man's books, but according to Dante, there's a place in hell reserved for said shitheads, where they suffer a million paper cuts an hour, for eternity. It's why I'm a man of faith."

"It'll take an hour to put all these back," Josh says.

I lift a particularly mangled volume from the floor, *Atlas Shrugged*, and smooth the pages. "He's either a communist or illiterate."

I leave most of the books where they lay and face the last door, burled oak stained straw gold. At four inches thick, the door's the strongest part of the trailer. I push it and try the knob. "No way in hell he got in there."

"Aren't you going to open it to make sure everything's alright?"

"No."

"What's in there?"

I remember a play I saw as an undergrad, *Where You Going, Red Ryder?*

"What's a matter with all of you?"

"You mean us here disaffected youth of the United States?"

"Yes…"

"We disaffected."

My disaffection followed the normal course, except I didn't bitch to the guy sitting next to me at work, or vote for the lesser of two evils, picking this or picking that. Instead I demanded a third choice: none of the above. I anticipated the moment of rebellion, as defined by Camus, where any possible future is better than the present. Josh knows I inhabit the fringes of patriotism, revere the citizen, scorn the state. But high school civics doesn't prepare young minds for the demands of revolt.

"Why don't you keep a lookout while I load these photos?"

Josh stands at the door for a few minutes, then goes outside.

A capitalist I know in Liberia sends spam email for a price; I contacted him while researching guerilla mass communication strategies. The site is still operational; with Liberian spammers, you never know. I log on to his website and review my account. It's too early to get him involved, but I like knowing he still accepts Visa.

I take the envelope from my pocket, scan each photo into the computer, and email them to a Yahoo account for storage. Any computer connected to the Internet now has the potential to unleash Virginia Rentier's worst nightmare: a billion iterations of her arched back, pursed lips, and shaved nethers.

The dearth of information on AZ Central's website about Prescott Delp surprises me. News like this doesn't happen every day, yet the site only has an archived story. I find Delp's address from Dex online.

Josh is still outside. I'm skuzzy all over and take a shower. The steam loosens my nose and I blow as much clotted blood out as I can without triggering another bleed, and scrub the puncture in my leg with Ivory soap and a washcloth. The pain is dull and I reach around the shower curtain, pull my flask from the commode lid and take a snorkle.

I park the Tempo across the driveway, blocking both cars nosed against the garage, and tuck my .38 under the seat.

"Maybe she won't think I'm a nut with you here," I say to Josh.

The front door has a metal security screen with vertical bars painted tan to match the house. Before I knock, the porch light flashes on and the door cracks open. A woman's voice croaks behind the metal mesh, "I got a gun, damn you. What do you want?"

"Ma'am, I appreciate that. And I'm sorry about your loss."

"Well?"

"Mrs. Delp? I'm sorry, are you Mrs. Delp?"

"What's your name?"

"Nat Cinder. This is Josh Golden."

"I'm Henny Delp."

"I met your husband on the day he passed, and he hid something in the library."

"I know you, Cinder. And he didn't pass. He was murdered."

She knows me? I recall the flowery script of the book notes, and study the metal door. Insects dart at the light above me.

"Who's that with you?" she says.

"My son."

"What'd you say you got at the library?" Her voice cracks.

"Your husband left an envelope in a book. When I saw the news I went back for it and found pictures of the governor."

"Rentier."

"They're not very classy pictures."

"I said she'd get him someday. But he had it in for her."

I wait through silence.

"Are you with the police or anybody?"

"Just a regular citizen, ma'am."

"Was that you prowling around outside the other night?"

"No, but I think I know who was—"

The rifle barrel clanks on the door.

"—because he's been trying to kill Josh and me for three days."

The door closes, a chain slides, and a moment later the metal screen opens. "Come in so we can talk without the neighbors seeing. Whole street's full of Democrats. You know their dogs always shit in my yard."

She backs away from the door. She's a round woman with short gray hair and haunches as wide as her shotgun is long. What they call roomy. She moves quickly and dabs her eyes with a checkered handkerchief. Josh nudges me and I follow inside.

The entrance opens into a small living room decorated with an old floral-patterned sofa, an end table on each side, and a lamp on each table. A closed television cabinet sits opposite. Baubles, doilies, and angels are everywhere. I wonder if Preston Delp married a woman a dozen years his senior.

Another woman peers from a stairwell.

"Come on down, Cora. They're mixed up with Preston."

Cora wears a robe and blue slippers to match her varicose veins. She watches us as she pads down the stairs and sits in a stern chair adjacent a bookshelf.

"Did you know about the photos of the governor?" I ask Henny.

"Did I know? Those and more!" Her laugh squeezes tears from her eyes and she wipes them. It's a reflexive move, and the skin is red from two days of it. Her eyes have dark bags underneath.

She's on the couch and I'm standing with Josh behind me. She leans the shotgun against the cushion.

"More photos?" I say.

She nods.

"Mrs. Delp, I wonder if you wouldn't mind leaning that Remington against the wall, or someplace it won't get bumped?"

She lays it across her thighs, pointed at my groin. I grin.

"Didn't the minority leader come around? Did you share any of this with him?"

"Clyman? I don't trust him."

"How did your husband get the photos?"

"Cora? Would you mind putting on a pot of coffee?" Henny looks at me and waves her arm at the sofa. "Go ahead and sit."

Cora disappears to the kitchen, but I expect her to peek around the corner. Josh and I sit.

"Preston began working for Clyman shortly after Rentier was elected, so it's been three years he's been gathering all of this … information … about her. He started poking through public records, old news stories, donor lists."

"What got him interested?"

"He worked for TetraChem."

"And?"

"He was a lobbyist. When the Democrats took control of the state government, they rammed a pollution bill through congress. TetraChem stood to lose big and it always costs less to buy a politician than pay taxes. Preston tried to work with the governor through the normal methods, campaign contributions, gifts, you know. But she wouldn't budge."

"That sounds like politics."

"Until TetraChem hired a private investigator to follow up on rumors. You know. That she goes with girls."

"So these photos are three years old?"

"Unh-hunh."

"Who'd they hire—the investigator?"

"I don't know. He didn't take the photos."

"What happened?"

"She got something in the mail the same day she planned to sign the pollution bill. She vetoed it."

"Your husband sent her the photos?"

Cora appeared in the kitchen entrance.

"Somebody did," Henny said.

"Somebody?"

"That's right."

"Then nobody used the photos for three years? She's signed all kinds of bad bills into law."

I mull it over while she leans forward like a third-grade teacher. "But bills are only bad if they hurt the annual report to shareholders," I say. I know Josh is eating up this anti-corporate shit.

"That's right," Henny says. "To a company the size of Tetra-Chem, politicians are a business expense. They didn't want to destroy Rentier; they wanted to buy her. That didn't work, so they had to raise the stakes."

"So they commissioned someone to take the photos?"

"I don't know how that worked. I just know that Preston wound up with them."

"Why did Preston take a pay cut to work for Clyman?"

"After digging in her dirty laundry at TetraChem, he wanted her out of government. He thought Clyman might have the power to get her impeached."

Cora rests two mugs of coffee on the table and stands beside Henny Delp.

"What else did he find to make him want to destroy her?"

"Aside from her being a crooked, corrupt murderer?"

Cora sits beside Mrs. Delp and places her hands on her lap. "Dear, should you be careful?"

"I thank God for Cora," the widow says. She wipes the corner of her eye with a cloth handkerchief. "She's a rock."

"I'm sorry to have bothered you tonight."

"Well, I guess you'll be the one to try to stop her. You know she's going to be the president unless someone hits her square between the eyes."

The way she says it catches me off guard. Choose this or choose that. "There's a website drafting her to run," I say.

"She set that up. It's maintained by a college student—her secretary's sister."

"And Preston—he didn't want her to sign the Vallejo bill?"

"Vallejo." She might have been spitting tobacco juice into a coffee can. "No, Preston didn't like Vallejo. He took the photos to Clyman. Just enough to show him how she was. I hope you don't think he enjoyed operating like this. But what else could he do?"

"Educate voters?" Josh says.

She faces him. "I suppose that's what they teach in school. Next time you're in the library look up *realpolitik*."

"You mentioned other things the governor was involved in."

"Prescott talked in his sleep. Mumbled on the phone. Complained at the dinner table. I haven't gathered up the nerve to go through his papers. He kept a box."

"Is it time?"

She blows across the top of her coffee mug. "What do you want with it?"

I search for a moment and what comes out is honest. "My view is that politicians ought to be held to a higher standard. Any crime that is an abuse of office—of the people's trust—ought to carry a death sentence. Instead, we assume politicians are crooks and just hope they don't hurt us too bad. I don't know if standing up to her means going to the press, the FBI, or putting a bullet in her head. I don't know. But I have to pick one of them."

"You see that desk?"

I nod.

She pads to it and rests her coffee mug on a doily on top.

"It was made in the twenties. Solid oak. My father owned it. It was in the back office of his grocery and when he died, it came to me. We moved it to the desert—Daddy lived in Houston—and the dry air cracked it. But Preston loved to work at that desk. He showed me a trick one time. Pull that drawer, there."

I pull the lower right file drawer. The slide allows a foot and a half travel.

"See how deep the drawer is?"

"Ah, there's a chamber back there."

"Can you see how to get into it?"

"Pull the drawer all the way out?"

"It's closed off from the front."

Josh comes close to study the mystery.

I crawl into the leg space below the desktop and run my fingers along the inside panel. "I can feel a door. Press and release?"

The panel sinks against my thumb; a latch releases and a spring engages. I relax and half the panel swings open, revealing a dark cavity about six inches wide and twenty tall. It has shelves. I marvel.

"You don't want to sell a desk, do you?"

"No, Mister Cinder."

"Do you have a flashlight?"

Henny goes to a hallway closet and returns with a two-dollar D-cell flashlight. "I think it works if you rap the side."

I aim the frail yellow light inside, withdraw stacks of papers, envelopes, and files, and pass them to Henny. She stacks everything on the coffee table.

"Is that all?"

"That's all."

A phone rings.

Josh jumps from the couch and flips his cell open.

"Merry?"

Chapter Eleven

Merry wiped blood from her nose, not realizing it also flowed from the corner of her mouth. She'd swallowed enough to be sick and had vomited on the carpet. Bandage Head stood holding the towel he'd used to wipe off his sex. She ignored him.

"Clean it up," he said, and nudged her with his boot.

She collapsed on the mush of carpet and lay with her naked torso stretched across bile and blood. Bandage Head grabbed a handful of hair and pulled her to her knees.

Merry rose in one last fury, screaming. She flailed at him with the sides of her hands and he batted her aside. She fell to the carpet with her hair tangled over her sunburned face. Her eyes were swollen.

"Clean it up," he said.

She rolled to her side. He tossed the towel on her; she gathered her strength and with clenched teeth rubbed his seed into her blood, pushing it deep into the carpet. The pink stain expanded.

Bandage Head stood to the side, pulling on a pair of black dress pants. He slipped a shoulder holster over his wife beater T-shirt, and opened the door a crack.

"Tony! Go to the van and bring me her purse."

He waited by the door and after a minute closed it with the purse in his hand. He dumped the contents on the bed, then went to the bureau top and opened a deck of Marlboros. He snapped the box and the cigarette shot to his mouth. He lit it.

He opened the cell phone and navigated to the stored phone numbers.

"Your boy. Josh, right?"

She said nothing. Bandage Head pressed SEND.

"Talk to him." Bandage Head held the phone to her ear.

She ignored him.

Bandage Head pulled the handgun from the shoulder holster with his free hand, and put the barrel to her temple.

She whispered, "…osh. Josh."

"Merry! Where are you? What—"

Bandage head pulled the phone away and put it to his ear.

"Hey, punk. Guess who broke your girlfriend's cherry?"

Josh falls to the couch, one hand on the phone, the other going to his eyes.

I reach and he slaps the cell into my hand.

"I understand you have Merry?" I say.

Silence. Then, "That's right. Say, I like my new Luger, Nathan."

"It's been picked up from dead bodies before. It will be again, unless you think this has gone far enough. You ready to make a deal? End it all?"

"The girl for the photos," Bandage Head says. "All of them—"

"Shut the fuck up and listen. Here's my deal. You bring Merry home tonight, in perfect health and none the worse for wear, and I won't track you down and hang you from a cactus by your nuts. That's my deal."

"You're some fuckin renegade. But what's to stop me from killing this girl right now, Cinder?"

"Nothing. You'll kill her one way or the other. That's why you better start running now, and never stop."

Josh tugs my arm, panic on his face.

Bandage Head says, "Put the kid on the line."

"I'm coming for you right now." I close the flip phone.

"What are you doing!" Josh presses his palms to his temples and spins a circle. "He's going to kill her!"

Henny Delp sits by the stack of files from the desk, looking them over with her head bowed away from me. Cora stands in the kitchen archway, face yellow and ugly like Stroh's beer.

"Josh, listen. I had to say that. Listen!" I cuff him and grab his shoulders. "Sit down. I had to take myself out of the picture with this guy. If I agreed to the swap, I'd have to be there, out in the open. Now he'll only expect to deal with you."

"But you told him to kill her!"

"I told him I believe he will anyhow. That's different. You call him back and tell him I've gone—tell him I took my bike, I'm after him, and I think he's in Flagstaff. Tell him you want to make the trade. Can you handle that? Just call him and set up a swap."

"What about you?"

"I'm gone, remember. Just call and set up a place to get the girl. I don't care where, so long as it's outside, away from people."

Tears stream from Josh's face and his lower lip bulges and trembles; he shudders without noise. I recognize a familiar mix of grief and guilt.

"He won't kill the girl," Henny says.

We both look at her. "The girl is useless to him without you, Josh. The only way he gets what he wants is to convince you to give it to him. She has to be alive for that."

"Josh, you got to be cool," I say. "No threats, no nothing. Just set it up. He has to trust that you'll play fair."

Josh presses a few buttons on his phone. "You have Merry?" Josh presses a button on the side. The volume is loud and I can hear the rest.

"I got her. Where's Cinder? I got a message for him."

"I don't know. He took off on his bike. Said he was going to Flagstaff to find you."

Bandage Head laughs. "Good. You have the photos?"

"He didn't take them."

"We'll meet north of Phoenix. Pioneer Road. Take it to the aqueduct and turn right before the bridge. Eight in the morning. You bring all the photos. If I suspect you're armed, or if cops come within ten miles, the girl dies. And if I see Cinder, she dies and I make it hurt."

I stand by the door and stare at the wall. Josh cries openly on the couch.

"This is my fault," he says.

"Don't waste time on guilt when you can still change the outcome."

"You should take this," Henny Delp says, pointing to Preston's notes on the table. "Take all of it. I can't use it like you can."

"I'll do what I can with it. But we've got to get this girl first."

"You'll know what to do with it."

Bandage Head dragged Merry to the door and opened it. Tony and Frankie and Johnny stood in the hall.

"You sleep out there tonight."

She sat on the edge of the bed.

"Come get this bitch," he said. Frankie came in, hardon pressing his pants.

Merry watched his feet; felt a slap across her face, the pull on her hair, the grope on her breast.

"I'm going to be the deadest lay you ever had," she said.

"You might," Frankie said. "You might."

Virginia enjoyed the Oasis because its patrons were liberal and the high-backed booths on the outside wall had privacy curtains. Men wore tuxedos and women gowns; the waiters draped white cloths across their left arms and wore gloves. Virginia smiled at two men at a table near the entrance, and drifted over the marble floor to the back of the mahogany-walled dining room.

Best of all, reporters couldn't afford a cup of coffee.

Marisol would be waiting for her in the third booth from the last, and if things tonight went as well as they had in Sedona, tonight would cement the relationship.

She left her security detail at a table and swept the curtain aside. Marisol simpered and gave a girlish shrug. Her shoulders were bare and she blushed from the spoon of her collarbones to the swell of her breasts.

"Congratulations, Madame Speaker," Virginia said.

Marisol held her wine glass in a toast. She touched her glass to Marisol's and they drank.

"A lot of people will have a voice because of your strength," Virginia said. "And they will turn to you with their needs in the future."

"That's very gracious, but everyone knows this is your signature legislation."

Virginia bowed her head. Indeed. "Teamwork."

"I've been thinking. This legislation will open a world of opportunity for the party. Not just here, but around the country," Marisol said.

Virginia watched a smile form on Marisol's lips.

"Of course, you've seen it all along. We need to get in front of it," Marisol said.

"I'm going to have a few key people up to my place in Sedona in a few days," Virginia said. "But here's a preview. Three hundred thousand new voters isn't a secret. I'm sure the Republicans are already taking steps to steal the Hispanic vote. They've tried—and have been partly successful in the past. But they haven't shifted their ideals to face the new realities, and as a result, have only won the wealthy Hispanics. The ones who need economic help, that's where we have to prevent their inroads."

"Will I be coming to Sedona?"

"Of course." Virginia touched her fingertips. "The Senate will pass their Vallejo bill tomorrow. You have to strike in the House with new bills, before the Republicans figure out this is a war of entitlements. I want you to dredge up every program you can find and sweep it into an omnibus. We need to include these new voters in all state-funded programs."

"I have staffers penning four bills right now," Marisol said.

"Good. Make them one bill and call it the Arizona Freedom Bill, or something like that. By Monday, I want you to introduce everything the Republicans are likely to think of on their own. Free English tutoring, business grants, everything. I want non-citizen Hispanics to feel like Arizona's Chosen People."

Marisol nodded. "That will bring more across the border."

"They'll vote for us. I hope you're watching closely. This will be your foundation when you run for my office in four years."

"We'll have a lot behind us by then." Marisol flicked the side of Virginia's index finger with her own; Virginia planted her hand on top of Marisol's.

"I'll be reelected in five months. The Republicans don't even have a serious contender. After the election, I'll launch a sweeping national platform. I'll reach out to other forward-thinking governors; we'll build an advisory organization, you and I, sponsored by my office, to assist other states enacting similar legislation."

Marisol nodded and brought her other hand to the tabletop.

"We're going to do everything. Healthcare. Education. Business grants. Civil Rights…"

The Governor searched the eyes of the Speaker of the House and took both her hands.

"Why don't we slip away for a few hours?" Virginia said.

"We haven't ordered anything to eat."

"I want you hungry."

They took a single Mercedes with tinted glass to the Governor's mansion. From the outside it looked like New York old money, but the southwest owned the inside decor. Entering through the garage, a pair of two-foot white horsehair vases rested on a credenza. The floor tile was red as the rocks of Sedona; a copper Kokopelli danced on the wall over Navajo rugs draped on a saguaro-wood ladder.

Virginia led Marisol by the hand upstairs.

"Won't your security see the light?"

"They treat me like John Kennedy."

In the bedroom Virginia poured a glass of chardonnay for Marisol. She filled a tumbler with Courvoisier for herself.

"The drink of Napoleon," Marisol said.

Virginia slipped out of her jacket and draped it across the back of a chair. She sat at the edge of the seat. Marisol stood behind her and kneaded her shoulders. Virginia groaned. "Dim the lights, Sweetie."

Marisol did so; a sliver of light entered the room between the drapes and split the room into halves. Marisol stepped through the narrow swath of light, beautiful and naked.

"I've been thinking about this all day long," Marisol said.

"Come to me."

Mick Patterson tossed a memo in the trash and followed a wisp of red, white, and blue from the corner of his eye. Two large photos hung from his wall. They'd been left by the previous occupant, a Republican. The photos were the kind bosses give underlings when they don't know how to encourage performance, and don't have the balls to kick ass. One said "PERSEVERENCE" and had a picture of an eagle and a quote from George W. Bush below.

"We will not falter, we will not fail..."

After thirty-five years serving the United States in one way or another, patriotism was rote. Of course he was a patriot.

The red light blinked—it was his 039 extension. Very few people had that number. Patterson lifted the handset.

"Patterson," he said.

"I thought it was inconsiderate of you not to have anyone waiting for me."

Patterson stood. "They let you out early. I was there at noon. Where are you?"

Leaning across his desk, he wrote the phone number from the caller I.D.

"I found a nice flat in the city. I have a bank credit card. But it isn't credit. Have you seen these things?"

"It's a debit card. You've been out of society a long time. Do you need money?"

"I have money. How do you think I got a … debit card?"

"Right. We need to get together. I want to make sure you have everything you need."

Patterson wrote the address on a notepad.

The deal with Bandage Head makes détente reasonable. We've agreed on a business transaction; each should get what he wants. Why go outside the deal? If his aim is to get the photos, tomorrow is his best chance. Unless he just wants us dead.

I bounce the Tempo up the driveway and skid to a stop in front of my trailer. A plume of dust billows in the dark and the car rocks on bad struts. I grab the shoulder rig with my .38 from under the seat.

Break the revolver, check the load, and close it. My finger is on the trigger.

Josh sits in the passenger seat. He hasn't spoken since we left Henny Delp's.

"Come on," I say, and tap the window.

Josh gets out of the car and follows like each step is a compromise with the Devil.

"You don't overwhelm me with optimism, Josh."

"He's going to kill her. You told him to."

"He'll only kill her if he kills us first. We have something to do with that. Fuck! Come on!"

I study the trailer until I am convinced it is unmolested, and inside, visit each room. At the computer desk I open the top right file drawer and pull the folder in the back, Janet Reno. I've taped a key to the bottom. In the library, a hardback of A Farewell to Arms sits innocuously on the top shelf. I open the cover. The pages are hollowed out and in the recess, a metal ring with fifteen keys.

I take the key from the Reno file to the knurled oak door and unlock it. The key ring is for what I store inside.

I flip the light switch.

"Good fuckin God," Josh says.

"Amen."

Twelve rifle racks are stacked two high, floor to ceiling, lining two walls. Steel bars and Master locks secure twenty AR-15s per rack. Opposite the door, three footlockers are open, displaying bayonets, thirty round magazines, and night vision goggles.

"I guess you could say I'm a gun collector."

He steps inside the room and touches one. "What for?"

"A day like this."

Josh turns and sees my pride and joy.

A wall mount above the third chest displays a Barrett M-107 .50 caliber sniper rifle. The bullet that goes with it looks like it should have ICBM stenciled on the side. It leaves the barrel at twenty-seven hundred feet per second—it can fly a mile in the time it takes a man to chirp a fart. Stories about snipers taking out targets at two thousand yards with this weapon are common.

What happened to all you disaffected youth?

We disaffected...

I lift the Barrett from the rack and exercise the bolt, view the empty chamber, and pass it to Josh.

"Heavy."

"Feels good, doesn't it? That'll punch a hole through an engine block. Imagine what it'd do to Bandage Head's ugly mug."

Josh holds it at the hip like Rambo.

"No, up here." I tap his shoulder.

He presses the stock to his armpit and struggles to get the barrel horizontal.

"What's this weigh?

"Thirty pounds."

"How do you shoot it?"

"Support it."

"You gonna take it?"

"Nah. This is for when you've got one target, a long ways off. An AR-15's better for close work. But there's nothing like a Barrett to remind a man he has options."

I take the weapon from Josh's unaccustomed hands and place it on the rack, unlock a stand of AR-15s and retract one, then take four thirty-round magazines from a foot locker, and a bucket of reloaded shells from behind the closet door. Sitting cross-legged, I toss a magazine to Josh and show him how to load it. Small work builds big confidence—the first step sets a man in motion. His hollow frown and empty eyes become the face of a young man who has made a hell-or-high-water decision.

"So what's the plan?" he says.

"These are mob guys. It'll be the four we dealt with at your gas station."

Josh's nose widens and his jaw sets.

"They'll ambush us. That's why he hasn't hit us tonight. He thinks it's a duck shoot. Plus, he told us his name at the gas station. He can't let us live."

Josh's eyes are focused somewhere beyond the wall. "Then we can't let him live."

"I'll get there before dawn. Hike in from a mile north, and stake a position to cover you when you make the swap."

"You've been there before?"

"It's hilly country; decent cover." I take a pull of Jack. "You want a hit to help you sleep?"

"No thanks."

I tilt my head.

"I'm sure." Josh says.

"Why?"

"It isn't good for me."

I grunt and take another gulp. "That makes good sense."

"Are you going to be able to shoot straight?" Josh says.

"If I'm conscious, I can shoot."

He shakes his head and his progression of thought is almost written on his furrowed brow. I'm filling magazines and he waits.

"What can I carry?" Josh says.

"If you don't know how to handle a gun, you're better not having one."

I finish loading my third magazine. Josh finishes his first. I rap them one by one on the edge to seat the shells—an almost useless ritual I picked up in the 5th Ranger Bat.

"I'll be leaving on the four-wheeler around three. You take the Ford by seven." I review the directions. "Write that down."

I motion for Josh to exit the arms room, then take a sweeping last look and lock the door behind us.

I wake to the thrum of a clock radio misaligned to the talk radio station. I've slept three and a half hours.

I gouge my eyes with my fists and fight a deep yawn. If I don't stand, I'll be asleep in seconds. Rolling from bed, I press my nose on the pillow and the pain shoots a jolt of clarity through my mind. My son has a godawful punch.

I'm foggy with Jack Daniels.

Mornings like this I tell myself things are going to change.

I dive into a black T-shirt and camouflage pants. Make a pot of coffee. Josh snores on a cot. I unload a magazine and refill it while the coffee drips; when it's done, I fill a thermos for the ride.

I reset the alarm and slide the button to the right so it'll shriek like an air raid in a couple of hours, eat a microwaved breakfast burrito, and grab my rifle and a pack of supplies. Blackness hides the terrain and I can barely discern the outline of the mountain behind the trailer. I sling the rifle across my back and drive the four-wheeler north.

I've parked a mile from the meeting place. Rabbit and coyote trails cut across the landscape and I follow their erratic paths, stumbling here and there on rocks I can't see. My nose is still clogged and I breathe through my mouth. The canal, two hundred yards distant, emits a rich humidity that teases my throat. I settle caffeine jitters with a snurgle of Jack and look down to the right. The exchange will take place farther up the dell.

I step carefully. Each footstep unlocks unknown perils. Even if I've only moved a foot sideways, the new terrain holds a thousand secrets.

Powdery dirt shifts under foot and I smell decaying flesh. I stop and test the land with my foot and take a step back. Kneeling, I press the grains between my fingers and move forward. The scent of rotten animal hits my gut hard as the slope becomes steeper and the emptiness of a mineshaft reveals itself in shades of shadows. I look from side to side and guess it measures eight feet corner to corner.

It's an abandoned mine, maybe the burial pit of a wandering cow. My gag reflex triggers and my eyes water as I choke to keep my breakfast burrito from joining whatever rots at the bottom. I back away.

The state has mapped thousands of mines like this, a hundred within Phoenix city limits, but no one has ever backfilled them, and the state has never cared. A child falls into one every year or two, interrupting the usual nightly news fare of children drowning in swimming pools. The newscasters paint their faces somber and tell the gruesome details. It is easy to hate the bastards.

Gretchen wasn't like that.

Avoiding the shaft, I climb the slope and circle the hill. A startled animal bolts through the brush. I move a hundred yards.

The horizon grows blue beyond the mountain ridge and eastern stars fade. Profiles of shrubs and cacti break into the sky. At my back, white and orange rays of sunlight pierce the sky.

I freeze. A shadow moves on the opposite skyline—the outline of a man cresting the hill. Thank God for little things like incompetent enemies. He lights a cigarette; the butane lighter flushes his brooding face. The cherry nub glows and I judge him worried or tired. In seconds I smell tobacco smoke.

Are there others who aren't smoking? The sun rises and I'll only have another moment to get in place. I'm hunched and scrambling. Only his nonchalance and stupidity allow me to remain unseen.

I track him by his cigarette and time my steps to when he takes a puff, mirroring his location until I've descended halfway to the road. He disappears behind a boulder. I take a concealed position where I have a fire lane at a downward angle, and rest the rifle on a rock. Partly hidden by a creosote bush, I recline against a flat stone.

Shapes emerge in vague morning colors. The man steps from behind the rock, lights another cigarette from the ember of the last, and stamps the butt into the dirt. He scratches his nuts and looks at the sky.

I shift the rifle and with slow movements pan close with the scope. His face is scratched on the side. One eye is bloodshot. He hasn't shaved in days; his skin is olive and his hair black. He wears loafers without socks and a green polo shirt with a pair of Ray Ban shades hooked over the V of his collar. He holds a snub-nosed pistol in one hand and his smoke in the other.

I align the crosshairs on his nose, imagining a burst of blood and brain on the rock behind him. One easy pull and the human gene pool suffers one less leech. I rest my finger against the trigger, and an electric charge surges through me like when I'm about to place an options trade. The moment is good, and may never be better.

Josh lay in darkness listening to unfamiliar sounds. Accustomed to the noise of the city, car stereos, Harleys, and horns, the desert quiet was a zoo of foreign sounds. Nat kept the windows open at night and amid bird cries Josh heard other animals, the rustle of rabbits in brush—who knew what else?

Light poured through the windows as if sprayed from a hose, bringing strange patterns to his eyelids. Yellows and reds swirled and became each other. Merry's face drifted through the strange scene, her mouth open, but silent. His stomach rolled and he waited for the alarm clock to sound.

Had some other man stolen what she saved for him?

Had they already killed her, and set a trap for him? He took a deep breath.

Josh stepped into Nat's room, afraid he would still be there, snoring, drunk. The bed was made. He crept across shards of glass to stand before the gun cabinet. A small pistol caught his eye. He reached around a jagged pane and extracted the gun, then held it like a sleeping scorpion.

Still in boxers, he went to the back of the trailer, aimed at a saguaro a dozen yards away, and squeezed the trigger. Nothing happened. He squeezed harder; still nothing. He twisted a lever on the side. Nothing happened. He touched the trigger, then thought to take aim. The gun exploded; the barrel snapped to the sky and a bullet smacked the cactus, blasting chlorophyll and fiber guts out the back. His ears rang. The boom echoed in the hills.

Blood rushed to his cheeks and his heart pounded. His mind was suddenly sharp. Crisp. The metal in his hand was the absence of helplessness, the return of control: a basket of options.

He pressed his left nostril and blasted a blood clot to the ground.

Josh Golden was ready.

Frankie's cell phone rang. He'd forgotten to set it to vibrate—not that it mattered out here.

"Hey, you there?"

"I'm here," Frankie said.

"So?"

"There's nobody here. Like I told you there wouldn't be. Just fuckin cactus."

"There's probably crosshairs on your chest right now. Call me if anything happens. We'll be there in a couple minutes."

Frankie closed his cell and rubbed his chest. He squinted to the opposite hillside; the sky was blue and the sun bright. He moved sideways behind the cover of the boulder and squeezed the grip of his gun.

The temperature climbed in the last few minutes and sweat stood on his forehead.

"Shoulda made the switch at the mall."

Witnesses never saw anything anyhow. But Buffa insisted on this location. "Just wait for the signal," he'd said.

To his right, the van rolled slowly over the gravel road; Johnny and Buffa peered through the windows. Frankie waved. The van rolled to a stop and Buffa stepped out and lit a cigarette. Tony joined him, eyes scanning the boulders and brush.

They spoke and the hollow carried their voices to Frankie.

"If he's as smart as you say, we're sitting ducks," Tony said.

"Once we see the photos, we kill them. Simple."

Josh had never driven a stick in a vehicle with a slipping clutch. It worsened as he drove because he didn't remember to skip first gear. He looked at the gas gauge. Plenty. Thank God for the little things.

At the turn from Pioneer, he crossed an aqueduct and followed a dirt road into a narrow valley. His handwritten directions sat on his lap. He'd stuffed the pistol down his lower back; as the car bounced on rotten shocks, the forward sight post dug a hole in the crack of his ass. It helped him focus.

He rounded a bend and two men stood at the back of a van. One was Bandage Head. Josh chugged in second gear, trying to crawl, but the engine was weak. Approaching too fast, he pushed the clutch. The Tempo coasted thirty feet and stopped.

He spotted a man in a green shirt to his left, lazily concealed amid the rocks. On impulse, Josh did a three-point turn and angled the Tempo away from the van.

The door creaked. He killed the engine and it knocked and rattled. He took the envelope of photos from the passenger seat and stood by the door, fighting the temptation to adjust the pistol.

Bandage Head smoked a cigarette at the left side of the van, and another man stood at the right. Josh saw a flicker of motion through the side mirror; a third was inside.

Josh unflapped the envelope and held the photos high. "Where's Merry?"

Bandage Head opened the van's rear doors. A crumpled shadow lay on the floor.

"I can't see her. Let her come out."

Bandage head tugged her to the edge of the van's bed.

"Let her go."

"Bring me the pictures."

"Come get them. And bring Merry with you."

"Don't trust him!" Merry cried from the van, her voice distant, faltering.

Bandage Head pulled his handgun from his shoulder holster and his arm fell to his side. He grinned, dragged deep on his cigarette and tossed it to the dirt. He grabbed Merry's hair and jerked her out of the van. She screamed and kicked.

Josh stepped forward.

She crumpled by the bumper. Buffa held her upright with one hand while he nudged her ear with the gun in his other.

"Bring me the photos. Now."

Josh stood.

"Three…" Buffa counted.

I'm pointing the rifle at my mirror on the hillside but I watch Bandage Head.

"Two!" Bandage Head says.

That's my Luger on his hip. My grandfather lifted it from a Nazi corpse in 1944.

I whip the AR-15 to Bandage Head and when the crosshairs align on his chest—a flurry of movement pulls my eye to Josh—and I squeeze the trigger.

Josh whipped the photos in the air and exploded forward with his longest stride, arms thrashing side to side, fingers outstretched and tingling.

"Agghhhhh!"

It was like a football play. Josh imagined the fringe of the next moment while fluid in the present. Bandage Head would level the gun at Josh and he would leap to the side, roll, continue and drive Bandage Head straight through the van and the windshield on the other side.

Bandage Head raised his gun. Nat's AR-15 fired and the shock wave cracked as the bullet passed. Two steps and he'd be there. A hole blasted through the back door of the van as Bandage Head shifted to Josh. Nat missed. Bandage Head swung his gun to Josh.

Josh lunged.

"ONE!" Bandage Head fired and the bullet cracked past Josh's ear.

Another shot from the right; Nat hit Bandage Head in the shoulder. Another shot, this one from behind, to his left. He didn't see and didn't look. It was the man in green.

Josh drove Bandage Head into the van and punched him as they tangled and fell. Bandage Head had blood on his shoulder and a crazed look on his face. Josh head-butted him.

Josh heard movement behind him and began to turn. He saw a shadow fall and felt an impact on the back of his head. Josh stared at outside into the sunlight, dazed, and felt another blow to his head. A man held a pistol over him, ready to bash him again, but Josh collapsed to the floor of the van and was still.

Bandage Head rolled him to the side, spat blood, then sat erect.

The man who'd stunned Josh leaped out of the van, grabbed Merry's hair and lifted, curled an arm under her legs and tossed her inside.

A lead slug cracks past my head. Too damn close. I duck behind the boulder. My mirror has stopped firing, maybe to reload.

Bandage Head and Josh are in the back of the van with Merry. The driver guns the engine. While my ears ring from gunfire I hear, *Come on! Come on! Come on!* I swivel the rifle barrel and scope the man who shoved Merry inside the van. Bandage Head jumps out of the back, holding his shoulder with his hand as the van pulls forward. He stumbles but catches his balance and plods toward the photos. I squeeze a shot at the other man beside the van and hit his arm, then aim at the running Bandage Head. They're moving too fast. This is why the Constitution guarantees full automatic.

My mirror fires and drives me to cover. The van backs toward Bandage Head and the second man jumps inside.

Josh lay on his back, head to the side. Merry's legs were bruised and scratched and blooded at the knees. She quivered with her eyes closed and her hands at her ears. Her skirt rumpled and showed missing panties.

The van lurched back and the driver chattered, "C'mon! C'mon! C'mon!" The man from outside jumped into the van, his bloody arm limp. He kicked Josh's legs aside and closed one of the rear van doors.

The van lurched. The driver slammed the steering column shifter and hit the gas and the brake going full on and full off; the van rocked and revved and swerved until after a few rollicking seconds it changed direction.

The van drives forward. My mirror leaves his cover and works his way downhill to the open. He points a pistol my direction but his eyes look lost. He finds me and pivots. I fire and the sound is like a ball bat hitting a two-pound t-bone out of the park. He drops into a bed of cholla, velcroed to a thousand lime-green needles.

Bandage Head picks up the envelope and crams photos inside. The van blocks my fire lane. I squeeze one off at the driver and miss. The van jumps forward, spitting dirt from the rear tires.

I fire at the driver again and smash the side mirror. I fire again and again. The driver slumps and the van drifts. Someone inside jerks the steering wheel and the vehicle turns to the road again. Bandage head runs to the passenger side. He's in the seat. "Let's go!" he shouts.

The driver moves sideways. A hand reaches out with a pistol and fires rapid, un-aimed shots. The van picks up speed and I shoot the forward left tire. The van jolts to a stop against a boulder.

I align the scope on the driver's head.

Exhale.

I fire and see a poof of red in the front of the van.

Bandage Head is in the passenger seat. I can't get a shot through the window because Josh and Merry are inside.

I race across the rocks.

Josh lay on his back. His vision shimmered and fragments of the picture trickled downward. He blinked.

Bandage Head was the only one left. The revolver's front sight post dug the small of his back. He shifted his weight, slowly reached back and clasped the grip.

The last man to occupy the driver's seat was slumped forward. Staying very low, breathing in sharp bursts, Bandage Head leaned over the one who'd chattered C'mon, pulled the door latch and pushed out the body. Bandage Head looked at Josh, then quickly to the gear shifter on the steering column. He pushed it into reverse and reached down to press the gas with his hand.

The van lurched backward.

Josh flipped the safety. He pointed at Bandage Head's left ear, blinked to steady his eyes.

"Hey FUCKNUT."

He pulled the trigger.

Josh held Merry. She recoiled from his touch.

"Hey baby, it's Josh, baby. I got you. It's over."

She trembled and no tears fell from her eyes. He touched her blood-matted hair and stroked her cheek with his index finger. She closed her eyes, released deep, heaving breaths, and finally clutched him.

"Josh?" Nat appeared outside the window; he studied the bodies.

"I'm here."

"How's Merry?"

"She's, uh…"

Nat opened the door and took a bottle of water from the console. "Give her a little. Wet her lips."

Merry opened her eyes and accepted water. "More."

Josh touched his head. Pressure radiated from a goose egg the size of a golf ball. He looked at Nat. His vision melted and warped. Pressure grew. "What do we do?"

"Are you fit to drive?"

"This?"

"The Tempo. You take Merry to the hospital. I'll take care of them."

"What do I say happened?"

"Hold off as long as you can, and then tell the truth. Don't lie about this or you'll be in a world of hurt. Just tell them you don't remember. Wait them out. Give me a couple of days, if you can."

Josh nodded. "What about you?"

"I've been saving for a rainy day."

"I'd call this rain."

I'm at the van. I know the area. Every day at about noon a white truck with a black driver follows the path along the aqueduct. I don't know if it's a security thing the City of Phoenix started doing after 911, but it'll be impossible for him to miss the bodies.

I change the tire on the van, load the corpse of the guy who mirrored me on the other hill and drive to Carefree, then cut back on a different route toward the cave where I took Josh—my Desert Lair. The radiator steams and the temperature gauge pegs red. I expect the engine to seize from the heat but it keeps running. If Chevy made a motorcycle, I'd look into one.

The road devolves from macadam to gravel to dirt to dusty tire tracks.

I've left the air conditioning off to help the tired engine and as the sun climbs the sky, the heat inside grows. I sit next to four bloody bodies—one loose shitter, one loose bladder, per. Whiskey burns the stink out of my throat, if only for a moment.

This is the first time in days I feel control over my life. The governor's henchmen are dead. I have restored the world to balance. Nat Cinder: holistic healer.

I park facing a pit similar to the mineshaft Josh noticed, about a quarter mile from its grey slope. This one spans fifteen by twenty feet and drops straight down thirty feet. At the bottom there's a rusted pickup truck with an engine in the bed, a pair of bicycles, garbage bags, and a yellow plastic Pennzoil bottle.

I shoulder my rifle, gather each handgun—three—and open the passenger side door. Bandage Head falls partly out and I catch him and prop him inside, unclasp his belt and unweave the Luger. I rub it against a clean part of Bandage Head's shirt.

A liter water bottle rests in the center console and the envelope of photos is tucked under Bandage Head's thigh. I take them.

I put the van in drive and hop out. It doesn't idle fast enough to creep forward. Standing outside, I press the gas pedal with the AR-15 barrel. The engine revs and the vehicle jumps forward. The front tires fall off the ledge and the van hangs half over the ledge. The rear tires are still on the ground and I depress the gas again. The tires spin and the van slides forward until it begins to pivot and the tires lose purchase. I scratch my neck. The sun beats on me. I go to the back bumper and strain and my lower back twangs like a string bass. The van flops over the edge and crashes to the bottom, where it lays upside down on the pickup truck.

The rear wheels are still rolling. It looks like another pile of rusted trash.

I take a prone position at the edge of the pit and point the barrel of a .45 at the gas tank. I fire, rupturing the tank. I fire again and it explodes.

I leave the envelope of photos weighed under a rock, visible from the pit. A pillar of black smoke reaches toward the sky carrying the scent of burning flesh.

Josh touched Merry's knee. She leaned against her door looking out the window. Her shoulders shuddered and she wept silently.

He drove southbound Interstate 17 with the sun bright through the driver's side window. The light shined on Merry, highlighting the contrast between the fresh blues and blacks of bruises—and blood smears—and her tan.

Blackness closed on his vision from the sides and the lines drifted alternately to the right and left. His hands trembled. He'd faced a man with a gun. The gun had been pointed at Merry's head. Merry had been beaten and probably raped. He saw death. He killed.

He swooned, laid his head against the rest and concentrated on keeping his eyes open. His stomach was queasy and he braked, then pulled to the side of the freeway. Before the car stopped he threw the door open and vomited.

Josh sat up. Revolving red and blue lights flashed in the mirror. He wiped his mouth with his arm and leaned against the headrest. He felt individual beads of sweat on his brow and his throat burned. A uniform approached through the side mirror, headless, footless.

"Can I see your license and registration, please, sir?" A woman's voice.

Josh passed his license through the open window. The officer leaned forward and made eye contact.

"What's the problem? Been drinking?"

Josh held her eyes. If she looked beyond him she would see Merry and would ask questions he wouldn't be able to answer. "I don't feel well. Bad breakfast or something." He forced a smile and clung to her eyes. Darkness invaded the borders of his vision.

"Have you had anything to drink lately?"

It took a moment for the words to come through the fog of his mind. "I don't drink." Blood rushed in his eardrums.

Her face turned to marble and the lines at the sides of her mouth froze. She reached to her holster.

"Who is your passenger? Mam, I need to see your face." She waited a second. "Mam I need to see your face!"

Merry was still.

"I'm taking her to—"

"I need you to step out of the car, sir."

Josh slumped as blackness overtook him.

Chapter Twelve

I've got to piss like a pecker-tied bronc but that's not what wakes me. I open my eyes to a foreign sensation: scales sliding across my outstretched arm and a slithering coil at my belly. A snake, maybe four feet unrolled, has snuggled against me for warmth.

I'm spooning with her.

I see the outline of her tail but in the dim light I can't be sure of the honey-dipper shaped rattle, nor can I see her head at the center of the spiral.

My pulse doubles and she must smell my fear. Her tail rattles against my forearm.

If I bat her away, I'll be sucking poison.

The Luger's in reach, but I can't toggle a shell with one hand, and if I could, I'm not wild about firing at a target a few inches from my body in a cave.

My right arm tingles; I've used it as a pillow. The duffel bag of supplies leans against the cavern wall, somewhere beyond my fingertips. I stretch my hand and feel the sack.

I can't quite get my fingers around the strap. I flick it, get it moving, catch it with my fist and give it a nice easy pull. The duffel tips, drags across the dirt wall, and topples on me. It rolls and the rattler is gone. Disappears.

On my feet, I look for my new lady friend but the shadows are thick. I grab the Luger and listen to the quiet. The cave insulates me from outdoor sounds; in here, it's easier to hear my heartbeat or the rustle of my clothes than a cricket in the brush.

"Hey, snakey, snakey. Woohoo."

I grab water and purification tablets, slide into the main tunnel, and then into the moonlit dusk. After downing a couple quarts of water, I feel halfway human again.

From the cave to the Carefree Highway is two miles. Cross-country to Pioneer Road, where I left the four-wheeler, is about thirteen. I sit on a rock, pull my boots off one at a time, and tug each toe until it cracks. Clean the jam between. Whiff my fingers and rub them dry on my leg. Bend the digits sideways and backward. God it feels good. My boots back on, I brush dust from my clothes feeling like I lodged at a four-star hotel. A plate of eggs benedict would make it five.

Voices come from the pit, melodious and low, like tree limbs rubbing in a breeze. The flames have died but a wispy black plume drifts skyward—and the deep awful vibrancy of the sky's navy black damn near brings tears to my eyes. Four wide-beamed flashlights dart back and forth.

By now, someone has seen the photos.

I settle into a long stride, sticking to an all-terrain-vehicle trail that winds northward.

In the quiet of the desert night I ask questions and get nothing but silent stars for answers. Why is Gretchen dead? Why do I live this way, in an endless self-medicated cycle of booze and coffee? Does she exist, right now, somewhere up there, out there, around me?

Or is dead, dead?

Miles evaporate under myopic scrutiny of unanswerable riddles. I reach Carefree Highway, probably named by some type-A asshole, and cross. The only headlights are a mile off and I set a course that will circle the hill behind Albertson's Grocery plaza. I've never walked this terrain but my eyes are sharp and the moon rises brighter as the night wears on.

Behind the hill, the valley extends several miles and a new road shoots through the middle. Houses spring on each side. In grey darkness, the shadowy development looks like a tumor on an x-ray.

I vector between the highway and 33rd Avenue, where a wild network of four-wheeler paths crosses the valley bottom. My compass is Interstate Seventeen, a string of white headlights on the left and red taillights on the right. It stretches from the bend of the hill behind me to the vanishing point ahead, north. In this broad expanse there are likely a half dozen open mine shafts, and though the quiet air encourages deep thoughts, they are not so deep I forget to watch my step.

The terrain roughens. Midway across a patch of rubble I catch a rock on its side and it rolls. I land with my elbow in my ribs and a chunk of cholla in my hand, but the sharp pain comes from my leg, where the whiskey-bottle puncture has busted open. I'm two thirds of the way to the four-wheeler. My Leatherman pliers make short work of the cactus quills, but my bleeding leg concerns me more.

Each step sends a jab of pain to my core, but after a hundred yards, it's background noise. My pant legs rustle, rocks crinkle underfoot, and my breath bursts in and out. Traffic thins on the highway.

Mind wanders.

"You've got to have some kind of government," my docile neighbors intone.

"The fuck I do."

"You can't throw the baby out with the bath water," another idiot complains. I say, "Throw the baby out too, if he's going to be a politician."

I entertain the shit out of myself.

The night air is cool after a day in the teens.

The east side of Pioneer road looms before me, a short steep climb, and I engage a chain link fence in mortal combat. I flop over and regain my feet.

I'm ready to be done with this adventure. There is a simple, final solution to our problems with Washington D.C: Let the people demand the death penalty for all crimes that abuse an office, from state representative to the President of the United States. Lower the standard from beyond a reasonable doubt to pretty damn likely, and delegate executive authority to roving bands of secessionists with forty-foot lengths of rope. The people will insist on it soon enough.

My four-wheeler starts like it's been running all night. Thirteen miles away, the stack of photos I left are probably exciting a lot of curiosity. Whoever finds them can sort things out.

I'm done with it.

Rentier glanced over the Senate version of the Vallejo bill. The wording hadn't changed and tomorrow the conference document would arrive at her desk. Things were coming together.

Striking the right tone with the media was imperative. A fortunate scheduling delay, which prevented her from utilizing the Chavez Center for two days, would provide ample time to prepare for maximum impact. The bill had national reach like no other during her first term as governor. After the signing ceremony she'd appear on Charlie Rose, and Jennifer advised her this morning that both Chris Matthews and Bill O'Reilly had expressed interest.

A few minutes ago she approved the outline of a white paper, ghost written by a grad student intern. The forty-page document detailed the record of non-citizen suffrage in the United States, and Vallejo's historical fight for passage. She'd convert it into a slide show and as high priestess of the cause, take the message across the country.

She hadn't always been adept at controlling her press image. Her first experience with a rogue reporter, Gretchen Cinder, ended badly. She was Small Time, assigned to cover an unknown Democrat candidate in a state House election—in a district that voted Republican—but she wanted to be Big Time. She wanted Virginia to be her red meat.

Virginia closed her eyes.

Party leaders assumed she'd lose but wanted to test her mettle. While the bosses groomed her for the future, Virginia ran a well-oiled campaign. She fought like hell and never intended to lose.

She crammed her days with speeches, interviews, radio appearances; she knocked on doors, held fundraisers and wrote op-ed pieces. When Gretchen Cinder called to talk, Rentier pounced on the easy publicity and scheduled a meeting at the closest fast food joint.

Virginia parked in the Burger King lot and rehearsed a few one-liners from her speeches. It was time to give government back to the people. No, it was time for the people to take government back. She ordered two large iced teas and found a table, watching outside through the window.

An Audi swerved into a space and a pair of legs swung from the driver's side door. She watched the body emerge. The woman was pretty in a Sixties way, no makeup, but natural assets. A flush on her cheeks and a lump on her abdomen. She was pregnant. Virginia studied her, and remembered ….

Shortly before her first congressional campaign, at the close of Brownward's 1988 losing presidential bid, Virginia met a woman reporter. They watched his televised concession speech at the Arizona campaign headquarters. Virginia spotted in her an aloofness that, combined with auspicious beauty, often hinted a troubled past.

Virginia identified potential lovers by such signatures.

Most women Virginia misjudged were embarrassed, as if being mistaken for a lesbian was an active sin. Oh, you're mistaken, I'm not—gay, queer, a fag, what? Abomination. But this woman pursed her lips as if to spout a lecture. Virginia left without learning her name.

At Burger King, running for congress, Virginia learned the woman's name: Gretchen Cinder.

They sat with cups of iced tea, and Gretchen placed a tape recorder on the table. Virginia took a deep breath and nodded; Gretchen pressed the red button.

"How do you address rumors you are a lesbian?"

Virginia stiffened. She stared into Gretchen's sunshine eyes. "This is over." She reached for her purse.

"My research has shown lesbianism is so integral to your campaign strategy, it ought to be a plank in your platform."

"What—"

"You've had relations with almost every woman in your campaign, staffers to benefactors. I've seen you court a judge—no pun. You're sleeping your way to the top. Carpet cachet, right? Care to comment?"

"No." Virginia left.

She drove without a destination and stopped at a pay phone to cancel her appearance at the women's Rotary luncheon in an hour. Arizona cowboys wanted their lady politicians to be pretty and attentive to their wants, submissive one on one but spunky in the ring. They sure as hell didn't want a dyke. Before it started, her political future ended.

But she could win. She had momentum. Dollars poured in by the thousands. She'd end one call and the phone would ring. Her calendar filled itself. She'd found the right formula; her message was earning a constituency. Crowds cheered when she took the podium and stood clapping when she left.

Three minutes after her call to cancel with the women's Rotary, she made another. "I'll be there. I asked someone else to handle it. Sorry for the confusion."

She spoke like a prophet. The women let their plates go cold, unable to eat. She made promises. She painted pictures. When they trembled with the sweet guilty agony of unsolved social problems, she stepped into the void and guaranteed a solution. She owned them.

When she left, she invited Gretchen Cinder to a fundraiser at an insurance agency owner's home in a few days. Gretchen would get one more chance.

Virginia opened her eyes. Patterson had entered her office.

"Where's Buffa?"

"I don't know. He hasn't returned a call since yesterday."

"Yesterday? What in God's name is he doing?"

"Little, in God's name. The girl was missing. We have police reports as of that night. Amber alert at eight-thirty. We've had no contact since the following morning. He assured me he'd make the trade. Since then, no contact."

"Do you realize it looks like my office coordinated all of this?"

"I tried to warn—"

"Find him!"

"Governor, we don't have a lot of options."

"I don't want options. I want one solution."

The sun burned Mick Patterson's face but stepping into Rudy Ging Theen's apartment, his sweaty collar turned cold. The air conditioner blew a stream of frigid air and Rudy sat under the vent.

"Good to see you," Theen said, and gestured to a sofa that came with the apartment.

Patterson took in the sparse decorations. A painting of Jesus, his famous Caucasian incarnation, with hands clasped in prayer. A small table with a typewriter and a stack of paper. A half-full cola bottle.

"Adjusting to the free world?"

Theen took the cola bottle and spit tobacco juice in it.

"You know, on death row, they don't much care about keeping the cell cool, and you'd think concrete wouldn't get that warm. But it did."

Patterson nodded and watched a gold crucifix Theen wore around his neck swing as he leaned forward. "I didn't think I would need to seek your help this soon, but I have a situation."

Theen nodded.

"A man is blackmailing the governor."

"You want me to pray for him?"

Patterson leaned closer. "I want him dead."

A clock on the wall ticked. A linen curtain rustled.

"I guess I was naïve to think the governor wanted a rehabilitated killer to walk the straight and narrow."

"I was straight with you from the beginning."

Theen nodded. "Of course, since I have a pardon, I'm free to decline."

"Why make an enemy when you could have this?" Patterson pulled a business envelope from his pocket and tossed it to Theen.

"Employment?"

"You're on the tab. A comfortable living touring high schools, pumping your fame and selling books."

Theen placed the documents on the writing table and weighted them with his spit bottle.

"Sure beats a shallow grave," Patterson said.

"You want me to trade redemption with the Lord for this?"

"The good thing about redemption is you can always do it later, and one more time."

I dial Josh's house. He doesn't answer. I went to bed thinking my part was played, but George Murray is still dead. The FBI is this minute looking for Tom Davis and a law professor from ASU that looks like me. I've also made a few enemies in the executive branch. Preston Delp's ditched Camry tells me the governor plays a zero-sum game. She wins, or I do.

I load a twelve-gauge Mossberg and step outside. The afternoon sun lingers in a hot orange and purple sky, and holds the temperature over a hundred and ten. The humid air ripples. The monsoon manifests in the form of a distant wall of grey rolling dust. It'll hit like a fistful of thrown rocks, and if this storm brings rain, the washes will flood.

I slide down a worn path to the bed of an arroyo and follow a narrow trail of loose stones. Dried cactus logs and storm-flooded debris choke the narrow turns. At the top of the wash I cross the hill. Jagged brown and black rocks litter the hillside; barrel cactus, saguaro, and cholla cooperate to make their domain all but impenetrable. The rocks tinkle like glass with each footstep.

Today my objective is to look like I am hunting. After fifty yards a depression morphs into another wash. I follow it toward my trailer.

I flush a rabbit and level the Mossberg, but don't fire.

A hundred and fifty yards from the trailer, shadows cloak a hollowed-out chamber in the side of the wash. I pause to drink.

In the back of the chamber, a wooden door is camouflaged with epoxied stones. A tunnel leads to provisions for a rainy day.

Or year.

The wall of dust in the east approaches faster than I thought. Already, short gusts throw handfuls of sand. The full storm will arrive in less than fifteen minutes. A flash flood would mean death to an animal trapped in the wash. I dig my heels into the sand and continue.

A few minutes later I am in my kitchen drinking water mixed with Jack.

They say admitting alcoholism is the first step toward recovery. This step is wide enough to pull up a chair and rest a while. I've preserved my brain in a skull full of alcohol. My body ages, but my mind is still the guilt-slogged mush it was fifteen years ago. That's my definition of loyalty.

On my desktop, unopened since I met Henny Delp, lay her dead husband's records. I have the same reservations as with the envelope form the library. The contents will demand action.

I check a local news website. Vallejo has passed the Senate and the governor will sign it at a ceremony at the Chavez Center.

At some point every radical wonders if he's a God forsaken jackass to believe in political purity. Every idealist debates the price he'll pay in service to ideals the rest of the world's forgotten. Every patriot questions the honor of spilling blood for something as incomprehensible as a just polity.

Each path before me requires compromise. Should I turn myself in, I'll be tried for five murders, if not executed in the basement, a la Oswald.

However, if I open the envelope, I'll find a sledgehammer that'll play whack-a-mole with every hot button I've got.

I rub my eyes. Gretchen parks her hands on top of her swollen belly; her face glows like pink wine. The image changes and she dangles in a car seat, dripping blood onto my face.

I pull my hands from my eyes and open the envelope.

Patterson rapped on Rentier's door and it edged open. He spoke before she spewed outrage.

"Buffa's dead. Sheriff McConnell called. His body is charred. Three others, too. They found him last night in a van dumped in an old mine pit."

"Why did he call this office, if the bodies are unidentified?"

"They found photos too. McConnell thought you might want to call the shots."

"What did you tell him?"

"Nothing."

She propped her chin on her hand and her index finger pressed her cheek. She closed her eyes. Opened them.

"Come in and tell me how you will make all this go away."

Patterson sat across from her. "I tell McConnell that Cinder photoshopped your face onto some Internet porn. Blackmailed you, and murdered this detail we had investigating him. Sheriff goes in guns blazing and the problem ends."

"McConnell isn't a blazing guns kind of guy. Where are the photos and who has seen them?"

"A deputy found them on the scene when they pulled the van out. Watson, I think. Him and the Sheriff. Watson isn't too bright. McConnell said he asked who the women were."

"Good thing I haven't already endorsed him for the next election." Rentier said. "Do it. But one thing… You go. And Mick?"

"Yeah?"

"It ends tonight."

Patterson nodded. "That's not all, Governor."

She took a deep breath. "What?"

"The girl Buffa kidnapped is in the hospital. Same with her boyfriend. Neither is conscious."

"Go on."

"She was raped. Repeatedly. Possibly by several men."

Rentier's face paled. "Buffa?"

"Has to be."

Rentier was silent.

"Governor, it's only a matter of time until they tie the girl to the van and Buffa. With those photographs, and the boy knowing everything, you've got a bigger problem than Nat Cinder."

Rentier stood and looked out the window. "Do it."

I pull a spiral notebook with dated, handwritten entries from the envelope. Look out the trailer window at the storm. Read a few scattered lines:

She thinks she's Stalin. Patterson's ex-military, some kind of Hitler. Himmler. Brown shirts.

Hires Joey Buffa for strong-arm work.

Harassment case dropped by ex-assistant in governor's office, Leonora Mayne, now lives in L.A.

Rentier will use Hispanic vote to get to oval office.

A rubber band secures a few folded pages of paper. Enclosed is a cassette with "Margaret Berry" penned on the side. The folded paper is a transcript and on the top in handwritten ink:

Her first tryst with a woman on the Brownward campaign—staffer from D.C.—coordinator for state campaigns.

Next is a stack of twenty-two black and white photos of the governor with three women, toys and tongues. One is a Rosetta Stone, with each woman's name in red marker.

Margaret Berry is not one of them. I've never heard of her.

Outside, rainless wind howls like bereaved wolves and throws sand that sounds like hail. It was worse an hour ago.

The envelope offers up a paper-clipped stack of newspaper stories with clothed versions of the same women shaking hands with the Rentier: the attorney general, a judge, and a Republican state representative. The governor enjoys a bipartisan sex life.

She's touched women in each branch of government. The attorney general enforces the law for the executive branch. The judge sometimes authorizes constitutionally sensitive invasions of citizens' rights. The legislator introduces the governor's pet bills into Congress.

Last from the envelope is a timeline that charts relationships and votes that favored sex partners' interests, and two vetoes of bills that would have hurt TetraChem, Delp's old company.

The transcript of Delp's conversation with Margaret Berry is typed—maybe because no one has cassette players any more.

Delp: *Margaret, this is Preston Delp. I work for Dick Clyman, the minority leader of the Arizona House.*

Berry: *I remember Dick. I guess he isn't still a Democrat, either.*

Delp: *Gave that up a long time ago.*

Berry: *Wonderful, what can I do for you?*

Delp: *You and he met on Brownward's '88 campaign.*

Berry: *Heady times. (laughs)*

Delp: *Do you remember Virginia Rentier?*

Berry: *(pauses) I remember.*

Delp: *What's wrong?*

Berry: *Nothing. She's your governor.*

Delp: *That's why I'm calling. I'm looking for background information. Low key. Dick's investigating a couple of things.*

Berry: *I don't think I'd be much help. I barely knew her.*

Delp: *Maybe. Dick said you two were pretty close, and he thought you might be able to help.*

Berry: *She was just an ambitious staffer. I don't know anything about her since then.*

Delp: *But you knew her then?*

Berry: *(pauses) I knew her. If I remember, she said Dick made a pass at her.*

Delp: *He didn't tell me that. (laughs)*

Berry: *(laughs) She was ambitious.*

Delp: *Uh-huh.*

Berry: *What are you investigating?*

Delp: *Blackmail. And anything else that comes up. She's dirty.*

Berry: *And this is off the record?*

Delp: *Yes.*

Berry: *Are you recording this?*

Delp: No, Margaret. Just looking for any insight you might have.

Berry: We went out for drinks. I wasn't yet saved. I took my solace
         where I could find it.

Delp: Sure.

Berry: (inaudible)… was upset and we went out to talk. Virginia
         was important to the campaign, doing a great job, really. I
         didn't feel I could fire her. We were losing, and everything
         was falling apart. It was chaos. Round the clock stress.

Delp: Who was she?

Berry: Another staffer. Easy on the eyes, going to change the
         world, just like Virginia.

Delp: What was she upset about?

Berry: (pauses) I really don't think—

Delp: Off the record, of course.

Berry: Virginia is a lesbian. Or was back then, at least. Ellen
         thought she was being pressured. She threatened to go to
         the press.

Delp: Was that a real threat?

Berry: Anything is a real threat in a campaign, you know that.
         Maybe she already had talked to the press. She had a
         reporter's name.

Delp: I suppose, yes.

Berry: I talked her out of it. Virginia apologized for the
         misunderstanding.

Delp: Just talked her out of it?

Berry: We're politicians, right?

Delp: What was the compromise?

Berry: (*pauses*) *What did you say your name was?*

Delp: *Preston Delp. You can Google me.*

Berry: *I am. Look, I'd like to help you, but I have reasons, here.*
What I'm saying is that what went on couldn't personally, I
mean couldn't possibly help you. You know she's a lesbian.

Delp: *I didn't mean to upset you.*

Berry: *It was just a difficult time for all of us. Pressure. And*
hopelessness.

Delp: *Were you involved with her in some way?*

Berry: (*pauses*) *That's an outrageous question!*

Delp: *You seemed to be leading there. Look. I'm not some holy*
roller trying to judge you. Lots of people have
experimented.

Berry: *Why are you investigating Rentier?*

Delp: *She's been blackmailed into vetoing legislation, and I think*
she has blood on her hands.

Berry: *Blood?*

Delp: *Murder. I don't think she did it herself. She hired someone.*

Berry: *Who?*

Delp: *A woman. A reporter. Maybe the one you were thinking of.*

Berry: *Maybe. I guess that wouldn't surprise me. She said things*
that made me think she was capable of something like that.

Delp: *You were with her?*

Berry: (*sighs*) *We had a short involvement. One night. I'm not*
proud of it. Didn't even like it.

Delp: *What did she say?*

Berry: *That politicians have to be willing to do whatever it takes. Whatever it takes. It's why I left the party—the whole Democrat vicious circle. People need your help, and you have to do whatever it takes to help them—including destroying them. Pretty soon there's nothing at work but your own ambition. The lines get blurred. Killing a person isn't murder, it's a personal sacrifice you're willing to make, so you can continue serving the people who need you. Know what I mean? They start to see themselves as the victims.*

Delp: *Some of these people are demented.*

Berry: *It's not just Democrats. They're just easier to spot.*

Delp: *What happened after that?*

Berry: *We lost the campaign and I came back to D.C.*

Delp: *After that?*

Berry: *I didn't leave the party for a few years. I didn't have any more contact with Virginia. I think it was a conquest thing for her.*

Delp: *Anything else come to mind?*

Berry: *I always thought she'd end up being the president. She's sharp, you know. Every ounce of her is ambition. You know how some women sleep their way to the top with men?*

Delp: *Yes.*

Berry: *She does it with women.*

Half drunk. Exhausted. I'm missing something big, but I don't know what. What I do grasp changes my understanding of the governor. She started out the victim, but I wonder.

The journal notes pollution bills Rentier vetoed early in her term. The first capped smog gasses and would have cost Tetra-Chem tens of millions in compliance to buy air scrubbers for its chimneys. The second mandated testing of desert land near industrial buildings for various poisons—and required mining companies to map and fill every unused mine shaft in the state.

Lucky me.

Henny Delp said her husband hated Rentier because she's a fascist. She desires limitless power and maintains a brown shirt police force. Fascism is corporatism, and she is a pliant servant. The notes state she's assembled a crew of thugs and Mafiosos under the leadership of her chief of staff, Mick Patterson. She has welded the separate branches of government together with bribes, force, or sex. Her connections usurp Constitutional protections and a stack of black and white photographs reinforces the ties.

Preston Delp worked with the minority leader to dig enough dirt to get her impeached, but Democrats control the House. Plan B—from early in the notebook, was to amass enough evidence to force the state attorney general to investigate. That plan imploded when Delp learned the attorney general shared the Governor's bed.

The whole thing is bigger than I thought. The notebook rambles page after page. I don't know what Plan C was, but the last journal entry says, "Cinder may be our man."

An eerie calm has replaced the storm outside; wildlife has yet to resume its rhythms.

I've been sitting for two hours and it's time to circulate Jack Daniel's. Out with the old, in with the new. I stand and stretch my back and neck. Something metallic glints in the window.

I drop.

The window explodes with a yellow flash. A bullet zips past my head and glass catches my face and neck. The bang of a hand-gun—high-caliber, slow slug—resonates in my ear.

I crawl through glass toward the Mossberg shotgun, leaning beside the door. I suspect my assassin will target that next, and I have to beat him to it.

The window frame splinters and holes pop through the wall. Books fall from shelves. Dust fills the air. Head low, I wriggle from the door as bullets pepper through it. He's berserk. My computer monitor explodes. I pull a flake of glass from my cheek.

Silence. The bad guy reloads. The burning monitor sits next to the evidence on the desk. The shotgun is on the floor with a split stock.

Now he's fucked with my Mossberg.

I dart to the desk and scrape the burning papers, notebook and tapes, clippings and photos, into a scrunched pile and ram them into the envelope. Pistol fire erupts outside and I jump for the shotgun. I've got an arsenal twenty feet away that could start a war, and one punk with two pistolas is dicking my day.

His shots have centered on the office. I retreat to my unlit bedroom. Out the window, a shorthaired man with glasses, sapling skinny, fires two pistols low and high. I raise the shotgun in one motion and pull the trigger, blasting out my window. I've got a walnut splinter the size of a toothpick in my hand. Half the stock falls to my feet but a quick glance tells me the weapon is sound.

My shot knocks him back, but he's still standing. I cycle a fresh shell. He swings his guns to me and I fire. He falls backward, arms splayed. His chest moves up and down; a foot lolls sideways.

My computer sparks and burns. I crawl under the flaming desk and unplug it, then grab an extinguisher from the kitchen and spray the flames with foam.

Fire out, I grab an undamaged AR-15 from the cabinet in my bedroom and check the chamber. Outside, the bad guy shudders. He's about twenty seconds from squaring up with the Lord.

"Hurry up, You."

I've never seen him, or his curious tattoo. He shakes and chokes on blood. His eyes find mine, and his communicate fear and mine say fuck you. When he no longer blinks or shudders, I go inside.

Smoke is heavy at the ceiling, but the fan draws air through the shattered windows. My throat is dry and my joints ache. I stand at the door, smelling the rich scent of Jack Daniel's dripping from my cabinet to the counter.

My eyes fall to a book on the floor. A bullet ripped through the spine, but I recognize the blue cover and the shape of the author's name. Dostoyevsky. Crime and Punishment.

Every man defines right and wrong, and if he submits to law for the higher good, he has nothing to submit to the *highest* good.

The distant sound of a helicopter grows until the rotors beat overhead. Like a dumbass I stand at the trailer door. The bird circles, and the sudden white beam of a spotlight lights me up like a singer on a stage.

Chapter Thirteen

Patterson arrived as police cars charged single file up the driveway, then spread to point every headlight on the trailer. He couldn't tell if things were FUBAR or on schedule. He still had to think of a way to get to Josh Golden in the hospital, but for now, the kid wasn't conscious, and Nat Cinder was.

Patterson parked behind a white Chevy Blazer. Deputies stood behind open car doors, pistols drawn. He took a Smith & Wesson .38 from his glove box. A helicopter hovered overhead, bathing the trailer in a spotlight. The commotion of stamping boots, rattling rifles, the helicopter, flashing lights—it was good to be in action again.

A body lay spread-eagle twenty feet from the trailer. The man's hair was short and his tennis shoes were new. Smoke drifted from broken trailer windows and a dozen sets of headlights revealed scattered bullet holes in the trailer's walls.

A man stood in the light directing other men. His board-straight body cut a V shape no matter which angle he turned. Patterson went to him.

"Sheriff McConnell?"

The man turned. Patterson offered his hand. The sheriff crunched it in his and barked at a deputy. "Get me a megaphone!"

"I'm Mick Patterson. The governor asked me to stop by."

"As soon as we have him in custody, I'll let you inside."

"Fair enough. I'll stay out of the way."

"You do that." McConnell looked at the .38 in Patterson's hand. "You best tuck that away."

"I have a permit."

"You have a concealed-carry permit, which doesn't mean shit on my crime scene. One other thing," McConnell said. "I'm taking this man to the station, not the morgue."

"Of course."

McConnell walked to the man lying on the ground and placed his fingers on his neck. He shook his head.

Patterson neared the body and recognized Theen. "I can't help wondering, Sheriff, why you're being so accommodating?"

McConnell frowned like he smelled hog shit. "Politics—like everything. And my wife just loves the governor."

McConnell stood and wiped his hands on his pants. A deputy slapped a megaphone in his hand and he barked, "This is Sheriff McConnell of the Maricopa County Sheriff's Department. Come on out with your hands in the air."

His voice echoed from the hill. Patterson watched the windows.

"From all those holes, he's probably already dead," Patterson said.

"He lived long enough to kill this guy." McConnell raised the megaphone. "Come on out, Cinder. There doesn't need to be any more bloodshed."

"I think he's dead," Patterson said.

McConnell motioned four officers forward. They assembled beside the steps. Two held an iron ram and the others stood with pistols drawn.

"You ready?" McConnell said.

A nod.

"Bust it down."

In a choreographed move, they climbed the steps and leveled the ram. About to heave, the closest deputy reached to the door-knob and pushed the door open. They rushed inside.

Patterson followed McConnell.

"What the hell do you mean he's not inside?" McConnell bellowed. "The lights are on, the car is here. Hell, the pilot saw him in the window!"

"The back room is locked," a voice said. "Hell of a thick door. He must be in there."

"Hold on 'til I get there," McConnell said.

The sheriff climbed the steps and turned his shoulders to enter. Splintered paneling and glass covered the gold carpet. A Zenith television with a thick layer of dust on the screen sat by the door. Papers and books covered the left end of the computer desk; the right was ash. Fire had left the monitor a burned-out shell.

"What've we got, boys?"

A deputy pointed to the back room.

The sheriff edged his way through the men. "Stand back." He pounded the door with the base of his fist. "Nathan Cinder. This is Sheriff McConnell, Maricopa Sheriff's Office. You're under arrest. Unlock this door and there'll be no problem."

Silence.

"This is not a negotiation."

Silence.

"All right. Knock it down."

McConnell cleared the hallway. Two men lifted a battering ram, swung it back and with a mighty heave slammed the blunt nose into the door. It bounced with a thud.

"Shit!" one said, and shook his hand.

"One, two, three!" They struck again, near the hinges.

"You got any dynamite, Sheriff?" The big one said. "This guy has an oak tree for a door."

"Keep pounding it."

"Maybe a crowbar." Patterson said.

McConnell turned. "Kohl, get the crowbar out of my Blazer."

A moment later Kohl appeared with the bar. McConnell rammed the flat end into the gap at the bottom of the door. He squatted and with the bar in the crook of his arms, strained with his thighs. McConnell's face reddened; neck veins bulged and sweat pressed to his forehead. The door bowed an eighth inch, but held.

"Get on the end of this bar before I give myself a hernia."

Patterson planted himself opposite McConnell, farther back. They lifted and groaned. The door bent a quarter inch. The floor under the bar gave and the bar lost the angle to pry the door.

"How about a chainsaw?" Kohl said.

McConnell and Patterson shared a look. "Get one," McConnell said. He stretched his shoulders and Patterson shook his hands loose.

They went to the office. McConnell viewed the bookshelf. "Libertarian?"

"John Birch Society," Patterson said.

McConnell grunted.

Patterson's hand found a file drawer. "You mind?"

McConnell nodded.

Patterson pulled it open and read the file tabs. "JFK, Vince Foster, Ruby Ridge, Waco, TWA 800. Clinton death list. 911—I told you."

"See anything that says 'Rentier'?"

"No."

"Then close the drawer."

Kohl entered with a chain saw.

McConnell signaled for him to wait and went back to the oak door and rapped on it. "All right, Cinder. We're going to cut you out of there. And if that doesn't work, I'm going to get my accident team out here with the Jaws of Life. I'll saw this trailer in half! Now come out!"

Silence.

"Cut the door out." McConnell waved another deputy forward. "Back him up. When the saw punches through the door, anything can happen. Cinder can shoot when Kohl pulls the blade out. He can toss a grenade through the open door. Any damn thing. Stay alert!"

The deputy drew his weapon and aimed over Kohl's shoulder.

The two-cycle chain saw engine filled the air with noise and blue smoke. Kohl looked at McConnell, received a nod, and touched the tip of the saw to the door. The teeth caught. Oak chips sprayed to the carpet, smelling like cat urine. Two-cycle smoke billowed into the hall.

After a few minutes Kohl rested. The saw idled and stalled.

"You through?" McConnell called.

"I'm better than two inches deep, but haven't punched through."

"You think he rigged a bomb?" Patterson said.

McConnell shook his head. "He'd die too."

McConnell strode to Kohl. "Here's your problem. Just run the tip through, none of this side to side business. Straight through, then up and down."

Noise came in waves; Kohl pressed and relaxed the blade as it bogged on the heavy timber. The tip punched through and he sawed downward another minute, and turned it off, coughing.

"I'm dizzy." Kohl stepped to the trailer entrance and took deep gasps of clean air.

"I didn't think to bring a gas mask," McConnell said.

Patterson looked through the hole in the door for light and found none. He ripped the starter cord and the chainsaw spewed smoke; he slid the blade into the slot and resumed where Kohl left off. After a foot, a deputy took over. Finally, only a two-inch section remained at the top.

McConnell tapped the deputy on the shoulder and waved his hand at his neck in a stop signal. He wedged the crowbar to the base of the door. Deputies lined behind him, weapons drawn and pointed past him. Patterson stood with his .38 ready. Kohl aimed a flashlight at the door. McConnell lifted. The door groaned and fell inside.

The flashlight cut inside.

"Fucking wow."

McConnell held the bar like a weapon and stepped forward. Deputies poured into the room behind him. Patterson flipped a light switch.

"I'd say he's guilty," Kohl said.

"These AR-15s?"

"Look at that," McConnell said. "The department just confiscated a fifty-caliber sniper rifle."

"Who the hell is Nathan Cinder?" Kohl said.

"Where the hell is Nathan Cinder?" McConnell said.

Patterson pointed to the closet. The deputies aimed.

"Come on out, Cinder," McConnell said. "It's over. Don't be a fool."

He stood beside the wall and pulled the door open.

The deputies' faces dropped as fast as their arms. McConnell looked and saw three stacked footlockers.

Cinder was gone.

A hundred yards from the trailer, a caravan of headlights raced up my drive. I grabbed the envelope with everything from Henny Delp and slipped out the back door while the chopper lit the front. Headlight off, I took the four-wheeler and followed a trail from memory.

A quarter mile from the trailer I killed the engine and stood on the seat. The helicopter's searchlight held steady on the trailer as police cars with swirling red and blue lights skidded in the driveway and officers swarmed the trailer with drawn sidearms.

Shadows moved in every room but the last.

The helicopter's searchlight leaves the trailer and circles in an ever-widening spiral. They've decided I'm not inside. I jump from the four-wheeler and run across jagged rocks, leaving no tracks, and leap to the bottom of the wash. My knees buckle and I roll into a rotted saguaro log. Adrenaline shoots through my veins. The puncture in my leg tears open yet again. Backing into the water-eroded recess below the bank wall, I brush the dirt with my shirt to erase footprints.

The grey light of the cavern entrance deepens to blackness at the back. Feeling along the contours of the rock, I pull a familiar ledge. A door swings open from the hinged top and I crawl through, locking it from the inside with a deadbolt in stone. I'm in utter darkness. The tunnel walls are dry and dirt falls to my bare neck when my head scrapes the ceiling. It's like a grave. I unlock the next door and enter a cool, musty chamber. My hands spread on cold concrete.

Echoes widen the sound of my scraping knees. I grope along the wall and ease myself erect and flip a pair of switches. A mellow glow illuminates the chamber and a fan hums from the left wall.

Built in cabinets line the north wall; one houses a small medical center. I pull the walnut sliver from my palm, clean the blood from my leg, apply a coat of antibacterial ointment, and wrap my thigh in gauze.

Money can't buy love or happiness, but it buys a lot of other cool shit. The grid has never heard of this place, yet I'm connected where it matters.

Miniature XanSol solar panels, hidden nearby in the desert, charge a power station at the far end of the room. An airtight maintenance panel hides batteries from sight, and a duct outgasses under a creosote bush. A well provides water and the cabinets store three months' food supply, and an Ethernet connection through a hidden antenna on the ground ties me to news and bank accounts. Filtered air cycles through a pair of vents, hidden on the surface between giant rocks. The vents lock in an emergency, and oxygen tanks will keep four inhabitants alive for days. I wouldn't survive a bunker buster, but damn near anything else.

I rest the envelope on a table and sit on a bunk attached to the wall. The low whir of the fan fades into a monotonous drone. My sinews twang when I move and my joints pop like firecrackers in a bathtub. The voice in my head comes across like a person sitting beside me.

A man in this kind of quiet can't ignore his thoughts.

Nine people have died, and the torrent of causes that rushed them to their ends sweeps me toward a single effect.

Sheriff McConnell sat on Cinder's four-wheeler looking into moonlit darkness. The helicopter had circled for an hour but left to refuel. A small detail of deputies secured the trailer. McConnell spoke into his radio.

"How far off?"

"Five minutes."

He said to Patterson, "We'll have the dogs soon."

Patterson drank coffee he'd made in Cinder's trailer.

"That smells good."

"He could be right over this ledge," Patterson said.

"You find anything in the trailer?"

"No."

"Those pictures of the governor…"

"Photoshopped. We tracked Cinder internally for a while. The governor chose not to validate him by discussing matters openly."

"So if there's nothing more, why hang out with the sheriff at three in the morning in the desert, with a multiple homicide suspect maybe twenty feet away?"

Patterson let the question hang.

"You figure he might get shot escaping?" McConnell said.

"I just want to be here when you get him."

"Right."

Car doors clunked at the trailer. McConnell switched on a strobe and a pair of flashlights approached. In a few minutes, two K-9 officers arrived with German shepherds. The dogs panted, tongues lolling, with a whimsical cant to their jaws.

McConnell gave the closest officer a plastic bag with a shirt from Cinder's dirty laundry bin and the handler let his dog acquire the scent. While the other sniffed, the first shepherd sprang toward the wash, ran down the side with officer trailing, found where Nat landed, and stood in front of the shallow cave. The second dog joined a moment later.

The two officers flashed their lights inside, tracing back and forth the length of it. One knelt and lit the rocky ceiling.

McConnell stood at the ledge. "They find something?"

"No. The fugitive hid in this little recess here, but must have thought better. Come on, Charlie." The handler pulled his dog away, but after sniffing the ground where Nat's feet imprinted the sand, the shepherd turned his gaze to the cave. Charlie pulled.

"He bury himself in there?" McConnell said.

"I don't think so. You can see where he went in, and covered his tracks a bit, here," he said, stooping and pointing, but it's all rock in there. He moved on."

"Charlie doesn't think so."

The handler wiped his brow. "Charlie's the best we got, but it's nothing but rock. Come on down and see, Sheriff."

"That's all right, Pete."

"I'll see if we can pick up the scent a little farther off."

He led Charlie up the wash, toward the hilltop. The dog sniffed, looked back, and found Nat's scent from earlier. The other dog followed.

"Why would a man ride a four-wheeler here, dismount, and take off on foot?" Patterson said.

"Not a very smart move." McConnell said.

"You saw his reading list. Misguided, but stupid?"

McConnell scratched his head. "Nah." He jumped up and down, testing the earth. "Nah."

"You think of something?"

"He had another vehicle hidden nearby, or something." McConnell kicked a rock into a creosote bush a few feet away, then scanned the earth with his flashlight. He paced. "That's about all I can think of."

I press my ear to the panel by the battery, and listen.

Chapter Fourteen

I wake. My watch says eight-thirty. I itch with sobriety and jump from my bunk only to find the external world is a mystery. This is how a submariner would feel without a periscope. No wonder they drank Listerine and aftershave.

In the mirror, my leathery skin is crow-tracked at the eyes and mouth. My hair falls to my shoulders in a tousled mop. I've been in blackout drive for so many years my sober eye beholds a stranger.

My belly pushes a wife-beater T-shirt and my arms wrinkle on the forward parts of my pits. The skin below my collarbone depresses in a feminine curve. Back in the day I could knock out a hundred pushups in two minutes. My shoulders cleaved with muscle.

Could I do ten?

I place a mug on the floor, go to my knees and brace my arms in a wide stance. My back straight in a perfect front leaning rest, I lower my chest to the mug, press to the start position, and count one. At five my arms tremble, my heart races, and a blood-pressure ache clouds the back of my brain.

I'm spent.

Years of booze have metamorphosed me from a stud to a study in decay. I sit on cold concrete heaving for breath.

A revolutionary ought to be in better shape. Somewhere in my years of losing myself I lost myself.

Disaffected...

There's a set of electric shears in the bathroom cabinet. I cut my hair to a fuzzy cue ball and shave a week's worth of stubble. I look different, but no better.

My empty stomach growls and I count back the hours on my watch. Ten hours since I had a drink. Reality tastes strong as black coffee. At the cabinet stash of Jack Daniel's, I pull a bottle from the shelf and open it. The smell rises, sweet and inviting. I dump the bottle into the sink and take the next. After the twelfth, I vomit into the toilet and drink well water to ease the hydrochloric sting in my throat.

Old habits mull about the entrance to this chamber, laying siege while I lick wounds inside. Habit rules day-to-day life but routine doesn't penetrate this place. I could hop on the Internet and research the latest Washington scandal. But the spare walls, the utter quiet, urge rest. I turn off the soft lamps and crawl on my bunk.

I wake clear, unaware of time. My body shakes and my mind floats high and distant. I want Jack Daniel's like I want air.

Water soothes but pisses me off. It has no taste. I drink more. My shaking hand spills most of it down my chest. Virginia Rentier stands in the mirror behind me, naked, holding a scythe. I blink and she vanishes. I piss in the commode, shaking urine on the basin and floor. I do better without my hand, without aiming. Rentier stands beside me; she reaches with one hand, her other behind her back. I swing my fist and it passes through her and I slip in a puddle.

My chest tightens as if God prays and I'm between his hands. I can't breathe and my heart stutters. I crawl back to my bunk and curl on my side. Panic recedes like an ocean wave, revealing a moment of stunningly clean lucidity just a few paces beyond where I stood before. I could die and rot to dust in this chamber with perfect anonymity. Not a soul would ever know.

Fighting addiction means fighting oneself, but my destiny strengthens me and I ignore the pleadings of my cellular self.

I must stop Virginia Rentier. Vallejo will ruin the country, and usher a murderer to the Oval Office. It doesn't have to happen this time. Not if one little man finds the courage to face himself and run no more.

Hours.

I sleep and wake, drink water and piss, until I stop shaking and my addicted body whimpers in submission. Then I rise and look for a bottle of Jack. I ransack the cupboards. None. I face the exit. There's booze in the trailer. Pain shoots in the back of my head and I drop to do pushups until they remind me how weak I am and how strong I must be tomorrow.

I don't know how many times I repeat the cycle. Each iteration brings strength, new awareness. Each takes me a foot from yesterday and closer to the morrow. I cling to the vision of myself as an unpolluted man. Calm in the storm. Like Bandage Head said, walking between raindrops.

I turn the light on and look in the mirror, surprised to find my head scruffy—then I remember. I shave and breakfast on canned fish and crackers. My watch says night has fallen, but which night?

I step in the shower and adjust the low-flow nozzle. Solar-heated water burns my skin and I scrub with a rough washcloth until fifteen years of stain swirl down the drain. The towel abrades my skin and reminds me I'm alive. Each breath fills my lungs with air and my power grows. I dress in shorts and a brown T-shirt.

Merry maintains a webpage with suitably goofy teen girl thoughts, last updated a week ago. Except a few local sports news stories, the Internet knows nothing of Josh Golden. AZ Central reports the governor will sign Vallejo—which the media has titled "The Right to Vote Bill"—at the Chavez Center on Tuesday. The computer clock says it is Sunday.

I prepare a small pack: Luger, field glasses, MREs, water, a radio, and a charcoal grey suit and tie rolled to prevent wrinkles, a pair of Rockports, and Delp's envelope. I leave the pack but take the binoculars and a shovel.

Outside the cavern exit, the moonless desert smells of creosote and humidity. The night is alive with crickets and birds and fluttering bats telling me no man waits above the ledge.

Crawling through the dirt works the stiffness from my leg. At the bottom of the wash, I turn full circle. My eyes adjust to the weak light and the outline of rocks and brush.

I circle the hill and lateral back to the front just below the summit.

The metropolis twinkles in the warm air and merges with the stars of the southern horizon to form an unbroken circle of lights. The moon breaks the horizon like a silver sunrise.

I level binoculars at my home. A Cave Creek Sheriff's Department Blazer, recognizable by the big bronze star on the door, sits in the driveway. I find a place on a rock. Government is everywhere. Down on my driveway. On the road into the city. In the air flying above me. I hate every bit of it.

I built the shelter thinking I would someday need to be unfindable. I didn't worry about a nuclear blast and I didn't try to build it to be bomb proof. My apocalyptic vision called for a government-proof shelter.

With the shovel, I dig until I hit metal, then clean out a square that is ten feet long, eight wide, and six inches deep.

Sweaty and alive, I reenter the chamber through the wash. Inside, I open a door into a twenty-foot metal conex, or shipping container. The roof lies six inches below the outside surface. With the dirt cleaned off, a trap door lowers and serves as a ramp. Inside I keep a Triumph Tiger—an enduro style bike with nine hundred fifty cubic centimeters of displacement and semi-knobby tires.

It'll flat out go anywhere.

After basic maintenance on the Tiger, I distribute the contents of my pack to the saddle bags.

Josh tried to answer through his parched throat. A nurse came from nowhere and held a plastic cup of water to his lips. She touched his head as if to cradle it, but he couldn't feel her fingers.

"Son, do you know your name?" the doctor said.

"Of course."

"Would you tell me your name?"

Josh thought. "I don't know."

"Bullshit!" said a man in blue.

The doctor flinched. He aimed a tiny light into Josh's eyes and said, "Do you know what year it is?"

"I don't know." He was warm under a blanket, and smiled with drowsiness. "What's your name?" Josh said. "Do you know?"

"I'm Doctor Shotwell. I worked on you a couple of days ago. Do you feel any pain or pressure in your head?"

"No."

"You're going to be fine. You should get as much rest as you can. You'll remember more later. It'll take some time." Dr. Shotwell turned to Josh's mother. "Miss Golden, I'd like to talk with you a moment." He said to Josh, "I'll be back soon, son."

His mother squeezed Josh's hand and followed the doctor into the hall. The man in the blue uniform prowled at the edge of his bed. Josh's heart thudded.

"Think you're pretty slick," the cop said. His deep-set eyes peered over cheeks that hadn't been shaved in two days.

Josh couldn't read the number on his silver badge.

"Why don't you just admit it right now? It'll make things go a whole lot easier on you."

"What do you mean?" Josh said.

"The girl."

What girl? He remembered getting a haircut. He smiled. Almost got a blowjob—but he didn't want to. Why? What girl? Did this cop represent the FBI?

"You're lucky she hasn't died yet. When she does, it's murder one."

Josh looked up.

"Tell me what you know. The guys waiting to talk to you ain't nice people."

The cop slammed his fist to the bed. Josh startled and pain stabbed his brain.

"You and your gang banger buddies raped her!"

"Who?" Josh said. "WHO?"

"Merry Paradise."

The door crashed open. "What are you doing?" Cyndi Golden entered like a mad mama bear. "You can't question him without me present!"

"Look, lady. I'm just checking on him."

"Get out!"

"I can't do that." He crossed his arms.

Cyndi pressed the intercom. "This policeman is disturbing my son. I want him out, now!" She marched between the cop and Josh, pressing her chest against his. He stepped back, and she filled the space. "Out!" She pointed to the door. "Out!"

Dr. Shotwell entered, mouth hanging with an unformed question.

Cyndi whirled to him. "He questioned my son without me present. My son doesn't even know his name. He doesn't know what he's saying. That can't be legal. And it can't be good for him. Look! He's upset. I want him out!"

Dr. Shotwell turned. "Officer?"

"I asked him if he remembers anything. Like you did. Every minute counts."

"You know he didn't do anything," Cyndi said. "You'll have his DNA back from the lab in a day. You're trying to trick him before he knows any better. Get OUT!"

Doctor Shotwell frowned. "As I understand it, you're a guard, not a detective. You can guard him standing outside the door."

The cop raised his finger and opened his mouth, then scowled. Cyndi followed him to the door and slammed it. Back at Josh's bedside, she said, "What did you say, baby?"

Josh peered at her. "What's going on?"

Cyndi glanced at Doctor Shotwell.

"I don't know, exactly, son." Shotwell said. "But my advice to you is not to talk to the police without your lawyer."

"What did she mean, 'they tested me'?"

"Do you know why you're here?"

"No."

"Recall anything at all?"

"No!"

"A police officer pulled you over. You had a girl in your car. She— You passed out and they brought you here. I found an acute subdural hematoma. Have you heard of that?"

"No."

"It's a fancy name for a blood clot between your skull and the dura, the lining protecting your brain. I drilled a small hole over your left parietal lobe—in your skull—to relieve the pressure. The bottom line is, although you were in danger, we caught it early and you're going to be fine."

"I've got a hole in my head?"

"A small one."

"Guess Mom was right."

"Do you remember Merry Paradise?"

Josh closed his eyes. He saw her face, smiling in the Mustang, and could almost feel her fingertips on his chest. He saw Nat, saw himself text messaging, remembered Merry's terrified voice on the phone, the shootout, the drive and the pain in his head, the dizziness, throwing up. And Nat—his father's—words ... *don't lie about this or you'll be in a world of hurt ... give me a couple days, if you can.*

Josh opened his eyes. The doctor and his mother leaned closer.

"How long have I been here?"

"Two and a half days."

"We can't trust the police," Josh said. "The governor is behind everything."

Josh began with the night he met Buffa. Doctor Shotwell nodded and frowned, then sat on a stool and took notes. "The hospital attorneys won't like me listening to this," he muttered, and prodded Josh to continue. When Josh told them of receiving Merry's phone call at Henny Delp's, Shotwell asked him to pause. He called hospital security and asked for guards inside each of Josh and Merry's rooms.

Josh asked for water.

Shotwell called his attorney.

"Lou, Hank Shotwell. Fine. I need to talk to you in your official capacity as the attorney general's husband."

I change into my suit in a gas station restroom two blocks from Mario's, where the Minority Leader is having coffee. VIPs flock to the café's patio, where suspended plastic pipes spray water mist that cools the skin like artificial sweat.

Dick Clyman sits with his back to me and reads the Times. I recognize his bison-like frame, wide shoulders, narrow ass. He sits alone at the table holding the paper in the air.

I check my tie in a window reflection. I look like I belong here.

We've met only once since Gretchen's funeral. He gave a town hall meeting asking the community's feedback on a bill that would have required state-funded organizations to turn away illegal aliens. The legislature decided that solving the problem would require conviction and balls, so being without each, they turned it into a proposition for the citizens to resolve with a direct vote.

During the meeting, a group in the back postured like Hispanic Sharptons and Jacksons, and hurled the usual salad bowl of accusations, racism, exploitation, yada yada. Some wore lapel pins with the logo of a Hispanic racial pride organization that seeks to reclaim the southwestern U.S. for Mexico.

Clyman weathered a verbal barrage, then did the unthinkable. He said, "Are you registered to vote in Arizona?"

"Racist!"

"Hate speech!"

I sat next to a lumberjack-sized guy I'd never seen before. He mixed "wetback" and "spick" with a few choice cuts of profanity. Red meat. The group in the back pressed forward, shouting; metal chairs dragged on the floor and people scrambled to get clear.

Lumberjack rose from his seat, spread his massive arms and waded into Mexicans, corralled four at once and pressed them back. I followed and covered his flank.

They circled us and fists flew. The skirmish ended in a few seconds when police pushed in from the back, cuffed my new friend and me, and hauled us away.

We drank coffee at the station until the Sheriff released us.

"No charges," the deputy said.

"Why?"

"Thank your father in law."

I didn't call him to find out why, and this was two years ago. Clyman and I have never spoken about illegal immigration, but now that I'm Plan C, the incident seems significant.

The morning sun rises in the gap between Mario's and Hooters. I grab a seat at Clyman's wire table. He lowers his newspaper.

"Nathan," he says. His jaw goes tight.

"Dick."

We're formal as two dogs sniffing asses.

"You look good with a shave and a haircut," Clyman says.

"Time to move on."

"I guess you're balls deep in this Vallejo thing," he says.

"Thanks to you." I open Delp's envelope and lay its contents on the table. Clyman places his newspaper on top.

"What are you trying to do, here?"

"You tell me." I pull Delp's journal from below the paper and open it. "This entry, in your former chief's hand, is from four weeks ago. 'Cinder may be our man.' What did he mean, Dick?"

"I don't know."

"Just pulled my name out of a hat."

"Something like that." He lifts his newspaper between us.

"Who killed him?"

"I'm in the dark. I hired him because he already had useful information. I suspect his death relates to that."

I rock against my chair, measuring him. I expected tension. My drunkenness killed his daughter and by rights he should be choking me.

"You knew about his ongoing work?" I say.

"He apprised me of a couple items that would hold up in court. The rest, well, I can't get my hands dirty, you know."

"Dick, trust me. They're dirty. You can't let her sign Vallejo."

He lowers the Phoenix Times. "What can I do about it?"

"Play hardball."

"I'm the minority. My party is scrambling to get on the chuck wagon. I can't stop Vallejo and I'll never get her impeached. If I release information to the press, I'm picking on a dyke. No one wins, but I sure as hell lose."

"It is all about you, after all."

"I have to stay in office to do any good."

"Tomorrow, three hundred thousand socialists get the right to vote. Their birth rate doubles ours. Within twenty years, they'll vote themselves another failed state."

"We're just going to have to earn their support. We're a big tent party."

"Stick your finger in the wind and vote."

"You don't know who you're dealing with. You ever wonder why I want to destroy her?"

"Politics. Power."

"No need to look any deeper than the pat answer." He waits, meets my eyes. "She had Gretchen killed."

Blood rushes in my ears. It doesn't make sense, and yet it does. All those black minutes I can't find, the suddenness of the accident. The driver who came from nowhere and disappeared. The big story Gretchen kept secret. I look to his face and for the first time see anger.

"Why?"

"Gretchen knew she went with women long before regular people would tolerate it. But that wasn't what Gretchen was into. She picked up a lot of stories about shenanigans during the Brownward campaign. She even put me up to trying to get a little friendly with Rentier just to see how she'd act. But it wasn't about her being a lesbian. It was how it figured into her politicking. Rentier was two weeks from her first elected office, and a story about her sleeping her way to the top *with women* would've destroyed her."

"Proof?"

"Did you keep any of Gretchen's work-related notes and such?"

I nod.

"Then you have as much proof as you're going to get. Gretchen had a safe deposit box containing a cassette tape of a phone call from Virginia Rentier promising bad things if Gretchen didn't back off. She played it for me and I advised her it wouldn't hold up. But it's clear as day."

"But after she died—you did nothing?"

"It wouldn't hold up. Her drunk husband didn't see a truck pull out. And she already had more connections than you could imagine. The sheriff's wife."

"This can't be."

He shakes his head. "It was personal between Virginia and Gretchen."

I rub my brow.

"Rentier wanted her. Gretchen rejected her, then investigated her. It wasn't just the risk of exposure, to Rentier."

I recall Gretchen brooding and angry, then cheerfully dedicated to a killer story.

"It's personal to me, too."

I leave.

I sit at a hotel bar with a ginger ale. My bike sits out front, visible through the window. The check-in is behind me, through the double doors. I'd planned to stay the night, but I don't belong here. I gulp my ginger ale and rap the glass to the table.

I feel like a proud man walking down the sidewalk who feels a pinch and finds some guy's tool in his ass. What can you do at that point? You're fucked.

What can I do?

I'll throw things so damn far out of orbit that suns and moons collide.

The television is tuned to CNN and the format is frenetic and scattered to appeal to its attention deficit audience. That's what they're making all of us. Camera shots jerk from side to side, then parry in for a close-up of some babe's perfect teeth. The screen attracts me the way a scrap of foil attracts a rodent.

The Director of the FBI, Beck Lancaster, shares a split screen with a still photo of Special Agent George Murray, deceased. Lancaster is the latest in a string of directors tasked with securing the country from men on camels. He's done a great job, but that's baseline performance in a police state, isn't it? I stand on the stool at the end of the bar and press the volume button.

"We have the evidence. The case is closed."

"What case?" I say. "Murray?" I didn't hear it and I don't want to believe it.

I get a refill of ginger ale and wait through another news hour for a repeat broadcast. This time, a photo of Charlie Yellow Horse appears on the screen while the babe with perfect teeth reads his short biography. Yellow Horse, it seems, is a Native American renegade, and leader of a small group of Arizona secessionists. An anonymous tipster to the FBI provided Yellow Horse's cell phone number, and they pinged it to find his location. He confessed within hours. The clip with Director Lancaster airs again. He states they have the murder weapon, fingerprints, and eyewitnesses. Case closed.

Fidelity, Bravery, Integrity.

The announcer cuts to the affiliate team for a local update. After the big news of four burned bodies being found in a mine pit, the announcer mentions Governor Rentier is heading to her ranch in Sedona with top state Democrats for long-range planning. She'll be back tomorrow, however, to sign the historic Vallejo bill.

Attorney General Jane Lynwood spoke into the telephone base, on intercom. "I told you, no interruptions. I'm unavailable."

Normally, Lynwood let the police do their work. When the evidence was in, she'd assign the case. But this poor thing, Merry Paradise, finally out of critical care and recovering from beatings, rape, and shock, deserved justice in a way the dead didn't. She was alive, and for her, the torture would go on and on. The only solace would come from knowing her assailants—her rapists—rotted in prison. If the rest of the world couldn't understand the attorney general wading knee deep into the investigation to make sure some Gerry Spence wannabe didn't free the rapists on a technicality, they could go to hell.

"But it is your husband," her assistant said.

Lou worked as a consultant to several hospitals. He made great money but he was needy. If she had seen Rentier rise to power as a

single woman before she'd met Lou, Lynwood wouldn't have
married.

"Tell him I can't come to the phone. My God, Sandy, why are you
arguing with me?"

"He says it's about the rape case. It's urgent."

"Put him through."

Ten minutes later Jane Lynwood wove in and out of traffic in her
Audi to the Deer Valley Hospital. Lou, sounding grave, said the boy
was conscious and remembered everything. He knew who raped
Merry, but also claimed he had information he would only give to
Lynwood in person. When Lou told her to come, he didn't phrase it as
a question.

She parked in the guest area and found a nurse station.

The elevator door opened to a hallway that looked the same both
directions. She turned left, toward a police officer mulling outside a
room.

"Officer, is this Mr. Golden's room?"

"Yeah."

"I need to speak to him. Let me in."

"No one goes in or out, lady."

"I'm the attorney general. Step aside." She pushed past him and
opened the door. Inside, a hospital security guard whirled. The boy's
mother sat bedside, and turning, Lynwood saw Lou watching her with
uncomprehending eyes.

I straddle the Triumph Tiger, still wearing a suit. The green tank has a pattern that resembles the slash of a tiger's ten-inch paw. It looks as edgy as I feel.

I assume my trailer is under close surveillance. I don't have a tunnel like some antebellum Mississippi mansion leading to my arms room, so I don't have my sniper rifle. That doesn't bother me. I have the Luger, and I want to be close to Rentier when she dies.

I know, without going there, that my trailer's been torn into a stack of toothpicks and paper. They've confiscated everything by now. A hacker surfs my hard drive and ballistics people study two hundred and forty AR-15s. Techs track my emails and analyze my financial records—the ones they know about. They're cataloguing my files of government atrocities to paint me a crazed killer.

But they aren't going to find anything that ties me to Delp or Bandage Head. They'll have to manufacture that evidence.

I pull in front of a car and run through three gears before hitting the brakes at a stoplight. Two more lights and I'm on my way to my shelter, then Sedona. The next turns yellow as I approach. The road is clear and I shoot under a red light.

I'm waiting in the left turn lane to catch Interstate Ten and the swirling red and blue lights of a City of Phoenix cop pull behind me. I'll take the ticket. Maybe someone, someday, will see it and hypothesize why the State failed to connect the dots. Fuck 'em.

I lift the visor on my helmet and the cop approaches. He's big and cocky like he expects he's going to find a Gen-X punk under the helmet.

I pull my helmet off.

"Do you want me to get out of this lane so we're not holding up traffic, or should we stay here, officer?"

"Here is fine, sir. May I see your license and registration, please?"

I love the courtesy. On an individual basis, these guys are the best. Imagine our bankrupt society without them.

"Yes sir." I retrieve my last identity from the wallet in my breast pocket. Today I am Hank Rearden.

"That your real name?"

"Sure is. Unless my mother didn't tell me something."

He smiles. "There's a famous book with a Hank Rearden. You ran a red light back there. I saw you check both ways. Should have checked the gas station. That's where I was."

"Guilty," I say, with genuine remorse.

"It was close, so I'm going to give you this one. Drive safely."

"Thank you, officer."

Jane Lynwood kept her eyes on the paper, but couldn't stay her trembling hand.

"You saw the photographs?"

"That's right," Josh said.

Lynwood studied him. His gauze-wrapped head accented his angular features. The blanket bulged at his crotch; not an erection, but a mound. Photographs! Her blouse felt clingy.

"When were they taken?"

"Our best guess was a few years ago. It had to be before she was governor."

"And there were three women?"

"That's right."

"How long before she was governor?"

"She didn't look too much younger, but the others did."

The hair on her arm stood.

"Where are the photographs right now?"

"I don't know. I threw them in the air when I rushed the man holding a gun to Merry."

"Why didn't he shoot you?"

"He fired and missed. Then Nat shot him. I tackled him and drove him into the van. Someone clubbed me and I blacked out."

"And this man—you called him Bandage Head—died in the van?"

"Right."

"From Nat Cinder's shot?"

"No, from mine. Nat hit him in the shoulder. When I came to, he was trying to get in the driver's seat to get away with Merry and me in the back. I had one of Nat's guns and I shot him in the head."

"Have you fired guns before?"

"That morning. I practiced on a cactus."

"Are you sure, baby?" Cyndi said. "It must be hard to remember."

Josh shot his mother a look that closed her mouth.

"Do you think it was necessary to kill him?" Lynwood said.

"You shitting me?"

"No. You could have stopped him without a head shot."

"The man killed Delp. He raped Merry. He was trying to kill us ...
What would you do?"

"You must have been very angry."

"After he had the photographs, he had no reason to let us live."

Lynwood swallowed and rested her pen on the yellow pad. "I
believe you."

"Do you have enough to arrest the governor?" Cyndi said.

"How can I find Nat Cinder?" Lynwood asked.

"I don't know," Josh said. "I don't know what his plans were."

"Miss Golden, if you talk to Mister Cinder, please ask him to
contact me. It's urgent." She wrote her cell phone number on the back
of a business card. She left one for Josh by the telephone.

"I have to run, but I appreciate your help." Turning at the door, she
added, "I would be remiss if I didn't advise you to seek counsel."

Lynwood stepped into the hall. He'd seen her naked. He probably
imagined her in bed, just then. The whole world would, if they didn't
get the photos back. But Rentier made it sound like an open
conspiracy—all women at the top shared the same common desires.
They all worked together. *The sisters would come together.*

She recalled Rentier with a glass of wine and a blush in her cheeks,
saying it was carpet cachet, an old-boy's network of up and coming
gals. It was equality—a network of women willing to help each other
get ahead, with a secret indoctrination that cleared the cobwebs from

the past and opened them to new possibilities in life, in sex, and in politics.

What was she thinking?

The door opened and closed behind her.

"We got to talk, Jane," Lou said.

"Oh shut up!"

The door swung closed.

"She isn't going to do anything," Josh said.

"Why?" Cyndi said.

"She's in the pictures."

"What!"

"Just what I said, Ma."

"Why did you talk to her?"

"I had to give the system a chance."

"Now you've got her bad guys gunning after you too!"

"Ma. Ma! There's a business card in my backpack. Could you get it for me?"

Cyndi opened the closet with his clothes and dug into the pack. "Earnest Whetton, Junior, Esquire."

"Can you dial the number for me?"

She pressed the digits and handed him the phone.

"Earnest?"

"He doesn't work here." The line went dead.

"Ma. Dial the cell number."

The phone rang through the receiver. A man answered. "Who is this?"

"Josh Golden. We met on the bus …"

Chapter Fifteen

Police and sheriff's deputies mull around my trailer. I drive past, a hundred yards away, without slowing. A mile farther I turn onto a Jeep trail and park in an arroyo, then trek to the underground chamber.

The sun sags toward the horizon, still hours from setting, but close enough to paint half the sky purple and orange. Saguaro stand bold against the colors, framed by jagged mountains on the right and a camouflaged city on the left. It is the kind of view that calls to mind a cowboy, riding away.

Inside, old Jack Daniel's reeks in the sink and reminds me of party days. I could slip away from all of this. Buy a bottle and let my mood and anger dissolve; allow the guilt to ride high again, the darkness to swell at the edges like black around a campfire.

Nothing prevents me from riding into the sunset. I don't have to be a hero. I can be meek and inherit the earth, go plug into a reality show on television.

On the Internet I retrieve the files from my Yahoo account, download them to this computer, and fire an email to my friend in

Liberia. Within minutes I receive his response, asking for my credit card number. I send it and the files.

If I fail to kill her, a couple billion global citizens are going to get the most interesting spam of their lives. It's prepaid, triggered by a week of silence.

Fifteen minutes later, I leave the conex. The Luger is in my right saddlebag, loaded with a nine-round magazine.

The padding in my helmet dulls the engine's steady whine and the landscape opens. Mountains loom personal and close; the brown crags shimmer through wavy heat. The sky burns with a nuclear sunset. I pass saguaro stands, then groves of cholla. The handlebars tickle and the whole thing is hypnotic. I see my past as if it belongs to some other maligned soul. I hear my story in a sober narrator's voice.

I rubbed Gretchen's feet on the morning of the day she died. I turned the corner of the bed and her foot caught my pant leg. She was eight months pregnant and had been complaining about her feet. I clasped one and she moaned. The alarm clock glowed green and I was running late, but I worked the side of her foot, the arch, the heel.

Five minutes passed and I dug her other foot from under the covers. She yawned and moaned and sighed.

I gave her left foot the same as her right, then kissed her belly and forehead.

"That's a sweet way to wake," she said. "Don't forget the dinner tonight."

A group of Democrats were having a fundraiser and Gretchen had to be there. The candidate had invited her.

"Are you seeing the doctor today?" I said.

"In the afternoon."

"I'll be home in time. I promise."

I drove to work late for having indulged my guilt and rubbed her feet. At Honeywell, my secretary refused to abort our baby.

"You're destroying my life," I said.

She sat in my office with her back to the glass wall. The door was glass, and employees on the outside paid no mind until Cyndi's shoulders shook with sobs.

"Imagine trying to support a baby without a job," I said. "Who's going to hire a single mother? Get used to food stamps. And if you come after me, I won't have a job either. No support for you."

I said the vilest shit I could think of. I wanted her to kill herself.

She looked through glassy eyes. "I have friends. I'm not afraid of you."

I was three years out of the Fifth Ranger Battalion. Friends? I'd take them on with a K bar. "You don't say something like that to a Ranger."

"You're evil," she said.

She went to her desk and filled her arms with personal items and walked out the door past gaping colleagues.

I didn't see her again until I ran into her fourteen years later. By then, I'd had fourteen years to meditate on the sixteen different kinds of asshole I am.

I left work early that day, blaming it on seafood from the cafeteria. I was a soldier; I'd been trained on how to solve domestic problems: I drank. Six hours later, I remembered the dinner I had promised Gretchen I wouldn't miss. I could barely see the road, but rushed home.

"Let me drive," Gretchen said.

"I'm fine."

"Think of the baby—your son," Gretchen said.

Drunk drivers can be fairly safe when proving they're not drunk. The fundraiser was at a tony house on Princess Drive. Marble floors and counters, brass balustrade, a poolroom, a pool, a library. Gaming tables from Vegas or Bullhead City filled the ball-room area, and tuxedoed men completed the gaming theme.

A Phoenix insurance agency manager lived there, a friend of Virginia Rentier's. When we entered she had a microphone and was begging him to sing an old Rod Stewart song, Maggie. I listened with a gin and tonic.

Only a few members of the press showed.

I sat in the great room pulling a steady supply of gin and tonics from the waiter's tray, keeping Gretchen's location roughly in front of my mind. Cheating men suspect cheating women. Looking around I saw serious money. Blue haired women, grey haired women, and women who washed the grey right out of their hair. All in gowns that cost as much as my Bronco.

Gretchen stood in a corner with an animated look on her face, talking to a woman partially hidden by a fluted marble column. This one had a shape to her. As the altercation waged back and forth, they advanced and retreated inches at a time. Rentier's gentle, black-gowned rump pressed out from the column, the curve of her lower back followed, then the athletic calves and finally, the full presentation. Virginia Rentier was stunning.

Gretchen marched away, spotted me, and veered. Rentier turned and it was the first time I'd seen her face that wasn't on a television ad. Her body seemed as inviting as sunshine, while her face was a chiseled block of ice. She turned to a glass cabinet that had an ivory and gold telephone, and lifted the receiver.

Gretchen led me from the room by my arm and a moment later, we walked to where I'd parked on the street. Though pregnant, she took full, angry steps, elbows working wide.

She didn't challenge me for the driver's seat.

"What was that about?" I said, and turned onto the freeway ramp.

"I don't want to talk about it."

A few minutes later I took the Seventh Street exit and headed south. Crossing Greenway, I saw headlights, heard a noise, everything went black. A bread truck rammed us from the right, driving us twenty feet. The Bronco rolled and I regained consciousness with Gretchen's blood dripping on me, her arms hanging down, forever short of a final embrace.

I've carried this for sixteen years. If justice was anything more than a human myth, the truck would have been traveling west, not east. Gretchen would be a happy widow.

I take the Sedona exit. The sun is a half hour from setting. The westerly display is the kind photographers dream of, but all I can think of is a black-gowned angel of death picking up the phone, dialing, and mouthing one word.

"Go."

Earnest Whetton, Junior, Esquire, took the southbound onramp from Deer Valley road to Interstate 17.

Holy Shit.

Talk about saving the job. How about making it irrelevant— jumping from law school to the biggest name in the country for a half dozen news cycles. If what the kid said was true, no more waiting around for the big bucks. His story should be easy enough to verify. The DA's office had been buzzing with the finding of Rudy Ging Theen's body at the site of an attempted massacre. Nothing had come out in the press, and with the governor's contacts, it might take a while. If he could get copies of the pictures and see the materials Delp had put together, this whole thing could blow open tonight. He'd be on Drudge by dawn, doing phone interviews by noon. Receiving job offers by dinner.

But how to get the photos? Nat Cinder had made copies, but he was nowhere to be found. The players in this case were so big, he ought to call the FBI. But they would take months to investigate, spend millions of dollars, and give someone as sophisticated as the governor all the time she needed to cover her tracks. And that could include killing more people.

He parked in a garage a block from his office and almost ran the distance to the front door. Before taking his jacket off or dropping his notepad to the desk, he pecked his laptop's password with one hand and found Sheriff McConnell's number.

"Sheriff, this is Earnest Whetton with the District Attorney's office."

"Hello. This Junior?"

"That's right."

"What can I do for you?"

"I'm working on the murder case associated with Nat Cinder."

"I thought Lynwood gave that to Luke Peters."

"It's turning out to be bigger than she expected, I guess. Got a minute?"

"Sure, but I already went over all of this with him."

"Right, I'm following up. Just a couple of things. We have a report that there were photos left at the crime scene, either in the van or up by Pioneer road, where the shootout was. Know anything about that?"

The line was silent. Earnest removed his coat and unbuttoned his sleeves. "Sheriff?"

"Have you asked Lynwood about that?"

"No. Should I?"

"You might." McConnell said nothing more.

"Rudy Ging Theen, the killer the governor pardoned just a few days ago—he was at your suspect's house?"

"I guess there's no harm in telling it."

"Know why he was there?"

"We matched both his nine millimeters to the bullets in the trailer. He fired forty shots before Cinder got him with a twelve gauge through the bedroom window."

"Who would have ordered a hit like that?"

"Listen, Junior. I respected your daddy. You're as tenacious as he was. But if you knew what's best, you'd move away from this line of thinking."

"I'm sure a lot of folks told Dad that, too."

"Yeah, and he didn't listen, either. Just like I know you won't. Good evening, prosecutor."

Sedona swells with tourists who come to see the red rocks and drink lattes. They wander from shop to shop, desperate to find a genuine relic to take home, something meaningful like a kachina doll or a turquoise belt buckle.

There's a parking space at the dirt bottom of a two-level garage behind the stores, and in a few minutes, I locate a hiking shop and buy a pair of replica Army BDU's, in a black, white, and grey camouflage pattern, and a tin of black Kiwi boot polish. The air smells of steaks and the jubilant sounds of a honky-tonk come from a third-story restaurant. Sedona sells illusions, cowboy boots and fringed leather jackets no cattleman would touch with a prod.

I find a pay phone and call Josh's home number. Cyndi answers.

"This is Nat."

"Hello."

"Where's Josh. How is he?"

"In the hospital. He almost died, Nat. Almost died."

"How?"

"They clubbed him on the head. What were you thinking?"

"He's a man; made his own decisions. I'm proud of him."

"Where are you?"

"Nowhere. I'm about to put an end to all of this. There's a lot you don't know."

"Josh told us everything. You need to call an attorney Josh found. He's trying to help and he wants to hear your version."

"I don't have a version."

"Nat…"

I mull it over as a fat man waddles by in a Hawaiian shirt and shorts. It would be nice to have vindication after all of this is over. "You remember my email address?"

"Snakcflag@gmail.com."

"Right. The password is 'Gretchen1991.' Have him log into my account and open the most recent email I sent to myself, and look at the attachments. I also left the photos by the bodies of the men that took Merry. Tell him to ask the sheriff what happened to the photos. That's his cover up right there."

"Okay." She waited. "Are you all right?"

"I am. For the first time in a long time," I say. "And Cyndi?"

"Yes?"

"I'm sorry. I was a total fucking piece of shit with you. And you've given me a lot of grace, just letting me near my son. I don't deserve him or you. And I'm grateful to you."

I hang up.

Back on my bike, I cross Midgley bridge and follow a pink Jeep with an extended back jammed with tourists, exploring the rugged beauty of the rocks and canyon on their dimpled asses. These are not seniors whose bodies have slowed; they are middle-aged, lethargic slugs.

Secession was a dream, I realize. Americans are too fat to fight.

These are the people who will condemn me.

Rentier's security element patrols the property perimeter. People in her line of work piss off a lot of people. They know it, and Rentier knows I am on the loose. Does she worry I've learned her role in Gretchen's death? Has she taken extra precautions?

My Luger shoots nine-millimeter slugs that exit the barrel at about thirteen hundred feet per second. Very slow, compared to a deer rifle, but the lead is heavy and a clean hit will convert her heart into soggy mush.

Before the Governor's gated drive, I turn on a road that crosses Oak Creek and winds into a rocky side canyon. It leads circuitously behind the ranch, and after a few hundred yards of driving on a road closed tight by maples, it slopes upward to a plateau, overlooking the noblest rocks in Sedona. I pull over and survey the terrain. An orchard spreads on the left and farther right is the back of the ranch house where the governor will entertain Democrat principals who gather tonight to celebrate the addition of three hundred thousand new constituents.

Helicopter rotors chop in the distance. The sun has slipped behind the rocks but a black dot and a flashing strobe grows in the grey sky. It approaches high and descends perpendicular to a blacktop landing between the house and orchard. My pulse quickens. I'm only a couple hundred yards away. One lucky shot into the pilot's head, or the engine…

The bird lands on a pad illuminated by floodlights. I watch through binoculars. The governor emerges with the House Majority Leader, the Secretary of State—a Republican, a man I recognize as a state Supreme Court judge, and a man who stands in a suit with his back to me.

I pull back onto the road and drive another mile, then turn into the first fissure that'll hide the bike. Cloaked in forest. The sun has set.

I change into camouflage, remove the Luger, study the magazine, and smack it in. I pull back the toggle and release, and hear the ambitious, satisfying sound of a round seating in the chamber. I check the safety—*GESICHERT*—and slip the pistol into my holster.

I swipe a finger of Kiwi on my face and rub it until my ghostly appearance disappears from the sideview mirror, then cover the backs of my hands.

Earnest made a chart with names, circles, and arrows in a rough chronology of the deaths, the rape, and the photos, based on Josh's account. He added information about Theen that Josh didn't know. Everything fit except for a few nagging questions, and a little problem of having no evidence and no witnesses, except a boy the Attorney General might charge with murder.

The phone rang. Caller I.D. said it was Cyndi Golden.

"Miss Golden, this is Earnest. Thank you for calling."

"I think Nat's going to get himself in trouble."

"What's going on?"

"He wouldn't say, but I think he's going to kill the governor. He called for Josh a few minutes ago."

"And?"

"He said he had business to take care of."

"Could be anything. Did you ask him to call me?"

"He said no, but he gave me something. Do you have a pen?"

"Go ahead." He copied an email address and password. "From what I understand of Nat Cinder, that sounds like him."

"He said one other thing. He left the photos where the bodies were found. He said that's all you need."

"Well, that's a start. But all that proves is that Cinder had the photos. A jury would look at that as evidence of his guilt."

"How's that, when the whole damn thing was set up to swap the girl for the photos?"

"I don't mean to be difficult, but how does a jury know it wasn't the other way around?"

"The dead men raped her, that's how. You've got Josh, Merry, and Nat, maybe, that are all going to say the same thing."

"Arresting the governor for every crime in the book takes a little more than a prosecutor knowing it. I have to be able to prove it. Especially when her orientation will incite every PC group in the nation to her defense."

He heard the soft sounds of a tired mother weeping.

"Look, let me get into this email and see some evidence. If you talk to Nat again, make him call me. *Make him*. He's got to trust me."

"Okay."

The line was dead. Earnest opened a browser window, went to Google, and logged in using Nat's email and password. He reviewed two-dozen spam emails, then Earnest double-clicked the first of twenty-two messages from Nat to himself.

He recognized three of the four women: the Governor, a judge, and Jane Lynwood, who had never looked so … intoxicated. The judge was on the sofa with a woman he'd never seen. Their actions were the pulp of male fantasies. They went down on each other, groped breasts, arched backs. The judge's mouth gaped in a frozen moan of ecstasy.

Governor Rentier's mouth was closed, her eyes planted, calm.

Earnest printed the photo and studied the women's faces and necks with a magnifying glass. The lines were smooth and the shading gradual. The silhouettes projected on the walls matched the women, both head and body. The shadows on their faces matched the shadows on their bodies, consistent with coming from the same light source. It would take the Stephen Spielberg of Photoshop to fake something like this.

Why else would the governor act like they were real?

The next shot gave a better profile of the unknown woman, who had come up from between the judge's legs for air. He printed it and opened the rest of emailed photos. They were all the same four women in various poses.

Something struck him. The governor always received attention from the other women, but never performed.

My finger rests on the trigger.

Gretchen smiles in a wedding dress. She sits in jeans on a tire swing; her belly just beginning to show.

She hangs above me, eyes blank, gone.

The north end of the cabin has a deck. The back corner, facing the woods, has a plate glass window. I crouch behind a garden shrub, check left and right, draw the Luger, and low-crawl to the house. Look through the window at an angle.

The kitchen opens to a rustic hall. A dining table extends into the right, where a wall eclipses my view. To the left, the governor and her guests sit on leather sofas and la-z-boys, snifters in hand, before a blazing fireplace. Rentier has aged since she destroyed my wife. Her edges have grown sharper. The group laughs as the judge tells a story that draws more boisterous responses every minute he continues.

Crickets chirp. They don't do that when people move through their territory. Where is her security?

Crouching, I pass under the window and at the corner of the house, hear low male voices coming from the deck. I peek. One adjusts a chaise lounge. A cigarette lighter flashes with a metallic click.

Two smoke cigarettes, standing, looking into the distance. Two more recline on chairs. Should they be patrolling, or stationed at doors? Almost on cue, one says, "I'm gonna take a round."

"Has it been fifteen minutes?"

"Close enough. Better'n smelling your ass."

He steps toward me. I shrink into the corner where recently tilled earth meets the house. The ground is black and the shadows are deep. His footsteps cross the deck. He hops down. Change jingles in his pocket. I close my eyes to slits. He steps past me, pivots two feet away. I hear his breath but if I turn my head, he'll hear me.

Has he seen something?

Is he in front of the window?

He takes a deep breath and sighs. I hear his zipper and feel the hot splash of urine on my calves. He's a slow pisser, and worse, a groaner.

"Ah, the governor," he says. "Not lookin' too shabby tonight. Ahh. And the Speaker. Wonder if they'll share a room. I'll guard that door."

I wonder how he can mistake the sound of urine on cloth for urine on dirt—but since he hasn't stopped mumbling the whole time, maybe he hasn't heard. The stream ends and he flops his meat before zipping his pants and walking away.

I'd always hoped to avoid this kind of intimacy with another man.

I lift myself slowly. The footfalls of another security man pound across the patio. I freeze in a push-up position. The piss on my leg is already starting to sting.

The man leaps from the edge, saying, "Hold up, Tim!"

He slips on the dewy grass and lands on his back. I'm frozen, six feet away, in a position I don't have the strength to sustain. He groans and the other two on the deck come to peer at him.

"I think I slipped a disk."

"He slipped his dick," one says.

"I'm not kidding. I can't get up."

My arms tremble at the elbows; I lower myself, contacting the earth as their voices continue. The other two leap down, and a man's heel presses against my leg.

Tim, the slow pisser, returns. "What's the commotion?"

"Ozzie broke his back."

"Can you move your feet?"

"Yeah. It's my back. I'm having a spasm. I've had em before. Roll me face down and pick me up at the shoulders."

The others squat beside Ozzie.

"You ready?"

"Do it."

They roll him.

"FUCK!"

"Gary—we only need two of us here. You mind taking a lap while we get him taken care of?"

One of them wanders off. I squeeze the Luger grip.

A door creaks and a pair of floodlights cast a hard light on the end of the building, deepening the shadow in which I hide.

"What's going on out here?" It is Rentier's voice. Others step beside her and heels click on the redwood deck. This is the moment a desperate man would seize—a blaze of glory, hail of bullets, kamikaze moment.

I wait and listen.

"Ozzie slipped, Ma'am. Sprained his back. Gary's patrolling, and as soon as we get Oz inside, we'll be back on post."

"It's a nice night. He'll be more comfortable on the porch."

"I need a doctor," he groans.

"Have Marcel drive him to the emergency room. Anything else going on out here?"

"No Ma'am. Quiet night."

"Fine." Her footsteps diminish and the door closes. From inside, laughter. Maybe her bodyguards will kill her for me.

They lift Ozzie at his shoulders and move him around the deck. The lights blink off.

The leader of the security detail included only the four of them in his rundown for the governor. The way Rentier treats her security, I wouldn't be surprised if she doesn't have any inside the house.

I stand and look through the kitchen window. They're in the same seats as before, except the judge, who pours amber fluid from a crystal decanter.

I pad across the deck to the door. Rentier is unmistakable. Blond hair cut short, spiked on top. An aristocratic curve from jaw to sternum. She sits upright; her stiff back props her head high. I am at a forty-five-degree angle to the glass door. Car doors slam from the front of the house. I lift the Luger and point at her head.

This is the woman who killed Gretchen. Killed Preston Delp. Hired men to kill me—men who raped a young girl. I don't know what else she has done.

A hand slaps the car roof twice, the universal "go" signal.

Rentier's head is half above my front sight post. The trigger is smooth. I can't help but run through a checklist. Yellow Horse is captured. I've apologized to Cyndi. I've finally told myself to let Gretchen go. Josh knows I'm his father. *We should stick together*, he said.

Two men approach the deck from the front, talking.

My ears ring. *We should stick together.*

Pick this or pick that.

Gretchen is gone forever.

Josh is alive.

The men circle the deck. They'd see me if they looked. Rentier holds her glass in a toast. My breaths come in long, slow cycles. Finally I have clarity.

Gretchen is gone and Josh is alive.

The men pass. I lower the Luger and slip across the deck.

In three minutes I work back into the forest, and in ten, I replace my camouflage clothes with my suit, clean my face with baby wipes, and pack the Luger.

At Sedona I find a pay phone and call information. The woman connects me to Mick Patterson.

"This is Nat Cinder," I say.

"This is Attorney General Jane Lynwood. Let me in."

"I'm sorry Ma'am. I have to check."

"Let me in!"

The intercom was dead. Jane thumped her steering wheel and watched an approaching car's headlights.

The male voice returned. "The gate is opening, Ma'am."

She stepped on the gas and slid on gravel as she took the wide turn by Oak Creek, and then skidded to a stop at the house. A guard stood at the front door and another on patrol rounded the deck at a run. There for her?

The door guard spoke into his lapel and the running guard stopped.

She marched across the gravel in her heels and fought to keep her ankles straight. The guard stood at the door, indifferent. She flung the door open and stepped into the great hall. To her right, the governor, the minority leader, Judge Wynn, and the House Majority Leader sat, each holding an amber drink, their faces flushed with merriment.

"Jane, how good of you to join us," Rentier said.

"We need to talk."

"Very well." She turned to her guests. "Please excuse me."

Rentier led Lynwood to a bedroom and closed the door. She whirled. "What the hell are you doing?"

After two hours of dress rehearsal in the car, Lynwood blanked. "The photos."

"I'm taking care of that."

"The boy in the hospital is talking."

"I see."

"You see? He claims you're behind that precious girl's rape, and Preston Delp's death. And what does Theen have to do with all of this?"

"What do you want, Jane?"

"None of this is a surprise to you!"

"Jane, we've shared a lot." She placed a heavy arm on Jane's shoulder. "Arrest the boy for murder. We'll draw Judge Wynn, and he won't admit the photos. You're a lawyer. Your name, my name, will never see the light of day. Case closed."

"I can't do that."

"You don't have a choice. You're in the photos."

"You're in them too."

"Of course I'm in them! I'm taking action, Jane. Something I always knew you'd have a problem with."

"That's why you had the photos taken."

Rentier sat on the corner of the bed. "Jane, we're on the edge of greatness—"

Photos in hand, Earnest dialed the phone with his pencil's eraser.

"Sheriff McConnell, this is Earnest. I'm looking at a black and white photo of the governor."

"Ah, hell."

"I know you or your men found the photos at the scene. What did you do with them?"

"You don't know what you're digging in."

"I have copies of twenty-two photos, showing a judge, my boss, and the governor."

"Shit. I gave them to the governor's chief of staff, Patterson. They didn't have anything to do with the case."

"How the hell could you know that?"

"Are you even a prosecutor anymore?"

"No. What else was at Nat Cinder's place?"

"You go after her, you'll find she's got muscle all over the place. You don't even have standing to ask questions."

"Her ship is going down. You can bail water for her, or you can jump."

"Cinder's computer burned, nothing there. Patterson went through his paper files. There wasn't anything there that could help you."

"Patterson was there?"

"At the governor's request. Because of the photos."

"You didn't think that was strange?"

"That's the way of it."

"I heard Rudy Ging Theen was there. Did Patterson have anything to do with that?"

"He didn't pay Theen any mind. He was looking for anything having to do with those pictures."

"Is that normal?"

"You listen, Junior. This is the way things work. I controlled my crime scene, but I allowed the governor to control damage. There wasn't any other way to do it."

"I appreciate that Sheriff; I didn't mean to get you riled. I need your help. Was Patterson there long?"

"All night."

"Sheriff, this is stretching … Why would he be there all night? Was he armed?"

"You'll have to ask him."

"I assume you identified the bodies in the pit?"

"Right."

"Did any of them own a black Jeep Grand Cherokee with a winch?"

"Yes, the one taken out with a shot to the head. Buffa."

"Thanks."

Earnest dialed Minority Leader Clyman's line. No answer. He called Clyman's home and got his cell number.

"Congressman, this is Earnest Whetton with the District Attorney's office. I apologize for calling you at this hour on your cell."

"Yes, uh, I'm—"

"Indisposed, I take it."

"Just a minute."

A moment.

"All right, I'm outside. Whew. Craziness tonight. You should come up here and get your boss."

"Up here?"

"The Governor's Sedona place."

Lynwood's there? What happened?

"She had a bitch session with the governor."

"About photographs?"

"You know about them?"

"I have them."

"Why'd you call me?"

"Where did Preston Delp get the photos?"

"I don't know. He got them before he worked for me."

"Listen to me. Give me what I need and the governor goes down."

"Joey Buffa."

"That explains a lot of things. Is Mick Patterson there?"

"No."

Earnest ended the call and dialed the governor's office. A late-working secretary answered.

"Where is Patterson?"

"Just left. I suspect he'll be joining the governor in Sedona, because he mentioned stopping at the Oak Creek Canyon lookout in the morning. I think he's shopping for Navajo gifts."

"Thank you."

Earnest pressed the toggle to disconnect and the phone rang with the receiver in his hand.

Last night I asked myself if I have what it takes to be the first man to die in a war.

I do—but I am not a romantic. General George S. Patton said you don't win wars by dying for your country. You make the other dumb poor bastard die for his. That is where I am right now. I'm willing to spend my life, but not for the show of it.

I am at Oak Creek Canyon, sitting on a two-foot rock ledge overlooking the precipice. From the corner of the ledge to the bottom of the canyon is six hundred feet of jagged rocks and trees. I'm at the top of the lookout, a peninsula with canyon on two sides. Wind whips up from the edge behind me.

Patterson, the governor's Chief of Staff, walks toward me from the entrance. His pug face holds arrogance I can read from a hundred yards. At the entrance, Navajo set up display tables of genuine trinkets, pine tomahawks and turquoise necklaces. Patterson and I will have all the privacy we need.

He stands a few feet away; his tan jacket bulges where he hides a pistol.

"Nice haircut," he says.

"I was ready to kill her last night," I say.

"Why didn't you?" He puts his fists in his pockets. "Come on, Cinder. You've been around the block. Your hands aren't clean."

He sits on the ledge a few feet away—out of reach. Not many fifty-year olds look like Chesty Puller. His politician's eyes are reasonable, warm.

"You have something for me?"

I take the envelope from my pocket. "This is the research Preston Delp did on your boss." I throw the envelope and he catches it. "Your henchmen—they stay dead. You don't have any leads on me. You drop everything."

He nods and waves the envelope. "How many copies have you made?"

"I figure close to six billion. It's on the Internet. If I fail to communicate with a spammer I know in Liberia in a week, he shoots those photos to every email list that exists. Prepaid."

"You know if the photos ever surface again, we'll kill you."

"Sure, you'll try. Rentier doesn't have to worry about photos. She has to worry about a black horse candidate willing to spend five million bucks to unseat her this November."

A flicker of interest crosses his eyes. "That so?"

"What'd she spend under clean elections last time?" I say. "Three point eight?"

"What about this?" He indicated the envelope.

"She has dirt; I have dirt. That's politics."

"You—? You're unelectable. Period."

"Then I buy a candidate who isn't."

Patterson looks past me. "I think your time's up."

Two state police cars approach with revolving red and blue lights. I glance at the cliff. The thought is flitting. The patrol cars stop a dozen yards away. Four officers step out.

"Mick Patterson?" The lead patrolman looks like John Wayne.

Patterson takes a step toward them. "This is Nat Cinder," he says, "right here."

"Mister Patterson, I am placing you under arrest for conspiracy and murder." He turns to another officer. "Search him."

"Mister Patterson, you have the right to remain silent …"

I stagger to the overlook wall. My heart pounds and my eyes are wet. I want to call God, but I don't know Him too well. The wind from the canyon is brisk on my sheared head, the kind of cold that raises arm hair and makes a man feel like something works beyond his reckoning.

THE END …

Baer Creighton Book 3 Available for Pre Order!

Luke Graves turned the family butcher business into an empire by cutting fat off the ledger as well as he cut meat off the bone.

He also learned many men sold beef, but few sold girls and boys. Demand was high—especially for the ones with brown skin—and supply, small.

Ten years later the family business included three sons and a distribution chain that delivered kids for any purpose throughout the western United States.

One evening, returning to Williams, Arizona from a pickup in Sierra Vista, the tire blows out. A chavo bolts the truck and runs for the plain. Cephus Graves takes him down with a deer rifle, then fires at a stray pit bull that catches his eye.

In the woods two hundred yards away, Baer Creighton looks up from his fire. He has a nose for evil men and he's found a clan of them. But he's met his match in Luke Graves.

Baer bleeds in Pretty Like an Ugly Girl.

Everyone bleeds.

When you read the end, you'll go back to page one to do it all over again.

Howdy. I appreciate you reading my books—more than you can know. If you've read this far, you and I are fellow travelers. I suspect you sense something is not quite right with the world. It's not as good as it's supposed to be. We human beings aren't as good as our ideals. Yet, we prize and want to fight for them.

I do my absolute best to write stories that portray the human situation with brutal transparency, but also I strive to tell stories that are not as bleak as the human condition sometimes seems. There's no limit to the darkness. Light is rare. But it exists, and I hope when you complete one of my novels, you find your values validated. I hope I encourage you to fight the good fight, just as you encourage me when you buy my books, review them, and join my Facebook group, the

Red Meat Lit Street Team. Y'all are an awesome community. It's good that we're in this fight together, and I'm grateful you're out there. Thank you.

Remember, light wins in the end.

Made in the USA
Monee, IL
22 August 2020

39017267R00208